EXPOSURE

MORGAN & JENNIFER LOCKLEAR

OMNIFIC PUBLISHING
LOS ANGELES

Omnific Publishing
1901 Avenue of the Stars, 2nd floor
Los Angeles, CA 90067
www.omnificpublishing.com

First Omnific eBook edition, June 2014
First Omnific trade paperback edition, June 2014

Library of Congress Cataloguing-in-Publication Data

Locklear, Morgan and Locklear, Jennifer.
Exposure / Morgan & Jennifer Locklear - 1st ed.
ISBN: 978-1-623421-21-2
1. Hollywood — Romance. 2. Celebrities — Romance.
3. Contemporary Romance — Fiction. 4. Divorce — Fiction. I. Title

10 9 8 7 6 5 4 3 2 1

Cover Design by Micha Stone and Amy Brokaw
Interior Book Design by Coreen Montagna

Printed in the United States of America

For Becca, Elli and Sue.

CHAPTER ONE

A slender ray of light from the floor-to-ceiling windows was slowly making its way toward the bed. The only sound in the room came from the clock on the wall. It was a noise that occasionally made it difficult for Michelle to fall back asleep if she woke in the night, but for now, she felt all too happy in the arms of her husband. She was naked, dozing comfortably, but still aware of her surroundings, and completely sated from their unexpected afternoon rendezvous.

There had been few moments like this during the past several months. Knowing her time with Kyle was rapidly drawing to a close, Michelle resisted the temptation to surrender to sleep. Soon she would have to let him go. He was catching a flight to New York City, and she would be leaving their Malibu home only sixteen hours later, boarding a plane for Houston.

Michelle was due to begin rehearsals for her next film the day after her arrival in Texas. The couple wouldn't see one another again for nearly a week. Eventually, when Kyle did join her on-set, she knew he would be all business and no pleasure.

Her mouth twitched downward at the thought, although her eyes remained firmly shut to the impending reality. Her head rested on Kyle's chest, her arm draped across his slick stomach. The room was still warm with passion, and she pulled him even tighter to her thankful body.

Kyle slept soundly, snoring lightly and offering no more than a mere grumble at the contraction of Michelle's embrace. She smiled in triumph. Usually, he rolled away from her when she pulled this move on him. He'd never been much of a cuddler.

In fact, she was surprised that Kyle initiated sex at all. She'd been sitting on the mattress at the foot of their colossal bed when he emerged from his closet, carrying a suitcase in each hand. She'd been feeling sorry for herself and sad to once again be left alone.

Even though a cool distance existed between them, Michelle still found his presence at home soothing. Kyle was one of the few people that she had known before celebrity found her, so despite the fact that their relationship was in an awkward phase, she held out hope that their foundation was secure enough to weather the storm.

As Kyle had approached, Michelle immediately recognized an expression that had long been absent from his face during their eight-year marriage.

He wanted her.

And she needed him, desperately.

She'd watched in perplexed fascination as Kyle set down his baggage and began unbuttoning his shirt. His lean body had never looked better, and his dusty blond Robert Redford hair shaded his hungry blue eyes. When he stepped toward her, she hastily began removing her own clothes, fearful he would change his mind before he could reach her.

He hadn't. Instead, he'd made love to her with wonder and passion. Kyle was even tender at times, running his fingertips along her toned, tanned belly as he moved his mouth along the parts of her body she'd kept groomed in hope of his return. Afterward, as she continued to linger in his embrace, she replayed those blissful moments in her mind. Making love with Kyle hadn't been this good in years.

Unfortunately, Michelle's reflections were interrupted a few minutes later when Kyle's soft snoring stopped. She knew her time was up.

"Just something for you to remember me by." He smirked as he sat up, forcing her off of him like he would a cat in his lap.

Michelle grimaced slightly as she resettled on their bed, but otherwise did not respond. She was already preoccupied by other familiar and intruding considerations. She'd been warring with herself for nearly a year about whether or not to end their marriage. In the space of an hour, she'd gone from sad to blissful to angry. Michelle realized her emotions were out of control, swinging from one extreme to another and quickly back again. She no longer trusted herself to make the right decision, let alone act on it.

Kyle's eyes drifted to Michelle's healthy breasts as he pulled his clothes back on. He'd repeatedly urged her to get implants and had even gone so far as to call her a saggy cow during an alcohol-induced argument the year before.

He only dropped the issue when she took a role as the lesbian lover of a sultry, twenty-year-old in a steamy movie. The two women shared several erotic moments onscreen, including what became an iconic scene of the girls shaving each other. When asked on the red carpet, Kyle was forced to agree that Michelle looked every bit as fine as her much-younger co-star.

To say otherwise would make him look like an ungrateful jerk. Which he was, of course, but at least he stopped suggesting ways for his wife to improve her body.

She stayed in bed, but did not cover up. He hated that.

Kyle easily traded the view of her for the one of himself in the bathroom mirror. He smirked as he carefully checked his hair. He was about to spend a week promoting a film he already knew would be a hit, and once the promotional tour was finished, he would skip down south to begin filming with one of the industry's up-and-coming directors.

Nathan McPherson had cast him in the sci-fi thriller after only one interview and no screen test, just the way Kyle liked it. Nathan was a smart young man, but Kyle would have to make sure the director quickly understood who was really in charge on-set.

Kyle left the bathroom without turning off the light. He looked down briefly at Michelle. She'd fallen back into the sheets and was resting peacefully amidst soft, champagne-colored bedding. Her long auburn hair was fanned out over the pillows.

He frowned as he retrieved his suitcases, a parting notion just then occurring to him.

"Don't make a scene if our trailers aren't right next to each other," he warned. It was the last thing he said to his wife before sauntering out of the room.

Kyle failed to notice Michelle hadn't spoken a single word.

He drove to the airport in his Bugatti Veyron Gabilier, feeling smug because he was one of only a handful of people in all of Southern California who owned the four-door sedan model. Most people didn't even know Bugatti made a big luxury car, and Kyle had strategically purchased it several months earlier at the frenzied height of the couple's latest paparazzi-dubbed "Baby Watch." The media was always speculating on when the duo would begin their family, and the latest round of predictions preceded a wedding anniversary jaunt to Cabo San Lucas. Despite the positive spin a baby would no doubt put on his career, Kyle had no interest in becoming a father, and Michelle returned from their vacation having enjoyed the margaritas almost as much as the fajitas.

He told himself that he was not the type of man who needed to drive a souped-up sports car or a gigantic Hummer to prove his worth. Even so, his Bugatti was a high gloss black with milk blue headlights. Kyle believed the severity of the lights and the blunt grill gave the vehicle a mean appearance, like a scowling ghost. He spent every second of the commute with the driver's side window fully down, knowing his appealing profile would only be enhanced in any photos the paps would inevitably snap of him. They always did. Kyle made sure of it. It was a tip he'd picked up from Kathy Griffin.

He parked his prized car in the short term lot and left it for his publicist to retrieve. It was not part of her job description to do such things, but Kyle Petersen made a habit of treating her worse than he did his wife.

Chapter Two

Shaunna Noble was born into a Hollywood dynasty. She was the only daughter of a grindhouse producer who struck gold with enough films in the late seventies to build a comfortable empire. After his wife's unexpected death, Gus Noble shifted his focus to television in order to stay close to his daughter. Although Shaunna was on the verge of turning thirty, everyone still recognized her as the little girl in the Noble Productions logo at the end of his shows and the beginning of his movies.

She was easily beautiful enough to be an actress, but had always been painfully shy. As a child, she hid under the polished grand piano during her father's lavish parties while Robin Williams and Gene Wilder looked all over the house to give her back her nose or, worse yet, to ask her questions about herself. With dark brown hair and honey-colored eyes, Shaunna often thought of herself as an autumn tree. She remembered playing in the woods near her home and wondering if she could just fade into the forest.

In school, she learned that with a pen in her hand, she was powerful. Later, she discovered that with a keyboard underneath her quick fingers, she was influential. Shaunna was a savvy observer of her environment, and after watching how her father closed one deal after another, she decided at the age of fifteen to serve the industry from the inside. She would help control the very public she feared so much.

With so many actors available and clamoring for any kind of attention, clients were easy to come by, yet they were mostly B-listers.

Usually, they were actors in their fifties who were celebrating the arrivals of their first grandchildren and who were not difficult to manage, from a publicist's standpoint. But she never took the job for granted and was always coming up with new ways to give her clients the kind of exposure their comeback careers desperately needed.

The keen application of Shaunna's first-hand knowledge of the industry quickly transformed her. She broke free from the image of a young girl trapped within the pull of her father's success and developed into a woman who was capable of placing herself and her clients in favorable positions. She was proud to stand in the light of her own achievements, and so was Gus, a busy but thoughtful father who often included her in his projects.

Kyle Petersen was not one of her most famous clients when she took him on. But when he landed the lead role in the book-to-film adaptations of a supernatural private eye, the actor turned into a superstar overnight. After the first installment of Kyle's blockbuster film series hit theaters, he single-handedly put her in a new income bracket. Shaunna assumed she would be forever grateful to him for keeping her in his employ and sharing his success. Thanks to the popularity of his films, she amassed a strong portfolio by the age of twenty-five.

However, Kyle's celebrity was accompanied by a creeping narcissism which turned him into an uncontrollable, ill-mannered beast by the time he was shooting the third film in the series. His character was a bit of a prick, and he began assuming those characteristics away from the set. Kyle even seemed to revel in his despicable behavior and perfected it, much to Shaunna's growing unease.

Shaunna dutifully picked up Kyle's car at the airport by taking a cab and using the key ordered solely for her. They'd run this routine before. She would catch a flight of her own later that evening and would assist him constantly in New York. However, they never flew together. Kyle made it a personal policy never to fly with the help, especially when his money afforded Shaunna her own first class ticket.

Kyle always flew in the studio's private jet. His attention-seeking ways had their limits, after all, and he refused to trudge through the terminals of LAX.

When Shaunna arrived back at Kyle's home, she pulled the car in past the security gate and into the Malibu driveway. After parking the sleek Bugatti, she removed the two big suitcases from the back seat. Kyle usually left his bags in the house for her to collect, but he must have put them in his car by accident. They were heavy, and she realized it would be a huge inconvenience at the airport once she added her own luggage into the equation.

Shaunna climbed back into her forest green Jaguar and departed. She drove to her own modest house in Yorba Linda and gathered her things for the trip to New York City. Her father grumbled about her choice of residence every time he drove out to visit, but it had no effect on her. Shaunna lived alone and didn't feel the need to live in a large home like the one Gus had raised her in.

Her personal life was simple, and she enjoyed the physical distance between her home and her demanding career. The quiet neighborhood offered exactly that.

There were six hours left until she needed to leave for the airport. It was a late departure and she would have to sleep on the plane, but Kyle wanted her there that night because she had his luggage and he would be appearing on several morning shows the next day.

Shaunna had a few hours to kill, so she did her favorite thing in the whole world: she went to Disneyland. Her home's proximity to the amusement park was no accident.

A twenty minute drive and a quick flash of her season pass later, and she was in the mid-week, late-afternoon line for Pirates of the Caribbean. Her favorite part of the ride was that first moment when the boat settled into the water. She closed her eyes and listened to the distant murmurs and clinking glasses from the Blue Bayou restaurant which overlooked the swamp as she and her few companions floated past. She then watched the electronic fireflies hovering in the trees while the recorded sounds of bayou life accompanied her. She always liked, but easily forgot, the smell of the water she floated on. It didn't have the odor of chlorine or bleach, but its aroma was nonetheless clean—pleasing, even. After two steep drops, Shaunna was on her way through a massive underground cave filled with the most amazing animatronics and pyrotechnics the 1960s could produce.

It was perfect.

She spent the eighteen minutes beneath the park looking for things she hadn't noticed before. This particular time, she found two robotic rats that were new to her, along with a pair of eyes peeking out from one of the ships forever engaged in battle.

She'd always been old school, but accepted the addition of Johnny Depp to the classic attraction, mostly because he was so very cool as an actor and a person.

Next she went to the Haunted Mansion, excited about how it had been completely redesigned for the holiday season as the Nightmare Before Christmas. She went through twice.

Big Thunder Mountain Railroad in Frontierland also got a double dip, and then she walked over to the Tiki Room and watched the show while drinking a pineapple smoothie.

Shaunna loved being in Disneyland. She was even a welcomed guest at Club 33, though she liked being out in the park too much and only visited the New Orleans Square establishment when the park became too crowded. It was a privilege she would always exercise and more than worth the yearly dues. Whenever she dropped by the club, there was always a hot cocoa waiting for her in the Trophy Room within a few minutes.

Disneyland was like a second home to her, but Shaunna knew it was never going to be a complete experience until she had a family. She was not lonely, but she was alone, and she knew the line between the two had a funny way of fading away.

She thought about heading over to Toontown, but decided she wanted a thrill and considered going on the one ride she'd never experienced, the Twilight Zone Tower of Terror in the California Adventure Park. She actually started walking in that direction, but chickened out before she even left the main gate.

Instead, she rode the Disneyland Express train all the way around the park and got off in Tomorrowland. Space Mountain was going to be her biggest thrill this evening.

Shaunna went home after a quick dash over to the Matterhorn, which was closed, and the final necessary trip through Indiana Jones and the Temple of the Forbidden Eye.

Dinner was a tuna fish sandwich and a glass of milk, and then she was back in her car and off to LAX with Iron and Wine's "The Devil Never Sleeps" playing on repeat.

Chapter Three

David Quinn was from Chicago. He grew up in South Chicago, to be precise, and the tough part of South Chicago to be more precise. He fell into acting when he accompanied a friend to an open casting call for extras in a zombie movie. He'd just turned twenty-one at the time and was a little drunk when he agreed to tag along.

The makeup artist didn't want to mess up David's beautiful face, and neither did the director, so David was cast as the wise-cracking member of the group of survivors and his character was kept alive as long as the director could reasonably get away with. He had most of the best lines in the film, as well as a gruesome death scene, followed by a few memorable moments as a zombie. He was a standout in an otherwise forgettable movie. The picture was called *Dead Heads* and had opened more doors for him than any other acting work he'd been able to land since.

David impulsively moved to Hollywood after his first co-starring role as a deaf veterinarian in *Dog Eared*. It'd been promoted as the next *Free Willy*, but had tanked worse than *Jaws 3-D*.

He stayed in town, mostly because he couldn't afford to move anywhere else, and found semi-steady work in commercials and underwear print ads. Eventually, even those opportunities faded away. He'd been nursing a dry spell that lasted eight months before he miraculously secured his next job.

To put it simply, David Quinn felt cursed. Directors just weren't casting no-name actors in leading roles, and they certainly weren't going to cast someone in a supporting role when he looked better on camera than their leading man. It was a frustrating place for him to be. His rich blue eyes were complemented by coffee-brown hair, and he had tiny comma-shaped dimples in his olive-skinned smile. His arms and shoulders were effortlessly lean, and his small waist only made his muscular legs all the more appealing.

The adult industry would have loved to nab him, but David knew there wasn't enough Purell in the world for that.

David's new role was that of a doomed pilot in a sci-fi thriller called *Sling Shot.*

According to the script, David's character was supposed to take an elite team of astro-scientists on a routine sling shot around the sun, which would then zip them all off to Iapetus, one of Saturn's moons. From a scientific standpoint, the moon was indeed interesting, but the government had a secret agenda which only the mission commander and the pilot knew about.

Trouble would ensue when the spaceship was struck and disabled by a solar flare and caught in the sun's gravitational pull. The crew would need to repair the ship quickly, or they wouldn't be able to survive even long enough to feel impact. Over the course of the movie, the commander would become paranoid and then kill David's character.

Nathan McPherson, who made his start in slasher films, remembered David from the set of the Chicago-filmed zombie movie where McPherson had worked as an Assistant Director. The casting director offered David just a walk-on part, but when he was reunited with Nathan, he was immediately recast as the handsome pilot who would meet his heroic demise at the end of the fourth reel.

David began to see it as good luck when he played a character that was killed on screen.

Nathan scheduled the death scene right at the end of the shoot because he had a thing about killing characters off.

"Once you're dead, you're dead…until it's time for ADR," he'd been known to say, referring to Automatic Dialog Replacement.

In *Sling Shot,* the commander would try to make the death of David's character appear to be an accident, but he would also be faced with the dilemma that his crew would then be deprived of their pilot. Fortunately, the ship's doctor—who was also his wife—would prove to be a capable replacement, and since the mission would be scrubbed, she would have to try to get them all home safely.

And she would, but not before she thought back to something David's character had said to her just before blast off, as their backs began vibrating and before everything became so loud that the count-down from Mission Control could no longer be heard. It was a line written by Nathan himself.

"We are all of this world, but brave the void to find another. Yet the whole time, we'll only be thinking of home."

The movie would end with a memorable shot of the sun reflecting on a slow-moving tear on the heroine's cheek just after the commander is confronted by armed men and arrested for the murder of David's character. The commander's undoing would come after the authorities received proof of the crime via an open transmission line—the murdered pilot's premeditated act of revenge.

The role was a significant upgrade, both in exposure and in pay, and David took it knowing he was only weeks away from quitting the business for good. Even if he couldn't afford to leave Los Angeles, he knew he couldn't continue on with acting. He had no idea what he would do with the rest of his life. All he knew was that the life of an unemployed actor was just too unstable for him.

Whereas others would have taken the new job as a sign that their star was on the rise, David took the news that he'd won a minor role as a sign that it was time to close out his lackluster days as a Hollywood actor.

There had been steady industry talk about *Sling Shot* for several months leading up to the shoot. David was going to celebrate the end of his career by playing a small role in what would hopefully become a summer blockbuster.

It was good enough for him. He gave up his small but sunny apartment and sold his futon to a neighbor. He was honestly more excited about the fact that the job got him out of California without costing him a penny he couldn't spare.

Chapter Four

David was standing outside the costume trailer and talking with Key Costumer Alix Crosland, who'd just fitted him with his ray gun belt. They were on location in Texas, and filming had begun a few days earlier.

David could not believe his luck when he realized he would be acting opposite legitimate A-list movie stars. Kyle Petersen and Michelle Cooper were Hollywood royalty.

David fondly remembered how Michelle arrived for rehearsals a week before her husband. Her hair was the color of a sunset just before the last bit of red was swallowed by darkness, and her eyes were green galaxies. She'd been wheeling her own bag and had beamed at everyone she'd seen, including him. She radiated beauty and confidence, and David's admiration of her was instantly secured.

On the other hand, Kyle had hit the set with a self-imposed fanfare, and when David attempted to introduce himself, he was answered with a glare of cool indifference. With that one look from Kyle, David Quinn suddenly felt like the butler's dog.

As he stood outside in the October sunshine with Alix, David watched as the script supervisor checked over the props and set dressings while the lighting techs looked for unwanted shadows or reflections.

"Do you wear a jacket in this scene?" Alix asked. Her slender legs emerged attractively from underneath a short, stylish skirt, and her cropped suicide-blond hair was smashed down by a plaid fedora. "Gary is going to come over and ask you any second now."

"Nope," he replied confidently.

"How many more days do you have?"

"I'm here for the duration. Nathan has my stuff pretty spread out because he doesn't want to shoot my death scene until we get back to California. I wrap just a day before Mr. Petersen does and two days after Ms. Cooper."

"Have you noticed anything about Kyle and Michelle?" David had already learned that Alix was the set gossip.

"No." David kept his answer short.

"When they're not in a scene together, they don't even look at each other. And I'm pretty sure they keep sending their publicist back and forth to communicate."

"Shaunna Noble." David spoke her name softly.

"You know her?" Alix looked surprised.

"No, but I've heard of her."

"Would you like to meet her?"

David swallowed. Since he'd first spotted Shaunna on the set a few days earlier, all he could think about was kissing her. Blessed with a figure that was a perfect combination of petite and shapely, in addition to a captivating, composed face, she was the kind of woman who made young, confused actors reconsider the reconsideration of their profession.

"Sure." David tried to sound casual and, adorably, believed he succeeded.

Alix smiled. As if on cue, Kyle's trailer door opened. Shaunna stepped out, carrying his costume for the scene they were setting up. It was media day, and flash bulbs started going off as Shaunna walked down the stairs. The photographers all stopped taking pictures when they realized it was just Kyle Petersen's publicist. She hadn't acknowledged the cameras either way.

Shaunna strode toward the costume trailer, and David intently watched her approach. Her long dark hair billowed softly in the warm air as she walked purposefully in his direction.

"Looks like you'll get your wish," Alix mumbled to David from the side of her mouth.

"Hi, Alix. Hi, David." Shaunna was talking fast. She was in a hurry, her voice uncharacteristically strained. "Alix, could you hold on to this? I don't want it getting damaged."

"Okay, but…" Alix began, but paused after Shaunna handed over the commander's uniform and quickly turned and walked away. She went back inside the leading man's trailer, slamming the door shut behind her.

Alix turned to a stunned David. "She knows your name at least."

"I know." David felt like he was in a dream. He'd never been formally introduced to Shaunna Noble, and he certainly wasn't famous enough for her to know any of his work. His mind began to race, wondering what he could've possibly done to make her aware of his existence. He sincerely hoped it wasn't anything negative.

"We'll catch up to her after the scene," Alix assured him. "Kyle runs her ragged sometimes. I can't believe she didn't bring an assistant. Shaunna has more important things to do than carry his costume over to me."

David looked at the clothes in Alix's hand, and his brow furrowed in confusion. "That's the costume he's supposed to be wearing for this scene. I wonder why she brought it to you."

Before they could speculate further, Kyle's trailer door flew open again and Shaunna stepped out, carrying a pile of loose clothes in her arms. She dropped only one sock as she stalked past the uninterested photographers and began throwing the items over the security fence which kept devoted fans within their designated area.

David recognized the pants Kyle wore to the set that day as they flew through the air. He also noticed Petersen's watch as Shaunna tossed it to a blond girl, who dropped her poster and ran away with it like a dog with a bone.

With the exception of the one sock lying twisted on the ground in front of his open door, Shaunna had just thrown every stitch of clothing Kyle stored in his trailer to the crowd.

His fans did not question the offering. They simply scrambled over one another to claim their prizes. Some immediately made a mad dash from the set and likely went straight to their computers to sell the items on eBay, while others departed and probably framed their tokens in shadow boxes. A few truly dedicated fans, usually referred to collectively as The Kyle Nation, would take their treasures home and reverently place them underneath their pillows.

The journalists and paparazzi assembled nearby went into a scramble of their own, recognizing the breakdown of a well-known and respected Hollywood publicist.

Alix's eyes grew wide in silent horror as she observed the destruction of some very fine designer clothing.

David Quinn's eyes were worriedly fixed on Shaunna Noble as she stormed away from the riot she'd started.

And Kyle Petersen was inside his trailer, humming to himself in the shower, oblivious to it all.

CHAPTER FIVE

Shaunna hated Texas from the moment she landed in Houston.

It wasn't the people. They were extremely nice and surprisingly bereft of the heavy southern accents her colleagues usually labeled as a liability. It wasn't the countryside, either. She thought the landscape was exquisite. She felt relaxed in the arms of the evening breeze, despite bugs that were as big as drink coasters and as loud as the car in *Chitty Chitty Bang Bang*.

The source of all her anxiety was Kyle. Since his arrival on the set, he'd been a complete prick to Michelle. It was impossible to ignore his cold interactions with her between takes. The two were cast as husband and wife in *Sling Shot,* and it should have been easy for them to act like a happily married couple. But when they filmed their first scene together, a sequence of their characters enjoying a fun picnic in a meadow, their chemistry appeared forced and lifeless.

Nathan recognized the friction at once, as well as the source in the form of Kyle's unwavering glibness, and adapted quickly. He began shooting close-ups of Michelle and long shots of the two actors sitting side by side on a blanket and drinking champagne. He even managed to capture a few good smiles from Kyle on film as he was telling the crew a story about his recent New York escapades.

Nathan reminded Shaunna of her father, who'd made his fortune duct-taping cameras to bicycles and following slow speed car chases down Mulholland Drive. Shaunna knew Nathan chose his campy pictures because they were fun, but he birthed them with all the love and attention of Scorsese.

For this reason alone, Shaunna felt compelled to help Nathan and made an effort to dissipate the growing animosity between his leading actors. Although it made her uncomfortable and was against her self-imposed rule of prying into her clients' personal lives, Shaunna asked Kyle about the state of his marriage later that evening over drinks.

She prepared herself for him to fly off the handle at her nosiness, but instead, he'd been ostensibly, uncharacteristically sweet. His response only compounded her concerns. He told her that his marriage was stronger than it had been in years. He then went on to discuss his favorite subject: himself.

After their meeting, Kyle returned to the penthouse suite he was sharing with Michelle at the Four Seasons. Shaunna was staying at a Radisson, along with Nathan and the rest of the cast and crew. She saw David from time to time, but they'd never spoken.

She'd first spotted him exercising one morning. She was about to wander into the hotel's gym herself, but reconsidered when she saw that even at six a.m., she would not be alone. It wasn't specifically David's presence that changed her mind. She was simply uncomfortable working out in front of strangers.

However, she was not uncomfortable about pausing to admire one. She was certain her ponytail would do nothing to hide her face should he happen to look up and make eye contact, so she went ahead and got herself a good eye full.

David hadn't seen her and was turned completely around. He was bending over to heft some free weights, and he was wearing shorts. Very short shorts. In any other context, they would have looked like something Olivia Newton John might have worn with roller skates, but on him, they were just a sexy, cruel barrier between her hands and his tight cheeks. These particular shorts were white with dark blue piping. Later on, it would be all too easy for her to accidentally remember them as underwear.

As she intently studied David's movements, Shaunna lost her sense of self and squeezed her water bottle hard enough to make it crackle. The noise was loud in the quiet hallway, and she quickly bolted down the corridor, suddenly determined to enjoy a bowl of Cheerios courtesy of the well-appointed continental breakfast.

Over the next hour, Shaunna convinced herself that David would not show up in the breakfast lounge, but she also opted for a second bowl of cereal and a banana, something she normally never did. And then she found herself hanging around to read the morning paper, which she also never did. As soon as she admitted to herself that she was stalling her departure, Shaunna laughed at her reflection in the napkin holder and returned to her room.

The cast and crew followed a hectic shooting schedule for several days because NASA gave the production more access to its complex on the weekends. There had been a night shoot on Friday, but Shaunna opted not to attend. As a publicist, she would never really be expected on any set and rarely ever ventured onto one. But this was the first movie shot with her two biggest clients, and the production was going to spend several weeks in a media heavy state.

This is what Shaunna told herself, at least. In all truth, however, she knew Kyle didn't want to be without his unofficial personal assistant for a month in weather that required at least twenty glasses of lemonade a day. Of course, lately, Kyle preferred a few fingers of vodka with all lemonades served any time after the noon hour.

Shaunna did have other clients and chose to spend the evenings catching up with her small, yet efficient staff in LA. She trusted their ability to handle the day-to-day minutiae, but even they felt better getting her input on high-profile matters.

For the following two days, Nathan had two units working simultaneously in and around the NASA compound. He pushed his cast and crew hard, but he got some good footage, and he needed to stay ahead of the metaphorical Indiana Jones rolling boulder that chased all directors from the first shot until the last splice.

As a result of the vigorous weekend, Monday was going to be light for everyone. It was the perfect time for Nathan to authorize a media day, where activity on-set would be minimal and set secrets were less likely to be leaked to the mainstream press. Michelle wasn't even scheduled to appear, and Kyle was only needed to complete a few scenes.

Shaunna received a text from Kyle announcing he needed to meet her on the set at ten thirty.

"Took you long enough." Kyle's voice was gruff as he stepped up into his trailer, wiping the makeup off his face with a baby wipe.

Shaunna had been two minutes early, but she held her tongue.

"We need to talk about Michelle." Kyle snarled his wife's name, and his tone made Shaunna's blood run cold.

"What's wrong, Kyle?"

"Nothing. Not anymore. Not after today."

"Is there anything I can do?"

"Yes." Kyle pulled his shirt over his head. He often undressed in front of Shaunna, so she'd long since learned to ignore it. "You can shut up and let me finish."

That was over the line. Shaunna stood up, feeling angry, and prepared to defend herself. "Kyle, I don't— "

He interrupted her, and what he had to say made her immediately forget her train of thought.

"I'm divorcing her."

Shaunna sat back down. Hard.

"I had no idea."

Kyle growled in annoyance. "Of course you didn't. Did you think I was going to let you tip her off?"

Shaunna was stunned and insulted, although she also knew he was right. Michelle was her client too, and she definitely would've spoken with her about how to handle the situation. Kyle's decision to end his marriage put Shaunna in an awkward position. She needed to understand both sides of the story in order to know how to handle the inevitable fallout with the tabloids.

"What happened, Kyle? Is it something specific?" Shaunna was trying hard to comprehend his announcement. She hadn't noticed any signs of stress on Michelle's part, even with Kyle's ever-increasing ego. Despite Shaunna's earlier suspicions and the gossip on-set, Michelle hadn't done anything out of the ordinary or said anything to indicate that the marriage was officially on shaky ground.

"Did you know that she keeps a journal?" He didn't wait for Shaunna to answer. "Stupid thing with buttons for flowers. And I check it every once in a while to see what she's up to."

Shaunna was immediately incensed at the invasion of Michelle's privacy, but she held her emotions in check. She needed answers, and blowing up at Kyle would not deliver them to her.

"You don't trust her?" Shaunna prodded gently.

"And with good reason!" he shouted. "She was thinking about leaving *me!*"

Shaunna couldn't believe her ears. Was Kyle really throwing his marriage away over some thoughts jotted down in a diary? She shook her head with disbelief.

"I'm sure most marriages go through tests like this. But she loves you, Kyle. I know she does. She was probably just using the diary to vent her feelings. Have you talked to her about any of this?"

He stared back at Shaunna blankly, his eyes narrowing to slits.

She pressed on and decided to steer the conversation away from the personal and back to the business of serving her client. It was the tactic that usually persuaded Kyle to see reason.

"This isn't great timing. You two have just started filming together, and the studio is banking on the fact you both will bring the movie positive press. You've committed to Michelle professionally for at least another year. The least you can do is give your marriage that much longer to work on your problems."

Kyle crossed his arms and tilted his head marginally, smirking as he began to speak. "Yeah, you see, Shaunna, I've already considered all of this. But we can't trust her. Not anymore. I need to control this. I need to leave her. If she leaves me first…she wins."

"What are you talking about?"

"By filing first, I just told the press that she can't even be lived with. They're all going to feel bad for me. They may not know what she did, but they will assume she did something to deserve it."

Shaunna shook her head emphatically. "You're dumping her! She'll get all the sympathy, Kyle."

He slammed his hand down on the counter. "No, they won't," he insisted. "Not if you do your job!"

His mind was made up, and Shaunna saw there was little chance of convincing him otherwise. Still, there might be time to put the whole thing off. She wasn't ready to accept what he was telling her.

"Well…let's at least work on a strategy, then. We'll map out the timing, and it will give you a while to think this over. Maybe you two can consider counseling, and if Michelle is all right with it, we can put the word out that you're working on your marriage. This way, even if you do decide to go through with a divorce, you can both emerge from it relatively unscathed. It doesn't have to be nasty, Kyle."

Kyle laughed in frustration. "What are you doing, Shaunna? Why are you are trying to spin this in her favor? You don't help her. You work for me. When I leave Michelle, you leave Michelle. Period."

Shaunna was again stunned into silence. He leaned forward and dramatically pointed his index finger at her.

"You're dropping her as a client. Today. She only—" Kyle began to elaborate, but Shaunna had found her voice and lost her temper.

"You ungrateful son of a bitch! She's bent over backward for you!"

Kyle opened his mouth to silence her, but she stood up quickly and stuck her own finger in his face.

"She let amazing opportunities pass her by when she thought it might interfere with your rising star. She's done nothing but think of *your* best interests!"

"You don't know what she's really like," Kyle responded softly. He was going to milk the moment for all it was worth. "She's so vicious to me when you aren't around." He took a shuddering breath. "I just can't take it anymore."

Shaunna turned her head away from Kyle and glared at the kitchen, her right leg beginning to bounce as anger flamed throughout her body. She was outraged, and not just because he was acting horribly. He was exhibiting a total lack of genuine concern for the end of his eight-year marriage, even though he had a wife who remained committed to him, despite her own misgivings. Shaunna knew their marriage wasn't a fairytale, but she'd considered it solid and even envied the couple on occasion for possessing the one thing in life that eluded her.

Kyle went into the bathroom and started the shower, leaving the door open. He continued to undress and tested the water. "I'm having her served with papers as we speak, and obviously I can't have you working for her anymore. I sent her out shopping so the bellman could move her to another hotel room before this evening, but I need you to prepare a statement."

Shaunna snapped back into business mode, realizing she now had a real and immediate issue on her hands. "Wait. You've already filed for divorce? In court?"

"Yes. It's being done in LA right now. That's why I really needed you here."

"Holy shit, Kyle! Why would you do that without talking to me? You know entertainment reporters are assigned to watch those filings as soon as they hit the public record. They're liable to break the story before Michelle can be served or before I can issue a press release!"

"I don't give a fuck when or how Michelle finds out. The sooner, the better. And she's not your problem anymore. Stop thinking about her and start planning a strategy that works for me!"

Kyle stepped into the water's flow and dropped back into the casual dismantling of his union with Michelle. "I'm just glad I got my favorite things out of the Malibu house in time. I've been sneaking my shit out piece by piece since August. In fact, you took two suitcases full of shoes through LAX for me. Thanks." She could hear him chuckling at his little joke.

Shaunna sat on his suede trailer couch, bewildered. Out of every shock she was processing, the slap in the face was Kyle's assumption that she would blindly tie her allegiance to him, despite the fact that he'd been using her as a shoe mule.

She knew the next few minutes would change her life. To her credit, she only hesitated for a few seconds.

Kyle kept talking, completely unaware that she'd exited the trailer with his Commander uniform and returned again. He was in the middle of explaining how he wanted to feign a mourning period before jumping back into the dating scene. He also made it clear that if Shaunna had any hot friends who were looking for a good time to be sure and send them his way.

For the first time since they'd met, Shaunna tuned Kyle out as she plucked his clothes off the floor, taking care to remove his wallet and cell phone. She was furious, but not stupid. The phone especially had sensitive material stored within it that could inconvenience many other people in the Hollywood industry, including her most important client: Michelle Cooper.

Everything else, she took, including his scuffed shoes and his prissy watch.

Kyle had already written down his plan of attack, an outline of all the ways he wanted to take Michelle down. He planned to give it to Shaunna soon, but he liked carrying on a conversation with the little prude while he was naked in the shower. He'd never been stupid enough to make a move on her in the past, but he'd always wanted to. He settled for undressing in front of her and having conversations with steam in the room. It wasn't the first time he'd asked her to meet him in his trailer after a shoot, and there was always the hope that one day, Shaunna would come to her senses and begin the affair he knew she really wanted.

Maybe telling her that he was leaving Michelle was all the motivation she would need. Kyle half expected to turn and see her stepping naked into the shower to take advantage of his newly liberated state.

(Shaunna had come in, but just long enough to remove his only towel from the bathroom and toss his cell phone into the toilet. On a whim, she knocked his toothbrush in as well.)

Kyle sensed her presence in the small space and remained silent. He wanted her to make the first move. Even after she left, he waited and took a moment to imagine a wet and slippery Shaunna pressed up against him. He stopped short of satisfying himself because he needed to get back to work and her skills were the key to staying ahead of the press.

Kyle needed to ensure that the media would sympathize with him, at all costs.

He washed his hair, and when he got soap in his eyes, he reached for his towel. His fingers found only the empty rack.

"Shaunna? Is my towel out there? Shaunna! Ow. Shit!"

Kyle turned off the water and listened. The only noise in the trailer seemed to be coming from the dripping shower head.

"Shaunna!"

He stumbled out of the bathroom blindly and, as he passed the open trailer door, heard the cameras and commotion. He'd completely forgotten about the media day.

Kyle opened his eyes wide, and the soap instantly stung with ferocity. His eyes quickly shut, but not before he saw flashes going off from far enough away to guarantee that every picture taken of him would look extremely unflattering.

He saw something else before he slammed the door and screamed in rage. He saw several fans wrestling madly over the remnants of his clothes.

This meant war. He was already prepared to screw Michelle royally, but now he was determined to fuck Shaunna over as well.

Chapter Six

Shaunna called Michelle from her car. She answered the phone crying.

"Where are you?" Shaunna asked.

"I'm at the Four Seasons...room two oh two." Michelle's voice was flat, but still awash in settling grief.

"I just left the set. I'll be there in a few minutes."

"He's leaving me, Shaunna..." Michelle uttered the words mostly to see if she could admit it out loud. But saying them was not as difficult as hearing them, and as soon as the words came back to her, complete with phone compression, her world became blurry with fresh tears.

"I know. He just told me and I quit."

"You...You're leaving him?"

"Left him," Shaunna corrected. "In grand style, too. But he deserved to be left by somebody today."

Michelle was silent for a while. "I'll make it up to you."

Shaunna spent her last minute on the phone telling Michelle she would do no such thing and that the two of them would be more than fine without a slimy peckerwood like Kyle Petersen.

Michelle's cheeks were dry but red when she opened the door to her new, much smaller room. She had a large envelope in her hands with the name of an LA divorce attorney stamped on the return address.

"Was it someone else?" Michelle asked. "Please tell me if you know, Shaunna. I just need to understand why."

Shaunna walked in and embraced her friend. "I was completely surprised too. He wanted it that way. He told me so."

Michelle sat down on the bed. It was still a very nice room and more her style. "What did he say?"

Shaunna sat next to her. "He read your diary."

Michelle pursed her lips and nodded. "So, he's hitting first."

"It's true, then?" Shaunna was surprised, but proud of her. "You were going to go through with it?"

Michelle nodded her head slowly. "I suppose it was inevitable. Yes, I was headed there."

"Good." Shaunna folded her arms, the one-word response hanging in the air for a moment.

"I'm sorry for how he treated you, Shaunna."

"Please. I don't want to hear you apologize for him ever again."

Michelle swallowed and rubbed her temple.

Shaunna did what she did best. "I'm going to use your Wi-Fi to put out your statement right now. Even if someone spotted the court filing, you're going to have the first word."

The women crafted a simple but sincere press release acknowledging Michelle's sadness that this chapter in her life was closing, but confirming her belief that it was the best course of action. The implied "good riddance" was about as subtle as train graffiti, and Shaunna made sure every celebrity blogger got it via a mass e-mail that would make a presidential campaign manager jealous.

The rags would have Michelle's announcement that same day, and the respectable entertainment magazines would work it into their earliest weekly runs.

Michelle's phone began vibrating every few seconds, and she told Shaunna to go back to her hotel to get some rest.

"I will never forget what you've done for me."

"Yeah." Shaunna laughed. "Neither will he."

"Did you leave him anything at all?" Michelle giggled. Shaunna had shared the whole story with her, and they'd even found an online video of the publicist flinging designer garments toward the camera. She knew her actions might be difficult to explain to her other clients, but she decided to remain focused on putting out one fire at a time.

"Actually, he could've used any number of things in the trailer, like the bed sheets, or the shower curtain, but I doubt he's intelligent enough to consider anything that isn't already shaped like pants."

"He *is* a dimwit!" Michelle exclaimed as if she'd just struck gold. "He's so dense that light bends around him!"

Shaunna appreciated the joke on multiple levels.

She went back to her hotel, but not before she asked Michelle one last time to stay with the rest of the crew at the Radisson. Michelle shook her head vigorously and told her friend that she wasn't going to give Kyle the satisfaction of chasing her out of the building. She knew it was what he wanted. He would wish to avoid confrontation from here on out if his pattern of cowardice was any indication.

"God help that pickled wiener if I get him alone in the elevator!" Michelle declared. "And I'll only need enough time to get to my *new room* on the *second floor!*"

Shaunna was proud of Michelle, but still felt the need to insist that calm heads prevail for the sake of the success of the blockbuster summer film. Michelle didn't make any promises, but told Shaunna that she would call Nathan herself and give him the respect of being in the loop. Both women knew where the power was on-set, and it was about four inches taller and ten years younger than Kyle.

Shaunna sat in her room for all of six minutes before deciding to take a swim. After the day she'd had, it seemed like the perfect way to unwind.

Many hotel pools had too much lighting, creating a harsh and unwelcoming environment. Therefore, Shaunna was delighted to find a Tiki Room feel to the area. She even felt a little homesick for Disneyland.

The pool was lit from beneath, but the area was otherwise dark except for the faux ground torches. She was little more than a smooth silhouette as she sailed through the warm water.

Shaunna wore a bikini because to do otherwise would only make her appear outdated and old-fashioned, thereby attracting even more attention. She had the body for the delicate white material, even if she didn't think so.

The water felt wonderful, especially on her scalp. She let it sift through her hair as her ears dipped below the surface and the world became muffled and forgotten. She wasn't buoyant enough to stay afloat on her back without swimming, so she got a nice workout as she alternated from her back to her stomach.

She swam like a frog for a while too, with her bottom up in the air and her legs spreading and closing. That was when she heard soft footsteps.

"Oh, hello, Shaunna. Nice night for a swim?"

David was standing at the deep end of the pool and smiling down at her. His tousled boyish hair was already wet, as he'd obediently taken the suggested pre-swim shower.

She immediately noticed that he was wearing different shorts. Tighter shorts. Wetter shorts. And she noticed with a tinge of envy that there was a towel wrapped around his shoulders.

He was going to get in with her.

"Actually," she said with someone else's voice and, very likely someone else's brain, "it's one of the nicest swims I've ever had."

David strolled to one of many empty lounge chairs and set his towel down. In doing so, he revealed the previously covered portions of his torso, and Shaunna watched his tight back muscles stretch harmoniously. When he turned around, she made certain she wasn't obviously staring at him, but she also wasn't about to miss the big reveal.

She wasn't disappointed.

David was toned, but not muscle-bound. He possessed a California tan which the Texas sun had only encouraged, and his tiny belly button was situated between the bottom two bulges that made up the six-pack of his abdomen.

He didn't strut around like other guys who had bodies like his, and she didn't think she would catch him looking down at his own biceps. He just looked healthy and happy. She liked happy.

A sign warned swimmers against diving, so David gracefully jumped in, being careful not to splash his pool mate in the process. When he came back up and broke the water's surface, his wet bangs ended below his eyes. He was forced to spread them apart with his hands like the sheep dog in the *Looney Tunes* cartoons.

David swam closer and stood with her in the five-foot section. They both wished the water was a little lower.

"I'm glad we got a chance to meet like this," David admitted. He was making a very concerted effort not to stare at her perky and barely covered breasts.

Shaunna wanted to tell him that she'd been hoping for exactly the same thing, but instead, she laughed nervously. To find herself alone with him in low-lit water, standing so closely so quickly, was enough to make her quiver, despite the warm temperature.

"As opposed to how we met earlier today?" she finally said, adjusting a bikini strap that didn't need adjusting.

"About that," David said. He didn't know what to do with his hands. They felt like they weighed a hundred pounds. "It's just that, we hadn't met before, and I noticed that you already knew my name."

Shaunna tilted her head. "Out of everything you noticed me doing today, knowing your name was the most memorable?"

David laughed. "Oh…did something else happen? I didn't notice. I was too busy watching this chick throw all her boss's clothes to the wolves."

"Ex-boss," Shaunna gleefully corrected. "I quit."

"Obviously," David remarked with a straight face, but it took tremendous effort.

"And I know who you are because Nathan talks about you all the time." Shaunna poked her finger out and touched a bead of water that was teetering on the edge of his shoulder. It leapt onto her and seemed to dissolve like a bubble popping in slow motion.

"He does?" David was surprised to have the attention of the director. The two had a good history together, but really didn't know each other all that well.

"Oh yeah, you and Michelle." Feeling encouraged by David's acceptance of her physical contact, she reached out to touch another bead of water. This time, the droplet was located in the center of his chest, right over his heart. "He's deliriously happy to have cast you both. Says you two are going to make the picture really hum."

David didn't hear a word Shaunna said once she touched his chest. There was something about Nathan and Michelle humming something.

"I think he's right," Shaunna told him. "I think you two are doing a brilliant job so far, and the way he draws the very best from his actors, even Kyle, should look pretty good by the end of it." Her expression darkened at the mention of her former client's name.

David noticed and put his fingers around her arm, gripping her lightly. "What you did today was one of the bravest things I have ever seen."

With his hot hand on her arm, she felt all the anxiety in her body melt away. She realized her natural defenses were coming down, as if his very touch was a cure.

She opened her mouth to thank him, but just then, the gate to the pool area opened and through it stepped two uniformed police officers. As they approached the couple in the pool, their gun belts and shoes squeaked in different keys. It sounded like an off-tune orchestra.

David and Shaunna watched curiously as the two cops paused near the pool's edge, just a few inches away from them.

"Are you Shaunna Noble?" the male officer inquired, peering down.

"Yes," she answered, completely baffled by their interest in her.

"Exit the pool, please," the female officer commanded. "We're going to need you to get dressed and come with us, ma'am."

Chapter Seven

In California, Shaunna might have been hauled off to jail in her white bikini with the press in tow, but in Texas, there were still some remnants of southern hospitality intact. Additionally, the arresting officers received strict instructions from their sergeant about how to handle this particular case. With one of the most famous celebrities in the world directly involved in the incident, their supervisor made it crystal clear there was no room for error in Shaunna Noble's apprehension.

The sergeant also made sure a female officer was involved in the arrest, and she dutifully followed Shaunna into her hotel room, watching impassively as the young publicist undressed completely and put on jeans and a blouse.

"Can you please tell me what I'm being arrested for?" Shaunna tried to keep her tone respectful, but she wasn't likely to come across as antagonistic while trying to slide panties up her wet legs.

"Grand theft," the officer replied, with no hint of emotion.

"What?" Shaunna was shell-shocked. How could she be charged with a felony? She racked her brain for the answer.

The officer removed a small notebook with a cacophony of more creaks and squeaks from her uniform. The action reminded Shaunna vaguely of a bored waitress about to rattle off the dinner specials. The woman was both pretty and fit, and she read with an airy voice that carried a hint of Oklahoma.

"You have the right to remain silent. If you give up that right, anything you say can and will be used against you in a court of law. You have the right to an attorney. If you cannot afford one, one will be appointed to you by the state. Do you understand your rights?"

"Yes." Despite the fact that she was chilly from the pool, Shaunna broke into a sweat. It was one thing to hear this speech in any number of TV shows or movies. It was quite another when someone was reading it directly to you.

The officer turned a few pages of her notebook while Shaunna struggled to put her hair up with a tie.

"Did you take Kyle Petersen's clothes and throw them to a group of fans?"

Shaunna was confused. How could that possibly constitute a felony offense?

"Yes, but..."

"And did you also throw his watch?"

Shaunna hesitated to respond as the reality of what she'd done finally hit home.

"It's okay, honey. We have it on video...from three different angles."

Shaunna said nothing. She understood she needed to invoke her rights and contact an attorney, as soon as possible. She sat down on the bed and slipped on her shoes, biting her bottom lip in an effort to keep her mounting fear at bay.

"It was a— " the officer referred to her notebook once again "—Louis Moinet watch." She whistled. "Says here it was worth about eight hundred thousand dollars." She flipped her book shut. Her case was closed.

The officer indicated for Shaunna to turn around, frisked her to be on the safe side, and then handcuffed the mortified young woman.

"That's a pretty pricy fit you threw at your boyfriend."

Shaunna was revolted at the thought. "He was my boss." Her words dripped with disgust.

The officer chuckled as she opened the door and gently nudged Shaunna out into the hallway. "Doesn't make it right."

Shaunna was taken to the Harris County jail. The booking took three and a half hours, and then she was inspected and given a blue jumpsuit. She was told she would be allowed to make a phone call after she was completely processed. Additionally, she would not be allowed any visitors until the next day.

There was nothing Shaunna could do but wait...and think.

David swept down various hallways of the Radisson with his swim trunks dripping and his eyes looking as frazzled as his hair. He was going to return to his room, dress, and then find Nathan. But first, he had something more important to do.

"Excuse me, Officer...Ryan?" David found exactly what he'd hoped for—a male cop standing outside a room door, waiting. David looked from the man's badge to his eyes, hopeful the encounter would go quickly and smoothly.

Ryan's response was heavy and wooden. "Yes?"

"Will you please tell me where you're taking her?"

The cop rolled his eyes. "Jail."

David smiled, hoping to convey politeness. "I'm sorry. I'm not from here, sir..."

"Office-sir," the cop interrupted with a grin of his own.

David began again, this time with a more serious tone. "This is my first time in Houston, Officer Ryan, and I don't know where the jail is. Perhaps you could—"

"And what are you going to write it down with?" Ryan interrupted again. He waited for David to eyeball the gold pen he kept in his shirt pocket.

David was an excellent judge of character and understood the officer wasn't just a jerk, but a brute that could be very dangerous if provoked. He looked down at their feet. Officer Ryan's shoes were more like boots, and his own bare feet looked shockingly vulnerable by comparison.

"Perhaps," David began again, "you could provide me with your business card. I know all officers carry them and..."

"I'm out," he said slowly. "But I'm sure you can Google it." Officer Ryan arrogantly folded his arms.

"Good one, Officer." David laughed cheerfully, but backed up to the other side of the hallway, where he leaned casually against the wall.

"Why don't I just wait for your partner to come out? They've got to be nearly done by now. I'll ask for her card. Surely you both can't be out."

Officer Ryan huffed through his nose. He reminded David of a bull, so much so that he briefly imagined the man might even charge. David had just enough time to wish he'd brought a towel to use like a matador before voices from the other side of the door confirmed his earlier prediction.

With a quick and practiced motion, the officer unsnapped the same pocket the gold pen was poking out of. He plucked out a thick "Government Cream" card with Sam D. Ryan printed boldly above a myriad of phone numbers, fax numbers, and e-mail addresses.

"Thank you," David said as he took it on the fly. He knew an exit cue when he heard one, and he was just glad that he was walking and not running.

David went straight to his room and grabbed his phone. He called his director while he slid his shorts to the floor, where they would probably stay for the next two days.

Nathan cheerfully picked up on the first ring. "Hello, Mr. Quinn. What can I do for you?"

"Shaunna Noble's been arrested."

"When?" Nathan's response was curt.

"Just now. They're probably walking her out through the lobby as we speak."

David heard only the click of the line.

He dressed as fast as he could and ran down to the parking lot, where he met a red-faced Nathan.

"Did you talk to her?" David asked, eager for any news on Shaunna's state.

Nathan nodded solemnly. "Just before the police took her away. She asked me to call Michelle."

David gave Nathan a business card with a gray sheriff's star on it. "I assume they're taking her to the county jail. Avoid talking to this guy if possible."

"Keep it," Nathan told him. "You're coming with me."

Chapter Eight

Nathan began walking briskly toward a royal blue El Camino. "Have you seen *The Mexican*?" he asked as they climbed in.

"With Brad Pitt and Julia Roberts?" David asked, somewhat confused.

"And James Gandolfini and Gene Hackman and J.K. Simmons. Well, this is the El Camino Brad Pitt rented when he got to Mexico. The one they shot half the movie in!"

David appreciated Nathan's attempt to keep the conversation light. After all, any discussion the two men had about Shaunna would only have to be repeated when they reached Michelle at the Four Seasons.

"Really?" David looked up at the orange fringe in the windshield. He then quickly opened the glove box. "No gun?"

Nathan laughed. "I know. I should find a replica to keep in there."

"I like the idea of practical movie memorabilia," David replied.

"In that case, you'll have to come see the rest of my moderately iconic vehicles."

"You have more?" David was intrigued. The car from an under the radar movie like *The Mexican* could only belong in a truly eclectic collection. "How many moderately iconic vehicles do you have?"

"Four!" Nathan crowed. "I also have the London hackney cab from *28 Days Later* and the nineteen-twenty-seven Buick Tom Hanks drove in *Road to Perdition*."

"That's only three."

"I know. I saved my favorite for last. It's the yellow paneled Jeep wagon Richard Dreyfuss kicked Bill Murray out of in *What About Bob*?" He was indeed proud of his acquisition.

The list did not disappoint, and Nathan only became more interesting to David as they spent more time together. David remembered being there the day Rick Baker taught Nathan a makeup trick by using a little motor oil to help fake blood retain a nice reflective sheen, even when the hot set lights started baking the corn syrup away. Nathan had always been a sponge, and he certainly knew his way around a camera as well as a sound board.

Nathan also apparently knew his way around the streets of Houston. They turned onto a wide boulevard, and David could see the tall Four Seasons a few blocks away.

"I know a guy in my old apartment building who owns the delivery van that Michael J. Fox surfed on in *Teen Wolf*," David mentioned casually.

"No way! Does it run?"

"It did a few months ago."

"What would he take for it?"

"I don't know, but I bet you could get him to bite on any fair offer."

"I was thinking eight thousand, if it's got documentation and runs well."

"Um…I was thinking more like five," David revealed. "It smells like tacos and it leaks oil."

"How about six? And you take a grand as a finder's fee?"

David blinked. "I'll shoot off a text."

Nathan and David took the elevator to the top floor. It didn't occur to either of them that Michelle would have been the one to vacate the lavish suite.

When Kyle opened the door, revealing an intoxicated sneer and a star-struck fangirl wearing a bedazzled cowboy hat, David knew they'd made an error.

"Oh. Hello, Kyle," Nathan greeted the actor tolerably. "I'm looking for Michelle."

"She's down in room two oh two." Kyle never took his eyes off David. "And what's *he* doing here?"

Nathan looked at David and back again. "He's with me, Kyle."

"Did you know," Kyle began slowly, but built steam as he tattled on David, "that while I was naked...with soap stinging my eyes... and trying to wave this guy and that hippie costumer of yours over to *help me,* they just waved back like we were passing each other in hot air balloons?" Kyle's voice leapt up an octave as he waved his hands dramatically.

Nathan smirked.

"I'm sorry about that, Mr. Petersen," David offered. "We really couldn't tell *what* you were up to over there. If you wanted someone, why didn't you just call?"

"Because that bitch threw my phone in the toilet!" Kyle shouted.

David's heart pounded and his nostrils flared. His complete urge to immediately mash his fist into Kyle's Beverly Hills-constructed nose was overwhelming...intoxicating. Instead, he allowed himself a few glorious gory daydreams as Nathan sternly concluded the exchange.

"I want to see you and Michelle on-set, day after tomorrow, and believe me, if I'm not convinced that you two can work together *better* than what I have seen so far, I will fold this production and go shoot my superhero movie."

"I'll be there," Kyle grumbled, even as the door was closing.

Nathan and David got back into the elevator.

"I didn't know you were interested in superhero movies." David began a new conversation in an attempt to calm their frayed nerves.

"Usually I'm not," Nathan answered. "But I had this idea for a funky period piece about a super heroine in the seventies. It's like *Jackie Brown* meets *Kill Bill.*" Nathan had a slight shudder in his voice from the rush of adrenaline in his system.

"So, it's a kickass girl flick in the age of disco?" David nodded his head. "I like it. Oh! Does she have a fro? She *has* to have a fro!"

"Hell yeah, she has a fro!" Nathan said. "And her signature move is to backhand the bad guys with brass knuckles!"

David shook his head with delirium. Nathan was going to score big with a campy retro romp, as long as he went for the R rating.

"What's it called?" David was almost afraid to ask. Titles were key with retro cinema.

"*BITCH SLAP!*"

The elevator doors opened on the second floor, and David's laughter preceded them into the hallway.

Michelle came to the door with her hair as soft as rose petals and her eyes just as red. "Nathan. David. What a nice surprise."

"We're sorry to come over unannounced, Michelle, but I wanted to talk to you in person. We wanted to see you. Shaunna was arrested, and..."

"He didn't!" Michelle's mouth and eyes flew open. "After all she's done for him! I should go up there and put a stop to this right now!"

"No!" Both David and Nathan spoke quickly.

"Shaunna asked for you," Nathan told her. "She needs your help, and going through Kyle is not the answer."

Michelle sighed. "I can't call my lawyer. Kyle's already retained him."

"She's going to need a good one," David supplied.

Michelle groaned. "I shouldn't have written down my doubts about our marriage. He was too proud to be left by his wife, so he lashed out and blindsided me."

David leaned in to address Michelle. They'd already filmed a few scenes together and were on friendly terms, but rarely spoke about anything except the croissants on offer at craft services.

"It's not your fault," he said softly. "I've seen the way he treats you, and frankly, you're lucky to be getting away so easily."

She realized just how right David was. The main reason she'd been so scared to go through with the divorce was because she knew Kyle would be insulted and would make things as difficult as possible. But now, he'd taken the initiative and the whole mess would be resolved quickly, because that was how Kyle always got things done.

Especially in the bedroom.

"Do you know where they took her?" Michelle asked them, redirecting her thoughts to the problem at hand.

"We assume the county jail. I'm sure we could find it, but this late at night, it will be a waste of time," Nathan remarked.

"Shaunna will have to spend the night in jail at this point, even if we do find a lawyer," David reasoned. "Don't you see? That's why Kyle waited all day before he called the police. With Shaunna out of the way, he can say whatever he wants about Michelle, and there is no one to contradict him."

"Of course!" Michelle fumed. "Even when it's about Shaunna, it's still all about *him!*"

"Do you want me to ask the studio publicist to pitch in and give you a call?" Nathan paused. "In fact, I'm surprised they haven't called me yet."

"Not necessary," Michelle told him. "Shaunna released my statement around lunchtime. We already beat him to the punch."

"Good." David nodded. "That just leaves Shaunna."

Michelle regarded the young actor. She saw something earnest and refreshing in David's passion to help her friend.

"Wait!" Michelle was suddenly inspired. "I know another lawyer! He used to be friends with Kyle—roommates, actually—and they had a huge falling out. Kyle still talks about how much he hates that guy. Every time he wins a case and it's in the papers, it gets Kyle going. Based on how often that happens, I'd say this guy wins a lot of cases."

Within five minutes, Michelle was on the phone. "Thomas? This is Michelle Cooper. Can we talk? I need someone I can trust."

Thomas encouraged her to continue, so she told him about the events of the day, starting with how Kyle had blindsided her and ending with Shaunna's arrest. Then she was quiet for a long time while she listened to his multi-pronged reply.

"I just want her out of jail as soon possible," she said at last. "Can you get any information back to me tonight? We don't even know what she was arrested for…Okay…Yes, I'll wait for your call…Thank you so much. Goodbye."

Michelle brought her attention back to the two men, who were now standing on her balcony.

"Well, she's screwed if they got her on a felony, but I can't imagine how that could be. He's going to find out what's going on and get back to me. And since he's certified in both criminal and family law, he's also agreed to represent me in my divorce. He promised to be a very visible activist on my behalf."

David sighed. "Well, that's a relief."

"Just the same," she concluded, "I'd still like to find the jail and check on Shaunna to see if there's anything we can do for her."

"I'll drive!" Nathan volunteered immediately and turned toward the door.

When they reached the El Camino, David volunteered to ride in the back of the truck, but Michelle insisted that they could all squeeze in together on the bench seat. Always the gentleman, David sat in the middle so Michelle could have the shoulder harness seat belt.

At one busy intersection, where music thumped and hummed in the air and the sidewalks were crowded with people milling from one block to another, Michelle turned toward Nathan.

"What are you going to do about the movie?"

"I'll tell you what I told Kyle, because it's the absolute truth," Nathan stated mildly. "I want to meet with both of you on-set Wednesday morning at seven, and if I am not convinced that you can pull this off together, then I'll do the studio a big favor and only waste thirty million dollars, instead of a hundred million, by closing down the production."

Michelle turned toward the window and looked through her ghostly reflection. Too much had happened in just one day. Her husband had left her, her friend had been arrested for defending her, and now her director was warning her that the biggest film of her career might also be taken away. There was nothing she could do about Kyle; he was a lost cause. She was already on her way to help Shaunna, and Nathan was waiting for her response. She turned to him with resolve.

"I can do it." Michelle sounded brave and one hundred percent believable. "I won't let you down."

Nathan didn't respond right away. Instead, he focused on changing lanes. When he pulled up to the Harris County jail, he parked and turned his car off before meeting her anxious gaze.

"I believe you."

Chapter Nine

Shaunna was a strong person, but after one night of incarceration, she was already beginning to weaken. She was cold. She was angry. And she was alone.

Her blue jumpsuit irritated her skin, and her hair was a dry, frizzy mess as she sat in the common room of the Harris County jail, awaiting her first visitor. Even so, when the giant of a man who'd been retained as her attorney appeared, he thought she was quite fetching.

"My name is Thomas Harper," he stated simply while he took his place at the only other chair at the small scarred table. "I'm a friend of Michelle's and an…ex-friend of Kyle's."

"Really?"

"Yes. I knew Kyle when he was a broke prick." Thomas smirked. "Now he's a rich prick." He shuffled through some papers and plucked out what he looking for. "But I'm going to see what I can do about that."

"How, exactly?"

"I'm also representing Michelle in her divorce." The attorney grinned broadly and laced his fingers together on the table. Thomas was wearing a light gray suit with a pale blue shirt that was open at the collar. She noticed a flash of silver against his tanned chest.

Her spirits were lifted considerably. She quickly realized that a shared acrimony would go far in cementing their relationship. "You have to take good care of her."

"Michelle hardly needs anyone to take care of her." Thomas laughed. "You're sweet to worry under the circumstances, but let's talk about you, Miss Noble."

"Please. Call me Shaunna."

"Shaunna," he repeated gently.

The windows in the common room were high up on the walls, and the chain link fence surrounding them cast crisscrossing shadows on her hands. She looked down at them and breathed slowly.

"You *will* make bail tomorrow, Shaunna," Thomas told her confidently. "The DA might say you're a flight risk because you have financial means to travel and you don't live in Texas, but I'll argue that you're still attached to the movie filming here in Houston and that you intend to immediately go back to work for Michelle."

"How is she doing? Seriously."

"She and your other friends have all been by, but they don't allow visitors for inmates, which is probably a good thing. It tells me the police believe you're going to make bail as well."

"What other friends?" Shaunna was slightly confused by Thomas's revelation.

"Nathan McPherson and some other guy named David."

"David came?"

Thomas snorted, then he laughed at himself for snorting. "Yeah. I think he likes you. Michelle had to convince him to leave."

Shaunna was surprised by the show of David's unsolicited devotion, but she liked it. She liked it very much. She decided not to ask Thomas any other questions about David, although now she had many.

"How long have you been in town?"

"I flew in early this morning."

"Will I have to stay in Texas until there's a trial?" She leaned back in her chair, a shadow slashing across her features.

Thomas shook his head. "I doubt it, but don't worry about any of that right now. As soon as your father arrives—"

"Gus is coming here?" Shaunna's mortification was evident.

Thomas nodded. "When I got into town, Michelle informed me that Gus would be in Texas by tonight."

The attorney watched Shaunna as she slowly lowered her head to the table.

Chapter Ten

By Tuesday evening, Kyle Petersen was feeling in firm control of the world around him.

His agent quickly replaced Shaunna with a new publicist, who had flown in from California first thing that morning. When she arrived, Kyle was pleased to see that the woman was the complete opposite of his former employee. Heather Lentz was tall and blond and projected a tough, albeit professional exterior. Shaunna, by comparison, had a natural girl-next-door approach.

Kyle quickly put her to work and found their lack of personal history suited his needs perfectly. Perhaps in time, he could expand their "relationship," but first, he had an image to protect and a career or two to destroy.

Kyle wanted to make sure the world knew he'd been ripped off by a former employee and that his soon-to-be-ex-wife had chosen to keep the thief in her employ.

Between the collapse of the Petersen/Cooper marriage and the resulting arrest of the publicist who had represented them both, Kyle, Michelle, and Shaunna were the talk of every entertainment and news program on television and radio. They were even trending on Twitter. The day went by in a blur, and Kyle had Heather working well past the dinner hour.

When his stomach growled loudly, he suddenly realized that without Shaunna or Michelle around to attend to his basic needs, he'd neglected to eat a decent meal in nearly two days. It was time to teach his new employee the ropes.

"Heather, let's put all this on hold for a little while. I need some dinner. You?"

Heather paused typing at her laptop and smiled widely, welcoming the opportunity for a break. "Actually, yes. Dinner sounds great. What did you have in mind?"

"I want some good ole Texas BBQ. There's this one restaurant, Hickory Hollow. I've been meaning to try it since I got down here."

"That sounds good. Should I make a reservation? Ask for a private section?"

He dismissed her suggestions with a wave of his hand. "No. I don't want to be seen out on the town tonight. You can call in an order and then go pick it up."

"All right. What do you want?"

Kyle gave Heather his request without bothering to check out a menu from the restaurant. As she located the number and placed their order, he settled himself on the sofa in the living room, covering his eyes with an arm. Within moments, he was snoring.

Heather organized her thoughts and then prepared to leave the suite. It occurred to her on the way out the door that he hadn't even offered to pay for the meal.

As she waited for the elevator, she checked the contents of her purse to confirm that her wallet was there. The doors opened and she stepped in. As they closed, she sighed heavily.

Kyle became aware of the fact that although he hadn't been asleep long, he'd been sleeping well. He was immediately angered when the knocking on the front door of his suite brought him back to consciousness.

"Goddammit!" he swore with a growl and hurled a sofa pillow to the floor as he lifted himself to a standing position. In no hurry to answer the door, he stretched and rolled his head in a circle.

Heather must have forgotten to take her key or, even worse, had her arms so full of takeout food that she couldn't be bothered to set it down to retrieve her key.

Kyle decided to wait a few more seconds, and much to his dismay, the knock came again, this time louder.

"For fuck's sake!" he exclaimed at the door as he stomped over to it.

He didn't bother to look through the peephole before he flung it open. He was ready to unload on Heather for being so worthless, but the words caught in his throat when he registered that his new publicist wasn't the source of the knocking.

He found himself holding his breath as his visitor blinked back at the stymied actor.

Gus Noble wasn't a big man. Actually, he was a bit on the short side, with unruly hair. Although he usually dressed casually, he stood in front of Kyle wearing dark trousers, a white shirt, and a black blazer. His mustache was something Sam Elliot would envy, but it didn't hide the thin line of his lips.

"Kyle." Gus spoke in a low, controlled voice, but there was no mistaking the anger in eyes so dark brown that they looked like ink wells.

The actor gripped the doorknob tightly.

When Gus ascertained that a return greeting was not forthcoming, he raised his eyebrows and tilted his head to peek into the suite.

"I've just flown in from LA." Gus locked his steel gaze back to the box office star. "The least you can do is to invite me inside for a drink."

Kyle nodded and mutely stepped aside to allow the producer's entrance before slowly closing the door.

Gus took a seat on the caramel leather sofa in the living room of Kyle's penthouse and waited for his drink. He was watching his obliging host closely.

Gus always drank scotch. Kyle brought him tequila.

"Look, Mr. Noble." Kyle remained standing as he began his monologue. "I hope you didn't come all this way to threaten me into dropping the charges against Shaunna."

"Actually," Gus said, already nodding his head, "I was hoping to reason with you. But I'm not above threats. Let's just see how reasonable you can be first. Now, tell me. What happened?"

"She humiliated me, and she threw away my Louis Moinet timepiece!" Kyle roared.

Gus sighed and took a large drink of his tequila before setting the glass loudly on the coffee table. He then pulled from his wrist a stainless steel watch and set it down just as loudly next to the glass.

"There. Now you have another watch." Gus picked his glass back up and drank while he watched Kyle's face turn red.

"She's been booked for felony grand theft." The smirk that crept up Kyle's face moved like a snake in a tree. "You'll have to do a lot better than that."

"Are you saying you'll cooperate with the investigation if I reimburse you? How much?" Gus reached into his coat pocket and brought out his checkbook and a pen.

"No," Kyle refused. "You aren't buying her out of this."

"You haven't caught up with me yet, Kyle, and that's okay. But I'm tired, so let's get the money part over with." He opened the checkbook and began to write. "Eight hundred thousand and change was what I heard on the news. Jesus, Kyle…how much do you pay for your coffee? Fifty grand? Let's just make it an even eight hundred thousand, for depreciation's sake. Either way, I hope you're prepared to go to court."

"What do you mean?" Kyle was puzzled.

Gus looked up from the task at hand and pointed his pen in Kyle's direction. "In cases like this, the DA will make the final decision about whether to proceed with a criminal trial, even if you choose not to pursue a civil case. Thanks to your knee-jerk reaction to Shaunna's knee-jerk reaction, this may all go on for a year or more, no matter what you do. But I'd like to think that without your support, the DA will also drop the matter."

Gus returned to signing his name. He then separated the check from his book and set it on the table. After he carefully placed everything back into his jacket, he looked at Kyle again. The producer expected a response, and the performer took his cue.

"And if I don't accept?"

Gus closed his eyes and shook his head. "Have you given any thought to what the media will be showing on TV and on the Internet and in every major entertainment magazine over and over and over again while they wait for developing news about the case?"

He waited for only the briefest moment before answering his own question.

"Your two-pixel peter, that's what. You think all the attention will solely be on her, Kyle? Perhaps. But I'm pretty sure you just shined a blockbuster spotlight on your little…problem."

Gus finished the rest of his drink in a single gulp and handed his glass back to Kyle. "And if you can live with that, then great. But I can also guarantee that you just shot your last PI movie unless things start going my way…starting with a scotch."

Kyle wordlessly retreated to the mini bar under Gus's watchful eye and retrieved the scotch. He took the time to gather his frazzled nerves, and when he returned to the sofa, he was once again wearing his famous smirk.

"You aren't producing my franchise, and you're not producing *Sling Shot*. Here's your drink, but that's all you're getting from me tonight."

"It's idiotic of you to think I don't need to be producing a film to influence its course." Gus took a small sip, and beads of scotch clung to his mustache. "And sit down…You're not intimidating anyone."

Kyle plopped in his chair.

"I've known your franchise's bosses since they were in film school. Who do you think gave them their first green light?"

Realization set in, and Kyle felt his blood rapidly cooling. He tried to wave off his increasing anxiety, unwilling to admit that he was losing his grip on the entire situation.

"So what? They aren't going to replace their leading man in a successful blockbuster series. They would sink themselves, and they aren't going to do that for anyone. Not even you."

Gus sighed again in mild annoyance. "How many actors have played James Bond?" he asked calmly. "Or Dr. Who? Or Batman? Shit, Kyle, they've already had four different guys play Danny Zuko in the stage production of *Grease*. Look…you've been at this for what? Five years now? Hell, you're already overdue to be replaced. All I'd have to do is suggest it, and I can get those two to cast Matt Damon to replace you."

"What do you want?" Kyle's voice was small, like a child being forced to apologize.

"You know what I want." Gus pushed the check across the table, then stood up. "You deserve to be compensated, and now you are. All the harm done from now on will be self-inflicted."

Gus let himself out of the suite without another word.

Chapter Eleven

Early Wednesday morning, Michelle walked over to the craft services trailer. It always served as the unofficial meeting place on movie sets, and it was where she saw Kyle and Nathan sitting at a table together.

She stopped and watched them.

They were talking, but not smiling.

It was the first time she'd seen Kyle since he had her served with divorce papers. She was not as angry as she thought she would be, but she was hurt. In fact, she worried that every step closer she took would only increase her despair.

Although she wasn't hungry, Michelle grabbed her requested usual for breakfast—a croissant she dipped in honey and a small cup of yogurt—then walked over to join them. She hoped the meal would provide a sense of normalcy and occupy her anxious hands while they spoke.

"Good morning," Nathan said evenly. Michelle knew her director didn't want to be too light about this meeting. He was young and could appear very childlike to others. She understood that his enthusiasm had a tendency to undermine his authority, and he clearly wasn't going to let that happen today.

"I'm very sorry that the two of you have lost your marriage," Nathan continued earnestly. "And I know that you will have your good days and your bad, but how much do the two of you want to finish this movie together? And please, be honest." He looked to Kyle first as he took a bite of his Pop-Tart.

"I think it's a fine picture," he began. "And I will gladly extend to Michelle all my courtesy as an actor." Kyle then looked at his estranged wife. "We talked about how much fun you would have in this role, and you haven't even gotten a chance to stretch yet. I think you need this, honey, and I want to help you grow."

Nathan paused chewing his breakfast and stared blankly at Kyle. Then he looked at Michelle, did a double take back to Kyle, and then looked at Michelle again.

Hearing Kyle call her "honey" made her feel like spiders were scaling her back. She looked down at her breakfast and wondered if he had soured her favorite meal forever.

"I can play nice if you can, Kyle, but I suggest we go no further with the litigation until after we wrap in order to avoid…fresh tension." Michelle held his gaze. Until that moment, she never realized how ugly he was.

Nathan nodded his head.

Kyle was frowning. He suspected a trap. A Michelle-was-going-to-clean-out-their-house-in-the-meantime kind of trap. He shook his head. "We can keep our private affairs private. I see no reason to prolong the inevitable."

"Look," Nathan interjected, "with all due respect, this isn't about your private affairs. It's about the movie. I've already told the studio that you both assured me you could work well together, and you have now each agreed to do just that. Is it going to be this easy? Are there no exceptions, or rules, or scenes to cut? Let's dissect this now and make sure we all know what we're getting back into."

"I'd rather not do the shower scene anymore," Michelle confessed.

"What?" Kyle shouted. "That's a horrible idea! It's one of the best scenes in the movie!"

They both looked at Nathan to make the final decision.

He puckered his lips and thought about it for a brief moment before turning to Michelle. "Kyle's right. It's a pivotal scene," Nathan told her solemnly before adding with a wink, "so, you'll just have to do it alone."

"What?" Kyle shouted again.

"I'm sorry," Nathan told him. "To be honest, I've wanted it that way for a while now. This clinches it."

Kyle pouted. He really wanted to have himself on film fondling his soon-to-be-ex-wife.

"Well then," he huffed. "Who is she supposed to deliver her lines to if I'm not there?"

"That's just it," Nathan explained. "She thinks you're there, on the other side of the glass, but you aren't. She gets to say the lines, but your character never hears them, and it will take the form of an omen that the audience will carry with them to space."

"Oh, that's brilliant!" Michelle was ecstatic. It was the first time since sitting down that she felt she could actually go through with it all.

"Fine," Kyle finally said, as if they were waiting for his approval. "But I have a condition of my own."

Kyle told them his one demand, which Nathan outright refused.

"It's childish and petty, and I won't allow you to— "

"It's my decision, really," Michelle interrupted Nathan. She was accurate in that Kyle's terms didn't technically involve the movie and therefore didn't require Nathan's consent.

"Well?" Kyle pressed. "Do we have a deal?"

Michelle's eyes were dry and steady, but she was furious at his cheap move. "Fine."

"I won't enforce it," Nathan added. "Do you both hear me? You can agree to this, but it's still my set and I won't contribute."

Kyle looked pointedly at Michelle.

"Don't worry," she said. "You'll get your wish, Kyle. You always do."

When Thomas returned to the jail, he brought an outfit Michelle had picked out for Shaunna's arraignment hearing.

"You like this get-up, then?" Thomas asked, his white teeth accenting his own smile.

"Michelle does," Shaunna answered. "She says it shows off my neck and shoulders."

"Only if you put your hair up," Thomas suggested.

Shaunna raised her eyebrows. "Watch this." She reached into the pocket of the black pants he was holding out for her and pulled out a hair tie.

Thomas was impressed.

"I always leave one in these pants, but I'll bet Michelle checked anyway." Shaunna's brow furrowed in confusion. "Michelle didn't send any shoes?" she asked the attorney.

Thomas shrugged in defeat and rubbed the back of his neck as he answered. "She did. But the jail has declared that women's high heels are a lethal weapon. I had to lock them up in the trunk of my car. Sorry."

Thomas remained in the common room while Shaunna was escorted back to her cell to change clothes. He hummed *Callin' Baton Rouge* and played drums on the table with his strong fingers. He had great rhythm, but possessed a singing voice that sounded like someone being beaten with a sack of cats.

When Shaunna returned, he nodded his head appreciatively, but not gratuitously. "You look very nice. How do you feel?"

"Tired."

"Are you nervous?"

She shrugged her shoulders. "Not really. I guess I believe you when you say that you can get me out of here today."

"I can." He stood up. "Let's get to it."

Shaunna was led to the nearby courthouse through a dimly lit and refreshingly cool tunnel that ran beneath the parking lot. She kept her eyes cast down at her jailhouse slippers and allowed herself to be escorted up three flights of stairs and into a brightly lit, high-ceilinged courtroom as large as a church's sanctuary.

She saw her father right away. He was facing the front of the courtroom, but it was him all right, no doubt about it.

Alix was there also, as were Michelle and Nathan. And there on the aisle, looking directly at her with wondrous eyes, was David.

He waved at her in greeting. Shaunna nearly waved back, but she caught herself and nodded a gracious acknowledgment instead. His cheeks grew rosy, and she understood that David suddenly remembered the formal and imposing setting. It wasn't the right time or place for flirting.

Shaunna stole another glance in her father's direction as she passed him to take her seat at the defendant's table. Gus's face was serious, but his daughter had long known his eyes were the key to reading his emotional state, and she saw that they were soft and warm. She had his support, and that, more than anything else, calmed her nerves as Thomas organized his papers and prepared for the hearing to commence.

Shaunna turned to face the empty judge's bench, and her gaze landed on the gavel resting there.

Very soon, its noise would punctuate the course of her future.

When Thomas was finished sorting his notes, he leaned in toward Shaunna and whispered in her ear. "Just be polite. Answer the judge's questions honestly but quickly, and let me take care of the rest. Your part will be very textbook, very black and white. You don't need to worry about anything else. All right?"

Shaunna nodded once and said nothing.

Suddenly, there was a buzzing of activity from the gallery behind them. Shaunna was well familiar with the annoying, swarming noise of the press following her former client's movements, so she kept her focus on the gavel.

Kyle Petersen strode gracefully down the aisle as though he were in the middle of filming a scene. His head was held high, and he was impeccably dressed for the occasion in an expensive, eye-catching suit. His face was serene and betrayed no emotion as he took in the sight of his soon-to-be-ex-wife, his current director, his former publicist, and her father.

Gus Noble glanced casually at the actor and then looked away.

As Kyle was taking his seat in the front row, directly behind the DA's table, Thomas turned slowly in his chair and raised his eyes to his former friend. The movement caught the movie star's attention, and when he made eye contact with Shaunna's attorney, he sneered and uttered a choice expletive or four.

Satisfied with the greeting, Thomas grinned and turned away from the actor, chuckling to himself.

Kyle angrily crossed his arms and glared at the attorney's back.

Michelle watched Kyle's reaction carefully and began clenching her hands in worry. If she had thought her idea through, she never would've made the phone call which invited that poisoned friendship and bad blood into Shaunna's tenuous situation.

"All rise."

The bailiff's booming voice startled Shaunna, and she gave him her immediate attention. Right on cue, a door at the front of the courtroom opened and an even beefier, middle-aged man with a full head of black hair and wearing a black robe emerged to take his seat behind the bench.

"Judge Phillip Barnes presiding over bail hearings seventeen-ten through seventeen-sixteen." The bailiff spoke with an experienced and even tone. "This is case number one-seven-one-zero, Your Honor—the State of Texas versus Shaunna Irene Noble."

Only the bailiff's last few words, spoken directly to the judge, indicated that the matter at hand was anything but routine. "This is the one they've been waiting for."

"So it is," Judge Barnes agreed as his emotionless dark brown eyes looked directly at Shaunna.

"You may be seated," the bailiff instructed as Judge Barnes turned his attention to the case file in front of him.

Everyone complied and settled into an anticipatory silence.

A tall woman with flowing strawberry blond hair was occupying the table next to Shaunna's. Her striking looks were accented by her crisp, black Ann Taylor skirt suit. Thomas Harper studiously looked her over as they stood up and sat back down.

Thomas nudged Shaunna and whispered in her ear. "That's Valerie Manchester, Harris County District Attorney."

Shaunna turned to Thomas, her eyes wide. She understood perfectly that the DA's attendance at a simple bail hearing was not a good sign for her. Manchester was as cool as an iceberg, and just as substantial, in Shaunna's opinion.

"So, this is the case of the girl who allegedly threw the movie star's stuff away," Judge Barnes declared to the quiet onlookers.

Thomas stood up quickly. "Yes, Your Honor. I'm representing Miss Noble. Thomas Harper, LLM."

"Oh." Judge Barnes sat back and crossed his arms. "A Master of Laws. Well, are we going to see some fancy tongue work from you today?"

"Not with my clothes on, Your Honor," Thomas quipped.

Although a few chuckled, most of those assembled in the gallery sat in surprised silence while the district attorney rolled her eyes. Judge Barnes nearly suppressed a smile.

"And how is it that a California lawyer is practicing law in the Lone Star State, Mr. Harper?"

"I'm here *pro hac vice*, Your Honor," Thomas added. "I believe the court processed the paperwork yesterday."

Judge Barnes was not visibly impressed as he turned his focus toward the DA. When his eyes met her iridescent blue ones, his face softened.

"Good afternoon, Ms. Manchester. You know, I don't believe I've ever seen so many sparkling personalities in my courtroom at once." When the DA merely nodded at his playful comment, Judge Barnes shifted gears. The sound of his creaking chair was audible as he leaned forward to examine the paperwork resting in front of him. The *pro hac vice* form was indeed included.

"I see here that the DA's office has charged—" the judge peered once again at Shaunna "—Miss Noble with Disturbing the Peace, Destruction of Property, and First Degree Grand Theft. Is that correct?"

"Yes, Your Honor," Manchester confirmed simply, her posture radiant with confidence.

"How does your client plead, Mr. Harper LLM?"

"Not guilty, Your Honor," Thomas answered.

The judge turned once again to the DA. "Do you have anything to add before I assign bail, Ms. Manchester?"

Valerie stood up. "She's a wealthy Hollywood insider, Your Honor, with the financial means to travel anywhere in the world. She must be considered a flight risk, and I respectfully request that bail be denied."

The audience immediately began to stir and mumble their disapproval, and Thomas capitalized on the brewing emotion in the gallery.

"Are you insane?" Thomas asked her directly.

Valerie turned her head sharply toward him. Her eyes flashed with anger, but she was interrupted before she could respond in kind.

"Order!" Judge Barnes commanded as he simultaneously struck his gavel on the wooden bench.

He deliberately waited until the spectators were calm before getting the proceedings back on track.

"Your client does have the means," Judge Barnes corrected Thomas, "and she resides in a very congested state over a thousand miles away from this courthouse. It would be very easy for her to disappear."

Thomas took a moment to grin. He then straightened his vest. "Miss Noble may be able to fly back home to California. In fact, I quite expect she will if a trial date is set several months from now. But what we are determining here is whether or not she'll return to Houston for any and all future proceedings, and I can guarantee you that she will."

"How can you do that?" Judge Barnes asked.

"Your Honor, my client wants to resolve this matter and cooperate fully with the court. Precedence in this county demonstrates it's commonplace to extend this kind of latitude toward a defendant charged with a first-time offense. Yet, that is inconsequential compared to the fact that Miss Noble is already prepared to discuss terms of a settlement with the DA's office. Unfortunately, they seem to have misplaced my number."

"We are not interested in any deals," Valerie barked. "Besides, she'd probably just throw anything we had to offer her to the gallery."

The retort produced a chuckle or two inside the courtroom, but Thomas was not deterred.

"Your Honor, my client has responsibilities here in Houston for the next two months. She isn't even going to be outside of the city limits until then. Also, I must stress once again that Miss Noble has no prior convictions, arrests, or even speeding tickets. In her two days in the Harris County jail, she was a model prisoner, and she has a community service record back home that would make a nun feel like a slacker."

Judge Barnes chewed on his thoughts before turning back to the DA. "What are the State's intentions?"

Valerie answered with a tone of strong determination. "She came here to flaunt the law, Your Honor. I want to see that she remains to sample the consequences. However, I'll only be asking for a sentence of five years, as well as full restitution and the usual fines."

The judge was nodding his head. He looked at Shaunna, and the fear on her face made up his mind for him.

"Bail is denied." Judge Barnes lifted up his gavel to the sound of more shocked gasps, but before he could bring it down with a decisive thud, Thomas spoke up.

"Your Honor, my client changes her plea to guilty."

CHAPTER TWELVE

The judge drew a deep breath before setting his gavel down gently on the bench. He laced his fingers together as he attempted to analyze the motive for Harper's tactic.

Under the table, Thomas grasped Shaunna's hand and squeezed. The gesture said *trust me,* and despite the fact that she could suddenly feel her heartbeat in her small jailhouse slippers, she did.

"My client requests the opportunity to apologize to Mr. Petersen and the court before sentencing," he stated.

Judge Barnes looked at Shaunna. "Please rise."

Shaunna stood on shaky legs. David had been watching her closely and actually twitched with the need to steady and comfort her.

"Do you understand what it means to change your plea to guilty?"

Shaunna nodded, and although she was terrified, she was also somewhat relieved. She had committed the act, and everyone with access to a television or the Internet knew she'd done it. How was she supposed to walk back into the courtroom and sit through a trial that would include video proof of her actions?

"Speak up, Miss Noble. We need your answer for the record." The judge spoke with an irritated tone.

"Yes, Your Honor. I understand."

"Tell me in your own words what you did," Judge Barnes requested.

Shaunna looked briefly at Thomas, who nodded his encouragement.

"I was angry at Mr. Petersen, so I threw his belongings to the crowd gathered on the movie set while he was inside his trailer, taking a shower. I didn't realize his watch was worth so much money, and I am deeply sorry for losing my temper and reacting the way I did. I should have just quit my job as his publicist and left it at that, but the argument we had hurt me, and I wanted to punish him. So, I deserve to be punished in return." Shaunna looked the judge in the eye the entire time she spoke, but she began to cry near the end of her statement as exhaustion and remorse began to break through the surface.

A deep and tense silence took hold of the audience as they waited for the judge's decision.

"That, Miss Noble, was an honest confession," Judge Barnes reassured the defendant. "And believe me, I don't hear many." He looked toward the gallery. "Kyle Petersen, step forward please," he ordered.

Kyle made his way to the aisle and stood between the two tables, placing himself in the center of the courtroom.

"Are you prepared to testify at what has just become a sentencing hearing?"

"No, sir."

"No?" The judge was visibly annoyed. "Well, enlighten me, Mr. Petersen. How much preparation time do you need to testify?"

"I don't need any time," he answered plainly. "I no longer wish to pursue the matter."

Judge Barnes looked perturbed. "Why not?"

"I've been fairly compensated for the items I lost..." He saw the judge sit up straight and added quickly, "By an outside party, Your Honor. I've had no contact with Shaunna or her...attorney. Anyway, given our history together, I would prefer it if the issue was closed." Kyle spoke with conviction, but appeared uncomfortable.

Shaunna was momentarily dazed by Kyle's reversal, and she couldn't stop herself from turning her head in his direction. Kyle was paying no attention to her or to anyone else in the gallery. He was fully concentrating his gaze on the judge, which could only mean he was acting and trying to draw the all-important audience of one into his performance.

Shaunna risked a roving glance in her father's direction, and his answering wink confirmed her suspicions. She quickly looked away and lowered her head before shaking it slightly. Gus had gotten to her former boss, and judging by Kyle's diligence in staying in character, Gus had hit the actor where it hurt most.

Judge Barnes inhaled loudly through his nose and just as loudly back out again. He turned toward the DA and spoke very deliberately. "Ms. Manchester, your star witness has decided to drop his civil interests in this case. Does the State wish to do the same?"

The district attorney was firm in her conviction. "Miss Noble is guilty, Your Honor. She said so herself."

"So she did."

He rendered his final decision with an autocratic flourish worthy of his own Oscar. "Shaunna Noble, you are hereby ordered to pay ten thousand dollars to the court upon your release from the Harris County jail this afternoon. Time served." The gavel came down quickly, and Judge Phillip Barnes was gone from the bench before the bailiff could instruct them all to stand up again.

Valerie Manchester frowned and gathered her papers together. She snapped her briefcase shut with an annoyed embellishment and turned on her high heel to escape the courtroom.

Shaunna slumped down into her seat and wept. She hated feeling grateful to Kyle, but in that moment, she truly was. She also felt grateful to Michelle and Nathan and Thomas, but when she opened her eyes, it was David she was looking for. When she spotted him, she was surprised to find he was emotional as well. The sentiment touched her in a way she wasn't expecting.

David was already staring at Shaunna, his eyes filled with relief. She moved toward him, trying not to rush. There was just something comforting in his eyes, something she needed.

"I'm sorry you've been mixed up in this, David. I know what you must think of me."

David laughed to keep from blushing. "I doubt that very much, Shaunna."

It was all they were able to say to one another before Gus swept in and hugged his daughter. Before he was willing to release her from their embrace, Nathan and Alix appeared at their sides, as did Michelle and Thomas.

Kyle had slipped out quietly, undetected by the celebrating friends.

"I'm going to stay with Shaunna while they process her release," Thomas informed the group. "It'll only take about fifteen minutes, if you all want to wait downstairs for us."

They all chose to wait, and Shaunna was taken back to the jail, where her clothes, pocketbook, and hotel key card were all returned.

"How did you know the plea change would work?" Shaunna asked Thomas as they were walking through the security barriers on their way out for good.

"Do you know what an even better question is?" he asked. "How did I know that the judge and the DA were sleeping together?"

"What?" Shaunna was shocked and stopped in her tracks.

"It was going to be my ace in the hole. There were no less than six nationally known television reporters in that room, staring right back at Barnes. If he were to invite such a high-profile celebrity media circus into his life, just how long do you suppose it would take for the press to discover and expose his affair with Ms. Manchester to his wife and to the public at large?"

"But how did you know?"

"I wish I could tell you I did something clever and covert, but the truth is, I bought a pretty intern a cup of coffee, and it turned out that she was the office gossip."

Shaunna looked skeptical. "So let me get this straight. You based my whole defense on hearsay?"

"Partly," he admitted. "But didn't you think it was a little odd that the district attorney was prosecuting a simple bail hearing?"

"Yes, but I assumed it was because this was a media-heavy case."

Thomas shook his head. "That's exactly why the DA would minimize her direct involvement in cases like these. Because she is an elected official. If things don't go her way at the most basic level, it can flush her whole career down the toilet. The only logical reason for her to have been in that courtroom today was because she felt her presence would influence the judge's decision. So I began watching them."

Shaunna's eyes lit up with recognition. "So, she figured that he would slam dunk this case for her and she would get on TV, making an example of a Hollywood insider."

Thomas nodded with enthusiasm. "But he backpedaled when I changed your plea and Kyle publicly stated that he would no longer cooperate with the State's case."

"How did you know Kyle would change his mind?"

"Honestly, I didn't, but your dad seemed confident enough for the both of us."

Shaunna entered the courthouse lobby with Thomas and the crowd began to stir. Some of those gathered outside could see her through the small windows, and word spread fast. Batteries were checked, microphones were tapped, and satellite feeds were wide open.

Gus approached Shaunna and took her hand. "Don't worry. We're going to use the back door."

"It's okay, Dad. They'll leave once Kyle's gone."

"No, they won't." He led her through a door and down a hallway, where Nathan, Michelle, Alix, and David were already waiting. Thomas brought up the rear.

"How are you feeling?" Nathan asked.

"I want a shower and a sandwich," she replied. Shaunna then snuck a peek at David, who was watching her and smiled when their eyes met. She also wanted a continuation of their swim, but she wasn't about to voice that openly in front of the group.

When everyone reached the door with a silver push bar across its middle, Gus stopped them.

"We're going to take the limo to the right. It's about thirty yards away, but if they're out there too, it's going to get pretty hairy. Just keep moving and don't talk to them."

"What's the big deal?" Shaunna asked.

"You are," he answered and opened the door.

The camera flashes were as loud as they were bright. She reached for her father's hand as he instinctively held it out behind him. The intrusive push of the press quickly surrounded them all.

The media mob was on the verge of stampeding Shaunna. The chorus of inquisition grew louder in volume as the precious seconds of their contact with her waned. As soon as everyone was inside the limo and the car door slammed shut, Gus issued a short command to the driver.

"Go, Benny."

As the limo smartly and expertly maneuvered past the throng of reporters, the group inside the car finally relaxed.

Chapter Thirteen

Gus invited David to join him and his daughter for dinner that night. Shaunna was beyond surprised at the inclusion of an additional guest, mostly because she was certain her father would want to spend the meal rebuking her for her foolish actions.

He did. And apparently he wanted a witness.

David sat mute as Gus addressed his daughter with love in his eyes and a twitch in his mustache. His words spilled out slowly.

"You know better than anyone that the hardest thing for people to forget is what they see with their own eyes." He appeared thoughtful as he chewed on his New York strip steak. "You're worried about what people will think of Michelle, but it's *you* they're all talking about." He put his napkin down on the table. "And it's not good."

Gus looked over at David, who quickly looked down. He then looked back at Shaunna, who was reluctantly meeting his fatherly gaze. "Your actions reflect on me as you know, but I'm not even worried about that." He lowered his voice, which wasn't very loud to begin with. "You could lose a lot of clients over this."

Shaunna swallowed, and Gus responded, "You already have."

Shaunna felt the weight of David's gaze as she nodded her head slowly. When she'd turned her iPhone back on after being released from jail, there'd been two messages canceling contracts, along with several requests from media outlets offering payment for her first interview.

"Are you going to stay in this line of work?" Gus's question was unexpected, but not as unexpected as what Shaunna heard herself say.

"I don't know."

"How are you set up?"

"I'm good, Pop. I could spend the rest of my days on Tom Sawyer's Island and still have enough left over to buy shoes every weekend."

Gus chuckled and then turned serious once again.

"I should know better than to even ask, but I will anyhow. Will you be coming back to LA with me?"

"No. Michelle is my friend and I'll be damned if I leave her here to deal with Kyle all by herself. I can work from Houston just as easily as I can work from home. I'm not going anywhere until she does."

Shaunna meant every word, and Gus acquiesced with a short nod. "Well, let's just get past this, and I'll tell anyone who asks that you were on drugs or something."

"Dad!" Her laughter was infectious and released the tension hovering over the table.

David laughed as well. It felt good to see Shaunna having fun and eating a substantial meal. Like her father, she'd ordered the New York strip steak. David had a Mandarin chicken salad, which was served in a bowl so large that at first he thought it was an upside down football helmet. Things really were bigger in Texas.

"So, tell me—" Gus put his hand on the back of David's chair "—how badly does it itch to have that zombie makeup all over your face?"

Shaunna's posture slouched instantly in relaxation, pleasantly surprised by the sudden change in topic.

"It's not the face that's the challenge," David answered. "It's the hands." He held up his own, as if Gus had pulled a gun on him.

"It itches your hands like crazy and you can't touch…anything." David looked down quickly at his lap, and Gus understood immediately.

"What did you do?" he asked the young man.

David turned to Shaunna and smiled. "We did what we had to do. And believe me, we all ended up with a bad case of zombie dick." He immediately regretted the revelation, not wishing to fill her mind with images of a diseased organ.

"It's not like there's a guy on-set who would hold it for you," Gus observed.

"I bet you could get a grip to do it," Shaunna offered as she forked a small dab of mashed potatoes into her wide grin.

Both men laughed, and the three of them decided to order another round of drinks.

Gus told them he was developing a few television shows and felt that at least one of them would spark into a huge success.

"Have you done any TV?" Gus asked David.

David shook his head. "No television, actually."

"Hmm, you'd be great on the small screen. More close-ups," Gus said gruffly.

David's composure faltered, but he quickly recovered. He wasn't expecting a compliment from the powerful producer, much less about his attractiveness. He was even more pleased when Shaunna nodded in agreement with her father, causing him to sit up straighter in his seat. "I like TV, actually, but I'm not the cop type. I don't have any interest in sitcoms, and I don't see myself as a doctor."

"I do," Gus and Shaunna said in unison, then laughed at each other.

"For the record, you would make a wonderful doctor, especially on a soap," Gus said with conviction. "You would also make a splendid rookie detective, hungry to prove himself but hiding some sort of addiction. And I know that if you did a comedy, you'd get to act more like yourself on camera, which I think you'd really enjoy." He took a sip of his dark red wine. "But what if I told you that I was casting for a western?"

David raised his eyebrows. Although he'd resigned himself to being a washed-up actor, he'd be a fool to immediately dismiss the opportunity to work with Gus Noble.

Shaunna pictured him in chaps and nothing else. She crossed her legs, and her thighs pressed together in delightful friction as her body reacted to her fantasy.

Gus continued on without a clue.

"You're a bit young for the part, but you have an intensity that could work, and I bet the camera would love you in a cowboy hat." He looked over at his daughter, who nodded her head eagerly.

"Didn't you see *Sacred Star*?" she asked her dad.

"Yeah…" Gus was already trying to place David in the B-picture.

"He was—"

"Don't tell me..." Gus was muttering under his breath as he thought. "Oh! You were that slimy little bastard...Larkin or Lincoln or...something."

David let him off the hook. "Layton."

"Yeah! Layton!" Gus sounded triumphant. "I hated that guy. You're good."

"Thank you, sir."

"Is your western role a good guy or a bad guy?" Shaunna asked, leaning forward.

"A bit of both," Gus said after some thought. "He's a complicated guy."

"Leading man?" Shaunna asked.

"One of 'em," Gus replied.

David took in a breath to say something, but then he felt Shaunna's hand settle on his thigh beneath the table. She squeezed the air right out of his lungs.

"Can you get him an early reading?" she asked, seemingly unaware of the effect the placement of her fingers was having on her dinner companion. Despite the barrier of his trousers, he savored the delicate sensation of her touch.

Gus smiled. "I can do better than that. I can get him a face-to-face with the casting director as soon as he gets back to LA."

Shaunna leaned back, smiling. She took her hand off David's leg, and he couldn't stop himself from wondering if she would repeat the contact later in a more private setting.

When Gus excused himself to use the restroom, David and Shaunna felt awkward at once.

"Thank you for that," David began carefully.

"It was nothing, really," Shaunna reflected. "Gus isn't usually such a pushover, not even for me. He wants you for the part. It explains why he invited you to dinner."

"Oh." David didn't know how to feel about her conclusion.

"I'm glad you came along," Shaunna added. "And anyway, I owe you for contacting Michelle after..." She trailed off. It was bad enough that she'd been arrested in front of David without having to say it out loud.

"Me too."

They sat quietly, their conversation having only made them more anxious.

A few days earlier, David had only known of Shaunna because he'd observed her from afar. But now, he was finding that her presence was like music in his heart and her absence like poison in his veins. Yet he didn't know how to sit with her at a table and recapture what they'd discovered in the pool.

That's when the idea hit him.

"Would you like to go swimming with me tonight?" he asked timidly.

Shaunna almost gasped. It was a wonderful idea. She thought of getting another opportunity to see David's bare chest and back and wondered if he was imagining her wet, moonlit skin as well. The thought of him undressing her in his mind was delicious, but she played it cool.

"Sure."

Inwardly, they were both dancing.

Chapter Fourteen

David picked up his dry swimming trunks from the floor of his hotel room and held them to his nose. He detected only the scent of chlorine. As he undressed and placed his one nice suit back on hotel hangers, he felt hopeful for his future for the first time since arriving in Texas.

He liked Shaunna's father, and the feeling was, by all appearances, mutual. Gus was kind to his daughter after his initial scolding and complimented her several times on her sense and her beauty.

David admitted to himself that he most likely would never have worked up the nerve to approach Shaunna on the set. But when he saw her being taken away by the police, the need to be there for her was too great to deny.

Just like the last time, Shaunna was already in the pool when David approached her. Mercifully, the area was protected from prying eyes, and except for one other couple talking in the hot tub, they had the whole swimming area to themselves.

Unlike the last time, Shaunna was wearing a black two-piece suit with flecks of aqua blue. She'd put her hair up in a ponytail with a hair tie that matched the highlights in her bikini.

David grinned as he set his towel down next to what he assumed was hers and kicked out of his Vans (he detested flip-flops).

"How's the water?" he asked.

"You tell me," came her playful response, accompanied by a small splash.

David thought about jumping in, but took the stairs and sat down with his chest and shoulders out of the water.

"Don't you want to get your hair wet?" Shaunna asked as she swam over to join him.

"I just didn't want to make a flashy entrance."

"Too late."

"How come I never get to see you make your entrance?" He made room for her on the steps, and she sat next to him.

"Oh come on, David. You know exits are my specialty."

He laughed at her quick wit. "That's true. But I'd rather you stay with me so I can admire you."

The duo finally fell into a comfortable silence as they contemplated their evolving attraction for one another. They listened to the rippling of the warm water as it nudged the edges of the pool and caught occasional murmurs from the lovers in the hot tub. Music from a car in the parking lot thumped for a while and then faded away into the muggy Texas evening. They sat a few inches apart, but they could actually feel each other, their bodies acting like magnets straining to touch. David suddenly found it hard to breathe.

"I think that if this movie doesn't put you onto the A-list, my father's show will do the trick." Shaunna meant it. David was gifted and gorgeous, two things most of the actors vying for a place in the industry wished they were.

"Thanks. I'm glad you were there." David looked over at her and liked how a strand of wet hair clung greedily to her cheek.

"I usually don't negotiate deals. I just write press releases and coordinate schedules, stuff like that. But I liked it, even though Gus is tough to deal with. He really did like you."

Shaunna thought she was babbling. David thought she was adorable.

"He really loves you."

David's words froze her tongue, but not her eyes. She looked at him and nodded her head.

"I know," she answered earnestly. "But he's not happy with what I did. I think you softened him up, so I owed you one anyway."

"Oh, so I guess we're even, then." David swam out into the pool, and Shaunna watched his powerful strokes.

She didn't wait long before following him.

"Nice try, David, but we're not even." She was surprised by how familiar it felt to talk with and be near him as they swam in the warm, soothing water.

"What do you mean?"

"For sending Michelle to rescue me. Thomas is her lawyer."

"I didn't. You asked Nathan to do that."

"Oh? Well, you're right, then. We're even." She watched him carefully, which wasn't hard because their faces were so close that they could see water droplets on each other's eyelashes.

They swam around the pool a few times discussing the progress of the movie while she was away, and when the other couple eventually vacated the hot tub, Shaunna sprang from the pool and walked toward it.

David watched her and sighed in appreciation of her stunning beauty, but quickly looked away, knowing an erection in those shorts would be about as subtle as a hockey punch.

He soon followed her, and she watched as he gingerly lowered himself into the steaming, churning water. His shorts clung to him in such a way that she was treated to a nice tableau of his manly treasures, and he noticed her nipples had begun to poke at the fabric of her bikini.

"Have you ever been in a hot tub while it was snowing?" David asked.

Shaunna answered with a smile that he was sure was capable of melting all the snow in the world. "I was in Idaho with some family friends, and one night, we went out while it was snowing. I loved it...until I got out."

David laughed. "I know. That's the worst. I used to surf, and on windy days, it was warmer in the water."

"You surf?"

"Surfed," he corrected. "I learned for a movie, and the only footage they got of me was wiping out. I'm horrible at it, but they let me keep the board, so I went out for a while to practice."

"Why did you stop?"

David shrugged his shoulders. "It's hard! Besides, surfers are very territorial, and just like George McFly, I'm not very good at confrontation."

Shaunna laughed. She liked a man who took his wisdom from the movies. She herself lived mostly by rules set by a certain Mr. Ferris Bueller.

"I also broke my board on some rocks," David confessed, looking down at how wrinkly his hands had already become from the water.

Shaunna's eyes widened with the horrific mental picture of an injured David in the rough surf.

"Don't worry," he said, scooting so close to her that their hips touched. Suddenly, his blood felt warmer than the water. "I won't *ever* break anything of yours." David's eyes were level with hers as they sat in the swirling basin, and he held her gaze.

"I believe you." Her response was tinged with hope.

As they continued to open up to one another in conversation, they were each required to go through their childhoods in detail. By the time their mutual biographies were recited, it was late.

David walked Shaunna to her door like the gentleman he was. When her towel unexpectedly dropped to the floor while she slid her key card through the slot, he carefully picked it up for her.

"Thank you, for everything." Before she could talk herself out of it, Shaunna leaned forward and kissed David on the mouth. She quickly lost herself in the delicious touch of his skin and moved in closer to his body. She felt her soft breasts press up against his hard chest. David kept his arms at his sides, but parted his lips and was rewarded with the brush of her tongue against his own. The kiss was short but succulent, and when Shaunna pulled away, she could see that David's eyes were still closed.

"Good night," she whispered as she stepped into her room.

"Good night," was his tender reply.

Shaunna closed the door behind her and reached around to untie her bikini top. Once it was removed, she stepped out of her bottoms and walked naked to the bathroom. She planned on rinsing off in the shower before reading herself to sleep.

There was a knock at her door while she was testing the water.

"It's David." His voice was muffled but discernible. "I locked myself out of my room. Can I come in to use your phone?"

Shaunna opened the door with a towel wrapped around her body and her eyes already halfway through their roll. "Isn't this how bad porn movies start?"

Chapter Fifteen

David stood in the doorway of Shaunna's room and swallowed, too enraptured by her state of undress to do anything more. Her towel had slipped away from her backside, and the mirror on the bathroom door was tilted in his favor. He glimpsed her round rear and gulped more air before running first one hand, and then the other, through his hair.

His own towel dropped to the floor, and when he bent over to pick it up, David found himself looking directly at her tight, damp thighs. He enviously observed several shiny beads of water attached to her skin, and he experienced a hint of disappointment as the most alluring part of her legs disappeared up into the cruel shadow cast by her towel.

"Thanks," he said as he stood up quickly. "I didn't want to walk into the lobby like this." He internally cringed as he spoke, knowing he sounded winded and nervous.

Shaunna couldn't help it—she immediately thought he was referring to the possibility of being seen and photographed by any number of curious vultures. The paparazzi scum might have snuck into the hotel and could be down in the lobby playing checkers in Hawaiian shirts, just waiting for a good shot of somebody connected to her fiasco of a life. She waved him into her room without a second thought.

David went to the phone and called the front desk to provide a replacement key. Shaunna watched in frustration as he hung up the phone. David's request had apparently been met with swift agreement, and that meant a hasty retreat on his part.

It was only because she was watching his slim, strong shoulders that she realized he was shivering. He wasn't paranoid. He was freezing.

"You're cold," she remarked. "Wait right here." Shaunna went into the bathroom with a motherly grin on her face. Prior to their pool date, she'd hung several towels over the shower rack, where they could be warmed by the heat lamp. It was a trick she'd learned from her father, and the result was a towel that felt like it had just come out of the dryer.

Shaunna walked back into the bedroom and right up to David. She plucked his damp towel from his shoulder and pushed the heavenly warm one right into his chest, wrapping him, arms and all, in a cocoon of relief.

In the process, her own towel fell completely off her body and slid to the floor.

They were standing very close to each other, and because David's eyes had drifted closed, he hadn't yet noticed the magnificent occurrence. Shaunna decided against running to the bathroom or, worse yet, squatting to retrieve her towel. She did the only thing she could think of. She threw herself into David's warm, shrouded chest.

David's eyes flew open. He didn't know what had happened, but he was sure it wasn't on purpose.

"My towel fell off," she confessed between pleasant-sounding giggles. Her voice was a song in his ear, and all at once, he could feel her, every inch of her, pressed into him. He was so acutely aware of her body's contours that the thin layer of cotton between them was easily forgotten.

"May I take this one back for a moment?" Her words were shy, slightly uncertain, and David was sure he could feel her heartbeat against his own.

"Of course."

She slowly, carefully wrapped herself in his towel and backed away, grinning. "I want you to have the warm one, so you'll have to let me walk you to the door, and I'll hand it to you once you get into the hall."

"Oh no, Shaunna," David responded, waving his hand in protest. "That's okay." Not knowing what else to say or how else to act, he began walking to the door. "I'll be fine. You really warmed me up." He smirked playfully. "Thank you."

She was hot on his heels. "I want you to have it. Don't be silly. I already have yours." She grasped the door when he walked through it. As soon as she could close it halfway, Shaunna removed the towel and handed it around the barrier.

"Good night, David."

"G-Good n-night, Shaunna."

David's stammers made her beam brilliantly from behind the door. With the nightmare of the past few days finally receding, Shaunna found herself in a happy, celebratory mood and was nearly intoxicated by sheer joy. Had he offered to stay with her, she might have just given in to the actor's charms. Instead, he was suddenly gone with one last sincere "thank you" and a smile that was just short of sublime, his blue eyes blinking slowly and his eyelashes briefly kissing his skin. She adored watching him while she was naked behind the door. It was thrilling to know that he knew she was naked too.

Shaunna drew a bubble bath, and when she recalled the moment of his sexy departure, she replayed the memory in slow motion. She thought about the way David's damp hair spilled over his forehead in small wisps and the way his muscled thighs supported his weight so easily. She remembered his white teeth and his tender eyes as he looked into hers. Shaunna was beginning to feel like she could look into those eyes forever.

Back in his room, David was happy. As far as Shaunna knew, he'd kept his eyes up the entire time he was with her. She was a vision of artistic womanhood, but he sensed she wasn't ready for a physical encounter with him.

He knew he would need to be patient, and he was a mountain of patience.

When David was lying in bed twenty minutes later, flipping past one TV channel after another, he found himself thinking about what it would feel like for Shaunna to join him.

He fell asleep with the remote on his stomach and his heart full of hope.

Chapter Sixteen

Michelle met Shaunna for breakfast at a little bakery in a section of town that obviously didn't come fully alive until dusk. The coffee was robust and the clientele was sparse, just the way Michelle liked it.

"How did you sleep?"

"Mmm." Shaunna nodded, her mouth full of sugary coffee. "Good. It was so nice sleeping with more than one pillow."

Michelle frowned.

"What's wrong?"

"Nothing. I'm just worried about you." Michelle covered well.

"I'm going to be fine. The mess is over for the most part, and as long as you continue to be pleased with my work, I'll be okay."

Michelle rolled her eyes. "You are the world's most gifted publicist and my best friend. If you say you're fine, then I'll believe it, but if you're not…"

"I'm fine, really. You're sweet, and believe me, if I thought I would have to move back in with Gus, I'd let you know."

The reassurance was good enough for Michelle, but now she had to find a way to deliver the bad news. She couldn't help but feel responsible for what happened to Shaunna.

"I want you to take the day off from me today and get in touch with your other clients."

"Already done," Shaunna chimed in cheerily. "I called everyone last night. Everything is in order. I have a layout to schedule with the EW photographer and a book signing to relocate in Minneapolis, but I can do both of those on the phone from the comfort of your trailer."

"Oh, well, I'm sure you must be tired. Why don't you just catch up on your sleep? And your, ah, reading."

Shaunna eyed her friend like an accusatory little sister. "Why don't you want me on-set?"

"Crap." Michelle tried to collect her thoughts before she continued. She saw no sense in backpedaling. "Nathan held a meeting with me and Kyle to discuss whether or not we would carry on with the shoot, given the recent developments.

"Kyle not only agreed to improve his attitude on the set, but after a visit with Gus, he also agreed to drop his civil charges against you. And he really has been doing his best work, although it's only been one short scene so far. But you're out of jail now, and that's all that truly matters."

Michelle lost her train of thought. She was scared to tell Shaunna what Kyle had insisted upon in exchange for his future cooperation, knowing how his demand had infuriated Nathan.

"As you know, publicists rarely spend any time on-set at all," Michelle tried again. "And in this case, you wouldn't even be here if Kyle hadn't insisted that you come. I just refuse to treat you like my servant."

"Just say it." Shaunna's request was firm. Being reminded of her father's involvement was enough to make her impatient for Michelle to cut to the chase.

Michelle swallowed and cast her eyes around the bakery before meeting Shaunna's once again. "You're not allowed on-set anymore."

Shaunna nodded. "I thought so." Among other things, this was going to make it harder for her to see David, a fact which instantly depressed her.

"Nathan refused, of course," Michelle told her immediately. "But I just thought you wouldn't really want to see Kyle anyway, and God knows I envy you. So I convinced him to let Kyle have his way."

Michelle watched her friend somberly pick at a cinnamon roll.

"I hope you understand that I only wanted to salvage the film and would never have considered the idea unless I thought you would have done the same."

Shaunna involuntarily nodded her head whenever she heard logical statements, and this time was no different. She reached across the table and took Michelle's hand.

"You did the right thing," Shaunna told her. She even believed it.

The knock came at David's door just as he was stepping out of the shower. Like most men, he hadn't bothered rinsing the chlorinated water from his body until the following morning.

Also like most men, he wrapped his towel around his waist but didn't tuck it into itself very well, dooming it to last for about thirty seconds or thirty steps, whichever came first.

When he opened the door and Shaunna saw what she was being greeted with, she couldn't help herself.

"How long have you been standing there waiting for me to come over?"

David played along. "My whole life."

Shaunna smiled, but her eyes looked sad.

David tilted his head slightly to fully meet her gaze. "Are you all right?"

"Yes, it's just…I found out from Michelle this morning that I'm barred from going on-set, but I just received a manuscript that she's been waiting for. I took a look at the call sheet and saw you weren't scheduled for makeup until noon. I wanted to catch you so you could give it to her."

"You can't be on-set?" David asked, holding out his hand for the script. His other was clamped firmly to the joined ends of his towel.

Shaunna shook her head and looked at his fingers as they grasped the white cotton towel.

"That's not fair." David was frankly surprised Nathan would allow such a thing.

"Well, like my daddy used to say, the fair only comes at the end of summer." Shaunna was trying to sound relaxed, but the joke only made her look more vulnerable.

"But it *is* the end of summer." David sounded hurt for her.

"Oh yeah, well, I guess I didn't make it to the fair this year." Her mouth was still smiling, but her eyes were hopeless and defeated.

"Well, I can certainly make sure Michelle gets this," David said with tenderness. "I can also give you your towel back." He let the towel fall into his fingers, which he kept laced together in front of him. She could now see his naked hips in addition to his abdomen, and it was a sculpture of temptation.

She played along and held her hand inside the door frame to receive the towel. David brought it up deliberately so that it was blocking her view of his completely naked body. If anyone had walked by in the hallway, however, they would have seen everything he had to offer. As she took the towel, willing herself not to whip it away like a magician's tablecloth, David turned around quickly and nudged the door closed.

The mirror on his bathroom door, however, was tilted in *her* favor, and she saw something with girth swinging back and forth between his legs as he scampered away.

Chapter Seventeen

"Are you thinking of taking the part, then?" David asked Michelle as he searched the craft services tables for the strawberries.

"Well, I have to read it first," Michelle responded, waving the manuscript David had passed on from Shaunna. "But if Marty is attached, how could I say no?"

David shrugged. He found the strawberries and took a bite of one as big as an apple and as red as a beating heart. "You've played every type of character. Since you have nothing to prove, you should choose projects that make you feel good."

"I should take that advice in choosing men, too," she observed wryly.

David laughed.

"How was Shaunna when you saw her?" Michelle asked.

"Not too good," he said honestly. "She feels useless, I think. Unneeded."

"Well, that's just ridiculous!" Michelle said.

"I know!" David agreed. "I wish I could do something for her."

Michelle gasped. "You can! I have a wonderful idea!"

"What?"

"My makeup guy told me about this amazing bar near the stadium. Why don't you and I take Shaunna out tonight?"

David opened his mouth, and Michelle supplied the answer. "Yes! Great!" She flitted away while he stood there with half a strawberry in his hand.

When he grinned, his lips were bright red.

Michelle texted Shaunna:

You & me tonight on the town, I insist.
Car will pick you guys up at 8.

Shaunna texted back:

Who's us guys?

Michelle responded:

David and I are taking you out
to a cute place we know
and no you can't say no.

Shaunna's response was simple:

Can I just ignore you?

Michelle laughed as she punched in her reply:

Too late for that.
I know you want to see him.
He talked about you,
in the makeup trailer.

Shaunna couldn't type fast enough:

WHAT DID HE SAY?

Michelle closed her phone and read through her new manuscript after she sent her final text:

I'll tell you tonight.

Shaunna tossed her phone into her purse and then fished it out again to see what time it was. She had just over six hours to get ready. To her discontent, it was more than enough time.

As promised, the limousine was parked outside the hotel at eight o'clock. David arrived before Shaunna, and he was standing outside, holding the door, when she emerged from the lobby. He kept looking for photographers, but didn't see any. He watched Shaunna with interest as she did the same.

"I swear it was all Michelle's idea," David admitted as he watched her walk toward him in a white strapless dress. A dress that was almost as short as the towel she had wrapped around her body the night before.

"Oh..." Shaunna acted hurt. She usually didn't do such babyish things, but couldn't help herself around David.

Normally, David would have felt self-conscious, but anticipating such awkwardness, he'd indulged in two bottles of Miller Genuine Draft before leaving his room and was feeling airy. He laughed off her reaction because he was already drawing her into a hug.

Shaunna smelled his sweet cologne, and his strong arms were wrapped in a soft dinner jacket that rested over a pale green dress shirt. His words were pleasant in her ear.

"I hope you plan on having fun tonight."

It was important for Shaunna to approach the evening with a positive attitude. She wasn't the type of person to go out with well-meaning friends only to cross her arms and resent the world for spinning. She hugged him back happily, and when she turned her head to answer, her lips brushed his cheek. It was a pleasing punctuation to her words.

"David, I plan on having a ball."

The duo toasted to Michelle's recovery and future happiness on the way to the Four Seasons to collect her. Halfway there, David reached out and took Shaunna's hand. He didn't say anything. He just held her cool and slender fingers in his warm, relaxed grip. She sat transfixed and was amazed by how intensely aware she was of the weight of his fingers laced within hers. Their hands fit so comfortably together that it felt like they'd been made for each other.

The limo driver had wisely chosen light, but upbeat music. David bobbed his head and sang along, but Shaunna was way too embarrassed to join in.

She did, however, have a second glass of champagne.

When the car pulled up to the Four Seasons, the doorman tipped his hat at the car and then disappeared inside the lobby. A moment later, Michelle strolled out, wearing a silver dress and heels. Her hair was up, and her long legs were bare.

David was out the door and standing with it open before the driver could so much as get his seat belt off. A half dozen cameras flashed from across the street as Michelle took David's hand and stepped into the car with a natural grace.

"Good evening, you two," Michelle greeted. She said "you two" in a way that made it clear she considered them to be on a date.

Shaunna felt a flutter of excitement in response.

"Hello, Michelle," David answered. "And thank you for tonight."

She touched his cheek. "You're welcome, and don't even think of trying to pay for anything."

David laughed. "Don't worry."

Michelle was pleased to see her friend smiling and tried to focus on Shaunna's newfound happiness, hopeful it would be contagious. Michelle was a good actress and projected a brave public face; however, she felt her moods shifting constantly, bouncing back and forth between feelings of incredible invincibility and intense vulnerability.

David found Shaunna's hand again, and Michelle nearly squeaked with joy. She'd never seen Shaunna with a date, and it made her feel like love and hope were still alive.

"We're going to a great little place I heard about. It'll have the fun-loving atmosphere we want and the privacy we need." Michelle wasn't wrong. Her makeup guy had made it sound perfect.

It was called Rim Shots.

A gay bar.

They secured a nice little booth by the dance floor where they would get up one at a time, or in pairs, to entertain the others with exaggerated hip swivels during Erasure's cover of "River Deep, Mountain High" and devastating pelvic thrusts to any song by Tom Jones. The whole place went crazy, actually. Apparently, celebrities like Michelle Cooper weren't part of the regular clientele. She was welcomed enthusiastically and, more importantly in Shaunna's eyes, respectfully.

"I spoke to Gus today," Shaunna told David during one of their resting spells. "He's going to have Nathan film a screen test with a few pages that he's e-mailing over tonight. They're not waiting until you get back to LA. They want the casting director to see you now."

"Oh!" Michelle remembered something in the middle of a sip of her Long Island iced tea. "I was with Nathan this afternoon when

Gus called. Nathan is going to shoot it this weekend. That way it'll give David some time to study the sides."

"Wow! Thanks." David was stunned. He didn't know what else to say.

"You're a natural," Shaunna told him matter-of-factly. "My father is a talent magnet, and it doesn't surprise me that you attracted his attention."

David had been given an enormous compliment from someone he greatly respected, but all he could think of was whether or not Shaunna would kiss him again.

"I'm surprised you don't pick up the craft," David offered, hoping she would take it as a compliment to her beauty.

"Oh, we've tried to talk her into at least doing some modeling, but she won't hear of it," Michelle interjected, and as soon as she used the word "we've," she felt a splinter in her heart. Early in their relationship with Shaunna and before a mysterious, confounding venom had consumed her husband, it'd been she and Kyle who repeatedly encouraged Shaunna to profit from her good looks and easy on-camera persona.

"I worked as a child, and it wasn't for me," Shaunna said simply.

"It's not for children," David retorted.

"No." Shaunna shook her head. "It's not. How did things go today?"

"Um, it was good," David supplied.

"Come on!" Shaunna teased, and her words were accompanied with a hand on his thigh under the table. She squeezed, and he jittered as if he'd been shocked. David was very ticklish, and Shaunna had just discovered that delicious fact. "Alix already sent me pictures of Nathan wearing one of the space helmets. What the hell did you guys do?"

Michelle looked at David and shrugged. "You tell it. I didn't see the whole thing anyway."

"Okay. Well, NASA let Nathan build a big long dolly track, and by the time the crew was done, it looked more like a roller coaster. I got to ride it!"

"You did?" Shaunna had seen an impressive bit of scaffolding in one of the photos. Now she understood what it was.

"Okay." David took a breath, clearly starting from the beginning. "You know how the storyboards show this left to right track shot of the hangars and the old sixties equipment? Well, NASA built these squatty cement buildings three months before we arrived, and they completely blocked Nathan's money shot."

Shaunna was nodding her head. She'd heard something about it during the first week of shooting, but she liked to listen to David talk. She was fascinated with the mechanics of his mouth, the way his tongue danced over his teeth, and the way his lips parted when he drew in a breath.

"The crew guys built ramps and ran the dolly right over the top of them. The roofs are flat, so it was an easy solution, and the shot even had a nice rise and fall to it."

"Why didn't they just shoot in front of the buildings?" Shaunna asked.

"Too close," David answered, having asked the same question himself earlier in the day. "The rounded tops of the hangars would be out of frame, and that's what Nathan wanted most."

Shaunna nodded. Nathan's movies were all about symmetry.

"Nathan was adamant that he be the one to risk it because there are no brakes on those things and those ramps are pretty steep. So they put a helmet on him and put him in the camera rig, and a bunch of the guys push him up as he rolls film. Everything goes great until he drops down the other side."

Shaunna was beginning to look appropriately concerned.

"The rig usually goes three miles an hour, and here Nathan flies by doing twenty and cursing the whole way because the camera is shaking so bad, his shot is lost. Then he comes to the curve."

Michelle knew what was coming next.

"Nathan wasn't slowing down at all, and half the crew was running behind him, trying to keep up. The curve was pretty wide, but it wasn't going to keep the rig on the track…so what does Nathan do? He wraps himself around the camera to protect it instead of jumping off and then closes his eyes and shouts, 'Tell Kelly Ripa I've always loved her!'"

"Is he okay?" Shaunna was laughing as she asked. She couldn't help it.

"Oh, he's fine," David concluded. "It stayed on the tracks, actually, but he went up on two wheels for a while, and I thought it was going to end badly."

"Did he ever get his shot?" Michelle asked.

"Yeah. He went right back on with a handheld, and the difference in weight was like taking a whole person off the rig. He let us all take turns after they made a few passes with the camera. They even widened the curve so we could go two at a time safely."

Shaunna sighed, thinking of her favorite theme park. "I wish I hadn't missed that."

"It's still up!" David said brightly, suddenly thankful he'd stopped drinking early in the evening. "Do you want to go now?"

She did.

Michelle had them drop her off first and told them not to stay out too late, although she secretly hoped neither of them would get any sleep until the sun came up.

She also insisted that they keep using the limousine, but David asked for them to be dropped off at their hotel, where he fished his own rental car keys from his pants pocket. He drove them to the NASA compound.

"We still have the helmets if you want one," David offered. "But I went with one of the crane guys, and we didn't even come close to leaving the track."

Shaunna inspected the course, walking along the track from back to front, and glanced up at David. "It's fine. We should have a fun and smooth ride."

"Oh, it's smooth all right, and almost completely silent."

He pushed the empty rig into position, and then they both took their seats. Shaunna laced her fingers through his.

"Hang on to your hats and glasses," Shaunna said in a cartoony southern drawl. "'Cuz this here's the wildest ride in the wilderness."

David laughed freely. "What is that?"

"You mean you don't know Big Thunder Mountain Railroad's announcements by heart?" Shaunna giggled.

"What's Big Thunder Mountain Railroad?"

Shaunna's giggle stopped. "Wait...have you *never* been to Disneyland?"

David looked down sheepishly. "Not yet."

She shook her head. "The minute we get back..." was all she said before David stuck his foot out and gave them a push over the edge.

It was indeed a silent ride, and it was as dark as Space Mountain, although Shaunna knew she couldn't tell him that because he wouldn't have any idea what she was talking about. They navigated the course three more times, and they always held hands.

When David drove her to their hotel and walked her to her door, he waited eagerly once again for her to make the first move. He wasn't disappointed.

Shaunna kissed him quickly before hugging him fiercely. "Thank you, David."

Her words were holding back a flood of emotion, and as her grip on his body tightened, she found herself saying them over and over in an effort to keep herself from sobbing.

David was silent, enjoying the smell of Shaunna's hair and the erotic sensation of her insistent breasts pushing against his heartbeat. He wrapped his arms around her and turned his head minutely to press his lips to her neck. Although he desired her, he yearned to comfort her anxieties even more. He worried that the act might be too intimate, but her hand on the back of his neck only encouraged him.

Shaunna hummed in delight and reflexively tilted her head to grant him more access. His lips were bold as they drifted over the soft column of her neck, and his hands rested firmly on her hips like guardians. His mouth moved against her heated skin for several long and delicious moments before she heard his whispered reply.

"You're welcome."

Soon after, much too soon, David released her.

"I'll call you first thing in the morning," he told her earnestly.

Shaunna laughed and entered her room with a practiced swipe of her key card.

David walked to his own room and slept so poorly that he heard the morning's complimentary newspaper hit the floor outside his door at half past five.

Thinking that at least he'd have something to take his mind off Shaunna, David rose and turned on the television. He was flipping through the channels when a glimpse of his own face forced him to stop.

To his astonishment, an entertainment network was talking about *him*.

He'd been photographed with Michelle, their faces smiling, their heads tilted very close together and their eyes locked on one another and glimmering with excitement. David recognized it as the moment when they were dancing to "Summer Nights" at Rim Shots.

His amazement transformed into concern, however, as an obnoxious reporter quipped, "Looks like Michelle Cooper is moving on..."

Chapter Eighteen

Michelle was sitting silently in the big trailer that had been modified into a conference room. She had her elbows on the table with her chin resting on intertwined fingers.

David was sitting beside her, double-checking his script.

Kyle had a printout of a blog post in front of him that showed the same picture David had seen on TV. In big letters above the photo was the article's headline:

No Wonder She Dumped Him!

Kyle was staring daggers at them from across the table.

David had discussed the rumor with Michelle as soon as he discovered it. He'd driven to her hotel, in fact, which proved only to fuel the fire. A few hovering photographers snapped David's picture on his way out. Nevertheless, the two had a good laugh about it. In the end, they agreed to simply explain the misunderstanding to anyone who cared to ask.

Kyle cared, but he didn't ask. He glared.

His irate scowl grated on Michelle's rawest nerves. Her sadness was a thing of the past. For the first time since Kyle had blindsided her with divorce papers and evicted her from their suite at the Four Seasons, she felt true, searing fury.

She was angry about everything he'd done since arriving in Texas. She was livid at herself for falling in love with and marrying the megalomaniac prick. And she was annoyed because she would be spending an entire day with the asshole, strapped to a harness, hovering above the ground and maneuvered into a number of dizzying positions.

It was clear to her that he'd believed that five-word headline linking Michelle to their new co-star. Word for pathetic word.

She met Kyle's cold gaze across the table and could see he intended to make her life hell over it, and this fact pissed her off most of all. Not because he'd been hurt by the thought of his soon-to-be-ex-wife with another man, but because the incriminating headline had shrewdly implied she found someone better than Kyle Petersen.

His glare hardened, and now Michelle's temper was on the verge of explosion. She opened her mouth to say something, when Nathan entered the room.

"Okay, everyone," he began the meeting before the door was even closed. "I know that this is going to be a physical shoot and that you'll be up in the rigs all day, but we need to remember that this is an emotional scene, as well."

Nathan looked from Michelle to Kyle. "As astronauts, you two know what separation from the ship means in a spacewalk. You're dead. Michelle, you're going to attempt to be the voice of reason as Kyle becomes irrational and crazed. But you have your breaking point too."

"Got it," Michelle replied promptly. In her estimation, truer words had never been spoken.

Kyle grunted.

"Now, we're going to be rotating you with wires that'll be attached to your legs in addition to the main support cables."

"We're going upside-down?" Michelle's voice caught on her last word.

"Not exactly," Nathan said. "But we can't have you both just hanging there like sides of beef." He peered at Michelle with a look of compassion.

Michelle nodded. She would do her best; she always did. "I trust you, Nathan."

"Thank you." He spun to face his ship's pilot. "David, as you know, you're talking to Kyle and Michelle on the radio, and even though we're doing your cut-aways in LA, we've set up the audio to get your vocal performance today. If you're up for it."

"Absolutely." David already had his lines memorized, even though his part of the sequence wouldn't be filmed until another day.

Nathan tossed a radio with orange tape and a big rubbery antennae to the actor. "Let's put David right next to me, and if this works like it should, we'll save everyone a week of mixing sound in post."

"Okay, what's next?" Nathan thought for a moment before addressing David and Michelle. "I want to see if we can beef up the emotion between your characters. You're both passionate people, and I want to capitalize on that. David, you're on the ship, and all you have are their voices on the radio. Michelle, you've got both their voices in your ears. I need you to go right up to the line of melodrama, tip-toe on it if you have to. Shit! Cross it if you have to. Your vocal performance is what's going to sell this scene. The strain, the fear, the fatigue. It all needs to come out."

"No problem," Michelle promised.

Lastly, Nathan picked up the flight suits from the empty chair he had put them in. "These are for today." Nathan handed his leading man and lady their costumes. "Alix made adjustments for the harnesses and for Michelle's effects pack. Plus, she put extra padding in the crotches."

Kyle nodded. He'd done enough harness work to join the Cirque du Soleil and could appreciate more attention to an actor's comfort. He looked over at Michelle and noticed that she looked every bit as nervous as he predicted she'd be. The frightening reality of the harness shoot alone had almost been enough for her to turn down the role in the first place.

Kyle couldn't suppress a grin. He was going to make this a very long day for her, especially after finding out that she had been slutting it up behind his back.

"Are we going to have any wind today?" Kyle asked innocently and watched Michelle's eyes widen and her mouth shrink.

"None," Nathan stated, eyeing Kyle suspiciously.

Michelle didn't look relieved, which only encouraged Kyle to keep at it.

"That crane looks about as old as Texas itself," Kyle supplied mildly. "I hope you didn't scrape all the rust off when you dressed it." He finally got a full-fledged flinch from Michelle and almost sighed with satisfaction.

"It's a two thousand and two *Greer!"* Nathan said sharply. "And I know what you're doing, Kyle." He looked at the man for a long time. "I will drop you from the scene. Keep it up and see if I don't. There's no reason why she couldn't be out there by herself. In fact, that's just like her character to do something like that."

Kyle closed his mouth. Nathan knew his weakness.

"I thought this was all behind us anyway," Nathan said in an exasperated tone to no one in particular.

"Why don't you ask David who *he's* been behind lately?" Kyle responded petulantly. He turned the printout so Nathan could see the headline and the accompanying photo of Michelle and David, nearly cheek to cheek.

David was incensed. "Now listen…" he began, but Michelle stopped him by taking his hand.

She gave David a quick apologetic look before standing up and addressing Kyle. "Since when do you care about me? Deal with it, Kyle. Who I see is none of your concern," Michelle scolded him.

She then walked out of the meeting, leaving everyone else sitting at the table.

With Michelle gone, Nathan and Kyle looked at David.

"Um. Sorry about that." He didn't know what else to say as he rose from his seat. "She probably just didn't get much sleep last night."

David left without another word, and as the door closed behind him, he heard Kyle attempt to roar at Nathan. The tirade was short-lived, however, as the door flew open a moment later and the director steamed past David, nearly knocking him over.

Kyle was left to fume alone at the table. He looked down, seeking his watch, but it still wasn't there. He'd formed a strong habit of checking it often, and it only succeeded in reminding him of what he lost.

It would've at least been something if Kyle understood that his departed watch was actually a metaphor for the woman he'd betrayed and therefore lost forever. But he just missed his watch.

When he finally did get up to take his costume to his trailer, he left behind a printout that had been ripped into pieces.

Chapter Nineteen

An hour after the tense production meeting, Kyle and Michelle were hanging twelve feet off the ground. It wasn't nearly as high as Michelle had imagined, but somehow, that made it seem worse. She couldn't help herself from looking down, but it was better than looking at Kyle.

Unfortunately, Nathan's crew was trying to light her face through her helmet, and she wasn't helping by not looking at her mark. He understood her fear as well as her anger and was trying hard to work around both. The sooner he got the thumbs up from his lighting chief, the sooner he could begin shooting.

"Why don't you use the lights inside the helmets?" Alix asked as she approached with a mango smoothie that had given her an orange mustache. "The ones we used for the power failure scene when we first got here."

"Son of a bitch!" Nathan exclaimed. "That's genius!"

"Thank you," she said sweetly.

"No, *thank you!*" Nathan replied. "Would you go get the helmets for us? I'll hold your smoothie."

Alix shrugged. "I can try. They were taken back to the props department."

"Then don't worry about it. I'll have one of the grips track them down." He should've known that his greedy geeks in the props department would've reclaimed them from the costume mistress.

Alix waved off his retraction. "I'm happy to give you a hand, Nathan," she replied before skipping away.

Nathan looked up at Kyle and Michelle, hanging like puppets in a closet. He held the radio to his mouth, but his regretful eyes said it all. "Sorry about this, guys. We're going to switch out your helmets."

Nathan raised his voice. "Okay, people! That's a ten!"

Kyle was staring at Michelle, willing her to tell him to stop. After all, she was his mark. "So, I guess David must be into older women," he mused aloud when the break was called.

Michelle ignored him. She tried to anyway, but he was clearly planning to needle her all day, quietly, so only she could hear him.

Alix quickly returned with the two helmets. She then found a chair and set it up on the other side of David. She leaned in to speak to him and detected his scent. It reminded her of being in a forest near the ocean.

She touched his arm lightly. "Can you help me think of a few things to do with Shaunna this week?" Alix spoke softly, but Nathan heard her anyway and nudged David's other arm before he could answer her.

"That's a good idea," Nathan remarked. "I don't want Michelle losing any sleep, and Shaunna deserves to have a social life while she's here."

David was concerned by Nathan's cool tone and wanted to straighten the record as soon as possible.

"Look, Nathan, about Michelle…"

"I want you rested this week as well," Nathan said, steamrolling over David's words. "If you can help Alix in looking after Shaunna, I'd greatly appreciate it. If not, then at least stay out of the Kyle and Michelle circus until we've wrapped and left this state in the dust cloud I found it in."

David really wanted to clear the air with Nathan, but realized the middle of a scene wasn't the time or place for it. He decided to drop the subject of Michelle altogether in favor of thinking of ways to entertain Shaunna every night. Maybe he wouldn't even need Alix at all.

One of the grips rode a cherry picker up to the actors, carrying the new helmets. He overheard them talking as he neared their altitude.

"...only money, Kyle. We already have more than we can spend."

"Maybe *you* do," he replied snidely. "Especially after you've robbed me blind with Thomas Harper, of all people!"

"Is *that* what this is about?" She focused her attention on the grip while he put her helmet on her. "You're mad because I picked your nemesis as my divorce attorney?"

Kyle took his helmet from the crew man and waved him down. "No, I don't care who loses your case for you."

"Is it David, then?" Michelle said sweetly. Maybe it had something to do with her general discomfort in the harness, but she was feeling feisty. "You really don't want to hear about David, do you?"

"No," Kyle confirmed. "I don't."

Michelle was sick to her stomach, yet she continued to look down. Her anxiety was evident beneath her sharp tone. Enough time had passed since the meeting that she was feeling embarrassment over her exit.

Nathan's voice crackled in their ears. "Michelle, I need you to be looking at your mark as soon as we call action."

"Okay." She knew Nathan was worried about her, but arguing with Kyle had given her something else to focus on, and she looked up with lava in her eyes.

"We're going to take it from the top and walk it to the edge. If you need a line, call for it, but then *keep going* until I cut. We need to make sure we're tracking you correctly all the way to the last pull out."

Both actors agreed with curt, military nods. Michelle loved live theatre and preferred to run a scene all the way through in order to better capture changes in tone and tension. Kyle hated it because it meant that he had to listen to someone else talk.

Nathan, who had accepted the rest of Alix's mango smoothie during the break, was feeling much better and winked at his AD, who was standing nearby and waiting for the playful signal.

"Cameras ready?" Arnie's voice rang out loud and clear, even from behind his clipboard.

"Ready," came a nearby response and two others from various other locations on-set.

"Crane ready?" Arnie boomed again as he tilted his head up.

Nathan looked up too. He envied the crane operator, a cranky fellow named Ralph who wouldn't let anyone else even sit in the big chair, even when he had the keys in his pocket.

"Ready," came his gruff voice from the cab at the base of the monstrous arm that loomed over the outdoor setup.

"Effects ready?" Arnie walked away after his last question in order to help guide Camera One.

From directly below the dangling actors and next to the second camera came an affirmative reply to the last check.

"Action!" Nathan yelled as he put headphones on so he could hear the actors breathing. It was going to be vital that their breathing become almost like a metronome in a scene that was going to build slowly and then rush down the tracks like the homemade roller coaster they constructed.

White and yellow smoke issued from tubes below the actors as two metal plated hoses were waggled tragically and strategically in front of the camera before being set down by two grips.

Camera One, the master shot camera with Jonathan riding the jib, moved up slowly and settled in the air in front of the marionette-like actors.

"Grant!" Michelle's voice for Amanda had a gentle Georgian accent to it.

"Amanda! Can you get to me?" Kyle sounded a little bored, but Nathan wasn't overly concerned with the lackluster beginning. He knew from experience that he was going to get his best stuff when they were both sore and frustrated. For now, he just focused on what the cameras and microphones were picking up the first time through the scene. Both actors swam frantically toward each other. As they did, the crane buzzed from behind muffled hydraulics, and both actors began turning sideways.

"Captain Edge to the Zenith! Come in, Zenith!" Kyle was a master at what David called *Come in, Houston* dialogue.

"Honey, I think we've lost power to communications and temperature control." Michelle's voice was steady, but she allowed just enough of a tremble to let the audience know that it was time to worry.

"Come in, Zenith! Our radios are out!" Kyle didn't skimp on energy when he delivered lines where he was allowed to yell at someone. Nathan had always thought the line was hilarious and summed up

Captain Edge perfectly. The fact that Kyle delivered it without a hint of irony, whether intentional or not, was a godsend.

Michelle was extremely dizzy, which only allowed for a more realistic portrayal of her character's plight. "Grant, this looks bad, but at least we repaired the shield and gave the crew a fighting chance to get home."

"Screw the crew! We're the ones who just got a death sentence!"

Alix nudged David and repeated the first part of the line under her breath, then added, "I bet that's Kyle's bumper sticker." David swatted at her playfully.

"We're not dead yet, Grant! In fact…I think I know how we can reach each other *and* kick-start the radio! Now, I have to make sure that I'm facing you directly and— "

"Why haven't they turned around? Every minute they waste is unforgivable!" Kyle played impatience well.

"Yes, but we still might be able to contact them. Grant, you need to get ready to— "

"You're crazy! We're dead! We should never have come out here!"

Michelle paused and took a good hard look at Kyle before delivering her next line. "You're right. We should never have come out here. But there's still something we can do to save ourselves…if we work together."

"We'll die together!" Kyle spat.

"We'll die apart." Michelle reached behind her suit and began unscrewing something on her pack.

"Cue effect!" Nathan called out, and a jet of gas issued from Michelle's pack and thrust her forward and into Kyle's arms.

"Amanda! What have you done?" Kyle was face to face with his estranged wife, who had a warrior's look in her eyes and gripped his arms with determined hands. "I had no idea you were so brave!" he finished breathlessly.

"It's not bravery, my love." Michelle didn't mean to deliver the line as sadly as she did, but she was also unprepared for the sudden proximity to him. "I just have nothing left to lose."

They both acted like they were linking their suits with multiple cables. They each had colored marks to touch on each suit. Digital tubes and hoses would be added later using CGI.

"All right, that does it. Life support is linked, but we don't have much time. When I said I wanted to spend forever in your arms, this is not what I meant."

"Oh, that's…uh…" Kyle made a face. "Shit! Line!"

Gary read Grant's line from somewhere near Camera Three. "How are you going to boost…"

"How are you going to boost the radio?" Kyle delivered his line far too angrily, unusable. It was too bad, because Nathan felt it was a decent first take so far. He said nothing and let the cameras continue to roll.

Michelle began typing on a futuristic wrist band with a touch screen. "I'm almost there…Zenith! Zenith! Do you read me?"

David spoke into his radio from his seat between Alix and Nathan. He was not reading from a script, and his voice took on a pinched quality.

"This is Zenith. What happened? Are you back aboard?"

Nathan loved the way that David's voice, as Nick, came through the helmets, and he shrugged one of the cans off his ears.

"The AG cable broke! We slipped completely off the solar shield! We're seventy seconds aft!" Captain Edge barked.

"What? Oh shit!…um…I mean, don't panic! We're reversing thrust! Can you ping us?" David's delivery was perfect.

"Yes," Michelle said. "I think so…No…Oh no…I can't…"

"We're dead." Kyle delivered the line like he was announcing that dinner was ready.

Nathan needed him to amp up his emotion, but didn't bother asking for it. He should have all the emotion he would need by take fifteen or so.

"Wait! Zenith, do you think you would be able to see a moon flare?" Michelle's delivery was, as usual, dead on target.

"We wouldn't have a lot of time to stop, but I think so." David was doing well, not upstaging, enunciating his words, and allowing his humanity to filter through the fuzz.

"Do it! Nick!" Kyle delivered that line all wrong.

Nathan sighed. He knew he was going to have to shoot the scene multiple times no matter what, but feared only that his leading man's performance was going to be stubbornly consistent.

"Stand by." Again, David's commanding tone filled their helmets, recorded by the same microphones that were picking up their voices.

This created a slight echo in their helmets, and Nathan loved the way that sounded.

"Zenith, we will only be able to get one shot at this. We're sharing life support, and we don't know how long the radio will last." There was a slight tremble in her voice at the beginning of her phrase and a bit of rushing at the end.

"Don't worry," came David's confident reply. "I'll only need one shot at you."

"I trust you, Nick. You've crashed me in a few simulations, but you've never let me down."

"And I won't." David put his radio in his lap. His part was done.

"When should we shoot the flare?…Zenith?…Zenith, do you copy?" Michelle looked at Kyle, who was late on his cue.

"Uh, we're down to life support power."

"We'll use that, then." Michelle lost none of her intensity. She stayed in the moment.

"We'll do no such thing!" Nathan knew that he would have plenty of good takes of this line.

"Grant, if they can't find us, we're dead anyway!"

Nathan wished that he was sitting closer to a monitor. He wanted to see Michelle's eyes. Her voice alone was tremendously engaging.

"Good. They'll be here any minute!" Leave it to Kyle to play glib, right on the nose.

"At best, they'll miss us. At worst, they'll hit us!"

Michelle was frantic, but not panicked. David didn't even know there was a difference until he saw her portray subtle steps to intensity.

"Good! I hope we crash through the bridge and kill them all!" Kyle didn't quite match her skill or her intensity, but he was yelling, and that was a start.

"Just fucking let me use the fucking radio for one fucking second!" Michelle played the line straight, but even so, most people on the set began laughing. It was funny to hear such language from a classy woman like Michelle.

"Settle down!" Nathan ordered after he snorted and actually slapped his knee. "Read the sweep, Camera Three; go ahead whenever you're ready, Grant."

"What do you want to say to Nick!"

"I just want to set a time to shoot the moon flare." She was pleading with him. A camera came rushing in from behind Kyle and shot Michelle as if she was somehow on her knees before him.

"Cue the crane," Nathan called out.

Both actors were bobbed up and down like fussy infants in a flabby aunt's arm.

"Too late!" Kyle said smugly. "That's their Whisk Shield! Fire the flare if you dare."

Michelle took out a prop that Nathan hoped avid sci-fi movie fans would recognize from the film *Blade Runner*. She held the gun above her head and recoiled her arm slightly, as if it had fired the small white orb that would appear in the finished print.

"Their main shield is going to push hard, Grant. We're going to have to hold on to each other as tightly as we can." Michelle let go of the gun, which floated away on a wire, and grabbed Kyle with both hands.

"You don't think the links will hold?" They were face to face again, looking into one another's eyes.

"Do you want to take that chance?" Michelle's performance had already been at times fierce and fragile, but now it was positively heart-breaking.

"No, it's not that…I just don't know if I'm strong enough to hold you."

"Grant, you act like we've already failed. Worse, like you wanted this to happen."

Michelle was crying. Nathan noticed it later as he was going over footage. Inspired, he decided to CGI tears that would float around in her helmet like diamonds.

"I didn't, believe me…but I guess I just get used to things too easily."

"Cue crane!" Nathan called.

The actors began to bob once more. David thought of a toddler toy that hung in the door frame when his little cousin came for a visit. They called it a Johnny Jump Up.

The camera operator watched smoke fill the frame as a shadow was cast on the couple by the big lid of an industrial recycle bin.

The actors were supposed to remain together until the end of the scene, but Kyle deliberately pushed Michelle away. She was the only one who saw it until Nathan reviewed the dailies that evening. From the moment the director first noticed the shove, though, he began watching for what amounted to hours of emotional abuse all day long.

"Cut! Reset!"

It was the first of many times Nathan said those words over the next six hours, and Kyle was single-handedly responsible for over half of them.

Chapter Twenty

Michelle used her vertigo as well as her rage and sorrow and turned in one solid performance after another.

Kyle's first take was brilliant compared to the next ten, where he stumbled over her name, yawned, laughed, and cursed at the Camera Two operator.

Only Michelle could recognize the look in his eyes. He was enjoying himself.

There were several delays as the smoke machines had to be constantly adjusted, and Nathan called for another break. Kyle and Michelle were lowered to the ground, but not unhooked. They were each brought some apple juice, but Michelle politely declined. She wasn't interested in taxing her bladder on top of everything else. She did ask for some Red Vine licorice and even offered Kyle a rope. He took it without a word of thanks.

By the fifth hour, Nathan was going to call it a day because Kyle's performance was only getting worse. But then the actor suddenly started turning in some compelling stuff. Not great, but better, and enough to fill in a few of the many holes he'd left in the first several takes.

After a few decent passes, however, Kyle once again began complaining loudly about everything from the dirty camera lens to the crane operator. He huffed at Nathan for taking too long with everything, even though he knew he only had himself to blame for the lengthy shoot.

As a professional courtesy, from one actor to another, Michelle tried to soothe him. It was a mistake. As a result, he turned his attention to her, berating her softly but menacingly.

"Maybe you should take some acting lessons from your new boyfriend. That is if you can stop fucking him long enough to have a conversation."

"What do you care who I see?" Michelle shouted, immediately drawing the attention of the entire crew. "Or how much more satisfying he is!"

Kyle roared. "It's hard not to notice when you're flaunting it all over town."

"You didn't want me anymore! Remember?" she countered.

"You're damn right. And I still don't!"

Michelle's voice began to falter. "If I find happiness without you, *despite you*, I am going to hold on to it!"

"Bitch! You couldn't find happiness—"

Nathan didn't need the megaphone, but he used it anyway.

"That's enough!" He was on his feet and walking toward them. When he was positioned directly below their feet, he raised the megaphone to his mouth again. "We had a deal, and you are both breaking it."

Michelle offered a soft apology to Nathan. Kyle sneered, but complied.

When Nathan returned to his chair, David tapped him on the shoulder and whispered something in his ear that had the director nodding his head like a kitten following a laser pointer. Nathan called for a reset and allowed David to borrow the cherry picker. He raised himself up next to Michelle and spoke with her during the long reset, gently tucking her hair back into her helmet.

It was such a sweet gesture that it nearly softened Michelle too much for the scene.

"Hey, I have a joke for you," David offered.

Michelle rolled her eyes, which David took as her way of giving him permission to continue.

"Why does Waldo wear a striped shirt?"

"I don't know. Why?" Michelle was already smiling.

"Because he doesn't want to be spotted."

He continued. "Why don't tigers eat clowns?"

Michelle rolled her eyes.

"Because they taste funny."

That particular joke got a loud groan from one of the camera operators.

David may have told bad jokes, but he was turning out to be a good friend. Michelle felt real affection for him in that moment.

David's chivalrous actions infuriated Kyle, however. He improved his acting and stopped complaining long enough to hasten the end of the work day. He just wanted to rid himself of the sight of them together.

The harder he tried to get the scene right, though, the more he messed it up, and his genuine mistakes were followed by world class hissy fits. His tantrums shook the crane arm, jostling Michelle and cheering him up momentarily. But David always reached out and took her hand, which immediately steadied her movements.

He even talked her into drinking a juice box. He made her feel more comfortable, encouraging and complimenting her performance between takes. Every joke he told was cornier than the last, yet she began laughing more. They both completely ignored Kyle.

Eventually, Nathan wrapped for the day and applauded everyone for their efforts. He took David aside and shook his hand. "Thanks, pal. I owe you one. You two are good together."

David was finally going to set the record straight about him and Michelle. "It's not exactly— "

"Nathan! We need you!"

"Oh shit!" Nathan said, looking over his shoulder. "Thanks again. Are you going out with Shaunna and Alix tonight?"

"Aren't you coming with us?" David asked.

"Sorry, not after all the footage we just shot. I have a lot work to get finished before tomorrow."

"Okay. See you then." David and Alix left together.

Michelle and Kyle were in their trailers for hours afterward while Nathan pored through the day's footage and witnessed Kyle's emotional abuse.

Michelle stopped by to see Nathan and say good night, her hair matted from the nap she'd just woken up from.

"Michelle." Nathan's voice cracked.

"Nathan, I hope you got what you needed today."

He stood and approached her with his arms outstretched for a hug. "I got exactly what I wanted, but at your expense." He ignored her puzzled expression and continued. "I knew he was fucking up my takes on purpose. But I had no idea how mean he was being to you up there. I promise I'll never let that happen to you again."

Michelle saw his pain and was touched. "I don't blame you for it," she added. "And as you know, most of the rest of my scenes are in the Earthlab. I can handle Kyle when my feet are on the ground."

"Go get some more rest," Nathan encouraged.

"I will."

He walked her to her car, and as he made his way back to the set, his stroll became a march.

Kyle came out of his trailer soon after, and Nathan was waiting for him.

Kyle didn't look very surprised to see him.

"Hello, Kyle. I've been expecting you."

Kyle didn't stop walking. "And why is that?"

"So I can kick your abusive ass."

Chapter Twenty-One

Kyle had walked out of his trailer, anticipating that he would be stopped and scolded. He certainly didn't expect Nathan to threaten him.

"Watch yourself, McPherson," Kyle snapped. "If you touch me, I'll have you hauled out just like Shaunna was."

Nathan was on him in an instant, his breath hot in Kyle's face and his hand like a vise on Kyle's startled balls.

"Let's get one thing straight right now."

Nathan was frighteningly strong, and despite the immediate queasiness Kyle felt, he still wondered if the man's other hand was going to clamp around his throat next.

"I don't care if I get arrested for fucking you up."

Nathan had just made his first point of the evening, and he continued. "I'll cooperate with the arresting officers, hire a good lawyer…Michelle's lawyer maybe—" he thought for a moment, as if he had all night to ponder the stars "—I'll make a deal, get a reduced sentence—" his grip tightened on Kyle's testicles "—and come back and fucking do it all over again."

All Kyle could do was squeak.

Nathan released his grip and held both his hands up. "Now, I won't touch you again tonight, or probably ever again, but that all depends on you. Don't *ever* think that I am not crazy enough to throw it all away just to make sure you'll regret *ever* getting the authorities involved."

Nathan sat down at the table. "Have a seat," he offered.

Kyle sat. It hurt his balls, but he sat.

Nathan crossed his leg by putting his ankle on his knee. "If you walk out on me before I'm done talking, I will chase you down and drag you back here by your swollen sack."

All Kyle could do was nod his head and try not to vomit. He had no intention of trying to walk anywhere for a while.

"I foolishly thought that threatening to close down the production would bring you into line." Nathan reached for his computer, and much to his amusement, Kyle flinched. "Look at this."

He turned his laptop toward the anguished actor. It was footage of him and Michelle hanging in their space suits.

"Stop it, Kyle," they heard Michelle plead between takes. "I'm scared."

"Good!" Kyle sneered. "A dirty little slut like you deserves it."

Nathan paused the video and turned his attention to Kyle. "If you try anything like this again, I will give all of this footage to Shaunna to show to the press. You're going through what promises to be a messy and media-heavy divorce right now, and I will gladly show the world exactly what kind of prick you are."

Kyle was quick in his response. "We were in costume." He sounded smug, despite still being semi-hunched over and cradling his nuts like a handful of flower petals in a wind storm. "All I have to do is say we were just acting. You'll only look like a fool."

Nathan shook his head. "Don't try to outsmart me, Kitten Dick. She called you 'Kyle,' as in, Asshole, not your character's name. Besides, that's not the best clip." He resumed the video.

The actors were still in the harnessed space suits, but this clip was filmed from a different angle with a much tighter shot of them.

"It's not just my time you're wasting, Kyle," Michelle was telling him. "It's the crew, the other actors, the studio and their money…"

"I don't give a shit how much money it takes or how much this thing shakes…" He began shifting forcefully in his harness, causing the crane arm to vibrate and Michelle to gasp in fright.

"It's your fault you're not good enough to do this scene without crying and carrying on," he said venomously. Their helmets were off, and the ugliness of Kyle's face was stark and biting. "You're the one wasting everyone's time and money. You're the worst actor on this movie. I hope you know that."

Nathan stopped the video and looked over at Kyle with renewed war in his eyes. "We still had boom mics on you, idiot," Nathan informed him. "I must have about a half hour of you verbally abusing your wife." He looked at Kyle and was not sure if he could stop himself from making a mess of the pompous actor's perfect teeth. "What do you have to say for yourself?"

Nathan let him squirm like a worm on a hook.

"You're only seeing one side of it…" Kyle began finally.

"Oh, you're a victim! Is that it?" Nathan interrupted. "Are you going to tell me what she has done to you to deserve such treatment?"

Kyle said nothing.

"Look." Nathan uncrossed his legs, and Kyle flinched again. "I'll make it easy for you. You slip, I slip. Got it?"

Kyle nodded. "Got it."

"Are you sure?" Nathan asked earnestly, leaning forward. "Because I can't tell if you're actually stupid or just too used to playing stupid, but you don't seem to get important messages the first time. I've already been fooled by your promises to conduct yourself in a manner befitting…a human." He looked at Kyle for a moment, then seemed to make up his mind. "Nope, you don't get it. You need a more permanent reminder." Nathan stood up with resigned duty.

Kyle fell backward in his chair and immediately began scrambling away in a crab walk. "I got it! I got it! I promise! I won't even talk to her." He stood up and didn't wait for Nathan to agree. He ran. It made his testicles ache with new pain, but he ran anyway.

"Stop!" Nathan's command echoed like a pinball among the set trailers.

Kyle was too scared to stop, but even more scared not to. He halted, but didn't turn around.

"Don't fucking bother Shaunna, either," Nathan warned.

Kyle started running again.

Shaunna was deep in concentration, typing and staring intently at her monitor, when the shrill ringing of her hotel room phone startled her. She'd practically forgotten about the cream-colored fossil sitting a short distance away.

Shaunna picked up the receiver and reminded herself not to come across as abrupt or angry, just in case whoever was on the other end was a reporter.

"Hello?" she answered matter-of-factly, as though she were even expecting the call.

"Hi, Shaunna." The familiar and welcome suave tones of a man's voice carried through the line. "It's David Quinn."

His voice caressed Shaunna's ear pleasantly, and she shivered in response. She also found it mildly amusing that David felt the need to use his last name to distinguish himself.

"Hello, David Quinn. I recognized your voice."

"I hope it's okay for me to call your room. I didn't have any other way to get in touch with you, and I didn't want to presume to show up and knock on your door…again."

Shaunna was marginally disappointed he hadn't done just that. After all, their other doorway encounters had gone so well.

"It's perfectly fine. No worries. How was your day?"

"It was good, but busy."

"Did everyone behave themselves?"

"Pretty much, but I'm glad it's behind us. Actually, that's kind of why I was calling."

"Oh?"

"Yeah, well…um…Alix and I thought we'd go out somewhere, get some dinner, maybe a drink or two, and we hoped you could join us."

Shaunna cringed. Logically, she knew she had no right to feel possessive of David, but the fact that he had made plans with Alix first and then called her to tag along left a bitter taste in her mouth.

"That's sweet of you to ask, but I don't need to be a third wheel. You two have fun." Her intention was to sound like a mature adult, but there was an edge to her tone that cut right through the line.

David picked up on it immediately. "What? Oh no. No. No. Don't get me wrong. Alix is great, but I'm not interested in her." David hesitated slightly before speaking again in a somewhat injured tone. "I thought you understood that." His voice was closer to the receiver, and the effect pushed his hurt but heated words into her ear, as if he had been in the room with her.

Shaunna fidgeted slightly and bit her lip as she pondered her response. She felt embarrassed at making the passive-aggressive comment and opened her mouth to apologize, when he interrupted her.

"I would really like to see you tonight." David spoke the words slowly, hoping to convey his true attraction for Shaunna.

She felt a discreet sigh escape her lips upon hearing his declaration. "That's sweet, David. I'd like to see you too, but the truth is, I'm pretty bogged down in work tonight." Shaunna put her elbow on the table and rested her head against the admittedly comfortable hotel phone. "It turns out there are tons of media outlets who ran with a story about your date with Michelle. I need to respond to them before the entire thing gets out of hand."

"Really?"

Shaunna could hear the surprise and disbelief in David's voice. It was clear to her that he wasn't yet aware how that one photograph had made the entire entertainment world take notice of him. He was completely ignorant of how close to worldwide fame he really was. Shaunna made a mental note to contact Nathan the next morning about finding David some representation from the studio.

"It's the truth. I've been working on this all day, and I'm afraid it will be late tonight before I'm finally done. Michelle's had to work such long and difficult hours this week that we haven't had a chance to get together and discuss our strategy. Just so you know, I'm being as vague and discreet as possible about the whole thing. We've found that denying things like this, even if it's the truth, just sprinkles more blood in the water. It's a fine line to walk, but my intentions are to protect you both."

"Do you think I need protection?"

Shaunna smirked. "You should always use protection, David."

"I'll try to remember that." David's chuckling was low and sexy. "So, you haven't talked to Michelle at all today?"

"Not really. Why?"

David didn't know what to say. Hell, he didn't even know what to think. Michelle had inferred to a room full of their peers (and Kyle) that they were an item. Now Shaunna was mounting a public campaign to address the rumor that amounted to a "no comment." Essentially, anyone could take that to mean whatever they wanted it to. He could see things were going to get worse before they got better, but with Shaunna recovering from her arrest and her banishment from the set, David decided to let it go for the time being. Rather than launching into all the ugly details of the day, he opted to simply summarize.

"I wanted to see how she was doing. Kyle was a dick."

"What else is new? He didn't make her cry, did he?"

"No," David said firmly, then gently added, "I wouldn't let him."

"You protected her," Shaunna said simply. "You see, we all need someone to watch out for us, and you, my friend, are being watched by a lot of people right now."

"In that case, I'd better get back to the gym to work on my lats and my glutes."

"What are lats anyway?"

He didn't hesitate to answer. "I don't know."

He was so fun and so willing to be himself around her. It made her trust him. Just talking with him made her feel better.

"I have an idea. Why don't you come join me here, and we'll order room service?"

"Really? That would be great. What time?"

"Whenever. Now's fine if you're ready."

"Sure. I'll need to call Alix and let her off the hook."

"Okay, break it gently. See you in a few minutes."

After their meal, a decent tri-tip with garlic mashed potatoes and white chocolate cheesecake, neither David nor Shaunna felt in a hurry to leave one another's company. Shaunna returned her attention to her laptop while David stretched himself across the sofa to watch television.

The programming was lacking, and he finally settled for a marathon of *Pawn Stars*. But the usually entertaining Chumlee was no distraction from the beautiful woman who sat a few feet away. As the minutes ticked by, David found himself watching Shaunna much more than the History Channel.

He was fascinated by the curve of her shoulder as it rose up to her bare neck. Shaunna's hair was wrapped up in a loose knot, and a few strands of her dark brown tresses had escaped to rest lightly against her skin. She mostly sat still while she worked, but would move her head slightly whenever she paused to think.

To his immense enjoyment, Shaunna twice stretched by raising her arms into the air before placing her hands on the back of her neck. She then slowly slid her delicate fingers upward to massage the muscles until she reached her hairline.

David silently cursed that he could only see her from behind, knowing full well that the side view would provide him the glory of watching her back arch…and her chest expand outward.

He wasn't sure how long he had been watching her. It could have been mere minutes, but it felt like a blissful eternity. He was completely drawn to her, and without thinking, he rose silently from the sofa and approached her chair. When he was close enough to touch her, David extended just one finger to slide ever so gently down the back of her neck.

Shaunna paused her typing upon feeling David's touch, but did not tense. He took it as encouragement to continue. His finger trailed a path carefully down to the neckline of her T-shirt and then reversed course, slowly but surely upward. When his finger found a lock of her hair and began drifting through it, Shaunna sighed and broke the silence.

"That feels nice." She closed her eyes as she spoke.

"Yes? I'm glad." Without warning, David lowered his head. When he spoke again, this time in a whisper, Shaunna realized his lips were barely hovering above her skin. "May I?"

Shaunna merely nodded her acquiescence, too dazed to speak.

David brushed his lips across the skin of her neck, but didn't linger.

Shaunna breathed her contentment, and David happily returned his mouth to her skin. This time, his kisses were more solid and aggressive. He was thoroughly enjoying his exploration of this alluring part of her body. When he unpredictably moaned his pleasure, Shaunna felt a jolt of desire ripple through her.

She was awed by his intense devotion, but she also felt guilty that he was standing so awkwardly, bending forward to reach her.

"You can't be very comfortable," Shauna suggested with a throaty giggle. She felt his smile against her neck.

"You'd be surprised."

As David continued to dapple her with sensual kisses, she turned her head minutely. Her brow arched flirtatiously.

"We can move this elsewhere."

This time, it was David who paused. "Is that what you want, Shaunna?"

She nodded and rose up from her chair as he took a step backward. He wasn't entirely sure what he had started with her, but he was more than willing to allow her to set the pace for the evening. He was grateful when she reached out to take his hand and led him toward her king-sized bed. When they reached it, she sat down on the edge and pulled David's hand so that he sat down next to her. Their fingers were entwined, and both of them fell quiet as they settled in with a nervous anticipation.

"Should I go back to my room for a condom?" David whispered, as though he was sitting next to her in a library.

"You don't need to. I've been on the pill since I was eighteen." After a moment, she added, "Even though I haven't had a boyfriend since I was twenty-five."

David allowed only a few seconds to drift silently by before he leaned toward her and touched his mouth to Shaunna's. One brief kiss swiftly led to another longer one. On their third kiss, Shaunna fully opened herself to David, welcoming his tongue to connect with hers. As she allowed her body to recline fully into the mattress, she pulled him down on top of her.

Shaunna hadn't been kissed in a while, but there was no denying what an exceptional kisser David was. His mouth melded perfectly to hers, exerting just enough pressure against her lips to indicate his true desire, and he moved his tongue gently, yet insistently around hers.

She never wanted the kiss to end, and David seemed to read her thoughts perfectly.

In a sign of encouragement, Shaunna slid her fingers just underneath the waistline of David's jeans and boxer briefs, resting them on the bare skin of his hips. She delighted in the feel of him under her touch and was intensely aware of his every muscle as David's body began to rock gently against hers in response. Through their clothes, she could feel David's arousal.

She hated to break their kiss, but there was something she wanted so much in that moment. Shaunna couldn't stop herself from requesting it.

"Take your shirt off, David."

He complied quickly and efficiently, doing so with just one hand before they began kissing again. Shaunna's fingers glided deliciously over his back, and she recalled the image of him from the first night they swam together. At the time, Shaunna thought things were never going to get any better than that with the handsome, yet humble actor.

Being wrong had never felt so good.

Shaunna was distracted from her inner reflections when she felt David's hand drift along the side of her left breast. His fingers were initially timid as he began to touch her, waiting for any hint of discouragement. When he received none, David began lightly caressing her, coaxing Shaunna's body to respond to him. When it became clear that she had no objection to his touch, David slid his hand down and then up inside her shirt. Shaunna was not wearing a bra, something David had noticed over dinner. He groaned his admiration, and she broke their kiss again to make a second request.

"Take my shirt off, David."

He immediately obeyed her, pulling them both up from the bed and swiftly freeing the material from her slender body. He took in the glorious sight of Shaunna's naked breasts for the first time. Shaunna watched David's face carefully and realized that no man had ever taken the time to gaze at her in such a way. She blushed as nervousness and desire flooded through her.

"They're not much, I'm afraid."

He blinked and focused his blazing eyes on hers. "You're breathtaking."

She swallowed reflexively and bashfully whispered her thanks.

David reached out for Shaunna and pulled her hair tie free. As her hair flowed over her shoulders, he swept his fingers through it with care and consideration. She felt herself relax under his loving touch, his efforts inspiring a pleasurable tingling throughout her core.

David waited until Shaunna pulled his head closer to hers and the two resumed their kissing, taking the time to bask in one another's touch. When their bare chests came into contact for the first time, they stared deeply into each other's eyes as they relished the feeling of their bodies pressed together.

Their bliss was suddenly interrupted by the ringtone of Shaunna's iPhone. She recognized it immediately: "More Human Than Human." It was the ringtone she had assigned to Nathan. She grimaced.

"I'm so sorry, David. I have to answer that."

He nodded and reluctantly released her from his embrace.

Shaunna crawled off the bed. Although she didn't cover herself back up, she turned her back to David as she picked up the phone and answered Nathan's call.

"Hello." She fought to keep her greeting as neutral-sounding as possible.

"Shaunna. We need to talk."

Although she was eager to get off the phone and return to David, there was no denying the tension in Nathan's tone. "Sure. What's the matter?"

"We need to set up a meeting first thing in the morning. I need to know how you're going to handle the whole David/Michelle thing with the media. The last thing I need is a constant swarm of paps trying to get the money shot of those two."

Shaunna felt relief that the bulk of their conversation could be delayed until the following day, so she didn't bother to point out there really was nothing to the whole David/Michelle thing. "I've been working on it all day, but I agree that we should meet. Do you want Michelle present?"

"I'll leave that up to you. But after the way they were acting this morning, I don't want to leave anything up to chance. It's difficult enough to manage Kyle without him being focused on Michelle doing David in her off time."

Shaunna felt confused by Nathan's severe reaction to the photograph and presumptive story. They'd all been in the business long enough to know that tabloids made false assumptions all the time when it came to celebrities.

"It was just one picture, Nathan. This will all go away soon."

"Shaunna. I know you're not on-set anymore, and so maybe you're not completely in the loop yet, but after what I saw and heard this morning, there's no doubt in my mind that Michelle and David have something going on."

Shaunna felt her stomach lurch and she instinctively covered up her breasts without being aware of it.

David sensed her sudden apprehension. He held his breath as he wondered what had gone so wrong so quickly.

"Perhaps you're mistaken, Nathan." Shaunna's voice was low and serious, almost as though she were in shock.

"I'm sorry Shaunna, but I don't think so, and it's going to make things that much more difficult."

Shaunna bit her lip and took a deep breath, feeling foolish and lightheaded. She informed Nathan she would have to call him back and hung up before he could answer her.

After she set her phone down, Shaunna pulled a shaking hand up to her forehead and issued her third request of the evening. "David," she said calmly. "You need to go now."

Chapter Twenty-Two

Shaunna's words pierced David's heart like a harpoon. He wanted to protest. He wanted to clear the air immediately, but he could see that she was closing down. Her command was an indication that she was fighting for control of the situation. So he stood up from the bed as soon as she asked him to leave and wordlessly put his shirt back on.

Shaunna's stomach twisted into a conflicted knot as she reached for own shirt and pulled it back over her head. It wasn't that she automatically believed Nathan's words over David's actions. Bad timing aside, the shockwave produced by the phone call had simply turned out to be the last straw on her heavily burdened spirit.

She had every intention of letting David explain the situation. As a publicist, she knew that there were always two sides to any story, sometimes more. She had pretty much pieced it together anyway, but this meant that everything was about to change.

He began walking toward the door, but her words halted him. "You follow direction well. I'll give you that much."

David spun on his heel. He knew she was bluffing. "I can explain everything."

"I know," Shaunna replied casually. "He saw the picture on a web site, and then Michelle said something to piss off Kyle, and then you protected her so sweetly on-set. How could they think anything else?"

David watched Shaunna carefully. He wanted to feel relief at her comprehension, but the impassive expression on her face kept him on his guard. "So, you're not mad at me?"

Shaunna's frustration creased her forehead. "A little, but you hardly know any better. You're like a puppy that knocks plants over and piddles on the kitchen floor."

After a few moments of silence, her features softened and she sighed. She didn't want to be cruel to him, and seeing his hurt expression made her feel guilty for ordering him away.

Observing her decreasing anger, he opened his mouth to speak, but she beat him to the punch.

"I've got a busy night ahead of me. This is something that will require a hell of a lot more than 'no comment.' If your director thinks you're sleeping with Michelle, then everyone on-set thinks you are too, and half of them have already told somebody else. I have to clear some things up with Michelle. Right now."

"I could stay," David volunteered eagerly, seizing the opportunity to clear up any misunderstandings. "You know...we could conference call."

"Are you on-set tomorrow?" Shaunna asked, evading his suggestion.

"Only in the morning," he answered quickly.

"Good. We'll have lunch." Her answer was curt, and David felt desperate enough to grasp at straws.

"Like...room service lunch?" His voice was hopeful, his wide eyes longing for her to smile once again.

"We'll go out to lunch," Shaunna clarified. This new development meant that their future was going to require sacrifices, and nothing about that fact made her happy. All she wanted now was to be alone with her thoughts, to figure out exactly how to manage their upcoming roadblocks.

"I'll call you, then," David told her. He couldn't escape the feeling that he'd dodged one bullet, only to jump in front of a bus. "Could I have the number for your iPhone? I don't want to have to keep calling your room."

Shaunna nodded and wrote it down quickly for him on a scrap of paper. As she handed it to him, she did so with a polite dismissal. "I wish things could have turned out differently tonight."

"Me too," he answered. Not knowing what else he could say or do, David opened the door and walked back to his room, his shoulders slumped in disappointment at the shift in their evening.

Shaunna carefully closed the door and walked back to the bed. She knew that if she fell backward onto the blankets, she would cry. She almost did it too, mostly because she'd been so sure that her decision to take David to bed was the right one.

Now she had been robbed of the pleasure by an unforeseen and colossal complication. The promotion and premiere of the film moving along in tandem with Kyle and Michelle's impending divorce would begin to dominate the headlines in the next few months. Michelle's every move would be closely scrutinized, and now David's newly established connection to the star only exacerbated matters.

She was feeling guilty, believing she'd failed Michelle and that she'd done so more than once. Kyle had been the more famous actor when he'd met and married Michelle, and as a result, she'd often been labeled as the less talented performer. Some had even suggested that her career remained viable only because of who she'd married.

To Michelle's credit, she never let the criticism affect her and she rarely worried about the public relations game. She'd always been content to let Kyle dominate the celebrity headlines, and Shaunna had allowed that to happen.

Building up Kyle Petersen's public persona had been her crowning achievement. And now, with his decision to divorce Michelle, she suddenly found herself standing apart from her creation and wondering how best to fight back against her own accomplishments.

Still, Shaunna knew the potential benefits to her client's career if the romance rumors grew legs in the tabloids. As a seasoned publicist, she understood the exposure David and Michelle would gain if she managed the media well.

It was now essential to Shaunna that Michelle emerge as the winner in the wake of the divorce. Shaunna believed in her client enough to know that her talents as an actor could easily propel her career forward once the divorce was finalized. She also knew she wouldn't have to resort to destroying Kyle's sparkling public image in the process. Even though she would have enjoyed doing it, Shaunna had every confidence that he would take care of that all by himself.

Looking back, Shaunna knew she'd set the entire mess into motion when she lost her temper and quit in such a sensational fashion. She'd failed so many by committing that impetuous act. She'd failed the studio, the director and his cast and crew, her clients, her father and, most of all, herself.

The time had come to get it all back under her control.

Her mind made up, Shaunna pulled out her iPhone and walked out onto the narrow cement balcony. The night was warm and not very humid, so she leaned against the iron railing and looked down at the traffic while she waited for Michelle to pick up.

It only took two rings.

David had been in a daze since leaving Shaunna's apprehensive arms. He was barely aware of his surroundings and couldn't bring himself to care. All he could think about was how wonderful she'd felt in his arms, what a perfect fit her soft body had been when pressed against his. As soon as that had been taken away from him, he missed the connection.

He showed up to the set the following morning and snapped out of his funk long enough to complete his takes. But as soon as the assistant director yelled, "Cut!" his thoughts went back to Shaunna.

The only thing that kept him moving through the day was the promise of a lunch date with her. He was counting the minutes, and the clock ticked off each one with agonizing slowness.

When his final shot of the day was complete, David strolled toward the costume trailer, only to find it locked. The obstacle should have been annoying, but David merely sighed and glanced over in the direction of Michelle's trailer. Seeing her door open, he made a spontaneous decision and changed direction, calling out her name when he reached the doorway.

"David?" Michelle's surprised voice echoed from somewhere in the back. "Come in. Please."

If David had bothered to glance around, he would've spotted Kyle standing near his own trailer, his features frozen in anger, watching intently as the young man entered Michelle's space. As soon as David disappeared inside, Kyle huffed before stalking off.

Standing just inside the entrance with no sign of Michelle, David went to place his hands in his pockets. When he remembered his costume had no pockets, he fidgeted and ran his hand through his hair in nervous contemplation.

"Um. Am I interrupting anything? I can go."

Michelle emerged looking fresh-faced and rested, but also slightly nervous.

"No. You're fine. Actually, I'm glad you're here," she announced as she reached to pull the front door closed. "I have something I need to say to you."

"Oh? Me? Really?"

"Yes. Do you have a few minutes?" She gestured to a chair located just across from the door, and David sat down. She noticed his tension as he leaned forward to rest his elbows on his knees, clasp his hands together, and begin to bounce his leg slightly.

Michelle was anxious to get him to relax. "Can I offer you something to drink? I have just about anything you could want in the fridge. Or I could make you some coffee?"

David's voice was appreciative. "A water would be great. Thanks."

She nodded and grabbed a bottle from the refrigerator, setting it down on the counter. Before she could retrieve a glass, David grabbed the bottle and quickly returned to his seat, breaking the seal on the cap loudly as he twisted it off.

Michelle watched thoughtfully as he took a long drink, her hands tightly gripping the countertop behind her. She waited until he swallowed before speaking again.

"David, I owe you an apology. My behavior yesterday was terrible, and it wasn't fair of me to drag you into my argument with Kyle. I'm very sorry about that."

His response took her by surprise. "Can I ask you something? Something personal?"

She nodded.

"Kyle…" David paused as he seemed to struggle with how best to proceed. "He…he wasn't always a prick like that, was he? I mean… not when you married him."

Michelle shifted uncomfortably and looked down the hallway of the trailer. She remained still and silent for several moments before blinking and walking to the back.

David listened carefully and heard Michelle open and then close a drawer before she reappeared in front of him. She was holding a picture frame tightly against her chest as she began to speak.

"I don't know when it took this turn for us. When we met, he was good-looking, hard-working, maybe a little cocky, but no more so than any other actor I've ever known. I've been thinking about it a lot, and I keep trying to find that one moment when everything changed, but I don't think I can point out a single incident. The transformation was slow, it was painful, and when it was complete, I didn't even recognize him anymore."

Michelle pulled the picture frame back from her chest and glanced down at it with a fond, yet sad expression before holding it out to David. It was a picture of Michelle and Kyle, hugging one another. The background was unconventional for such an intimate pose. The couple was standing in a hallway next to an elevator, but they had the happy and relaxed appearance of two people enjoying each other's company.

As he looked at the photograph, David realized he'd never seen Kyle like this in person. Not even in the course of acting out a scene.

It was as though a genuine smile on the face of Kyle Petersen had never existed.

"How old is this?" David couldn't contain his curiosity.

"About five years old, I guess. It was when Kyle was promoting the first movie of the PI saga. His big break. He was in a hotel, giving one interview after another, and I stopped by to say hello while he was on a short break. The picture was taken by Shaunna, actually."

Hearing this information made the photograph even more intriguing to David. He studied it for a few more moments, trying to find some glimpse of Shaunna. He looked for her shadow on the wall and even looked at the reflections in the eyes of the celebrity couple, but there was no sign of her to be found. Michelle noticed the tight, pained appearance on David's face as he rose and carefully handed the picture frame back to her.

Michelle set it down on the counter, flat but face up, before returning her attention to David.

"Have you talked to Shaunna today?"

He shook his head and tried not to let his sour mood overtake his features.

"She told me a little bit about what happened when Nathan called last night. I feel responsible for that."

"Don't." David's tone was firm. "We talked it over last night. Shaunna understood what happened."

Michelle shook her head. "I acted like an idiot yesterday. I hurt you both, when all I really wanted to do was hurt Kyle. And I'm not especially proud of that, either. It was a weak moment for me. And then you were so sweet to me during that damn harness shoot."

David fidgeted, but didn't interrupt her.

"I don't know how I would've gotten through yesterday without your help. I want you to know I appreciate it. It won't surprise me when we get called in for re-shoots. I was a wreck."

David searched Michelle's eyes. "You were brilliant yesterday. If there are re-shoots, it will be because of Kyle. And I doubt Nathan is going to risk losing such great footage of you. You were incredible."

Michelle blushed slightly at the compliment. "Do you really think so?"

David nodded emphatically, his voice tinged with praise. "We were all impressed. Kyle was the only one who seemed to be clueless, and if I'm being honest, I don't think he totally was. I think he saw it too, and I think he was threatened by it. You're so much better than he is. In every way possible."

Michelle's eyes grew wide and took on a glassy sheen. She was rendered speechless for a few moments as a large lump formed in her throat.

"Thank you for saying that, David. You have no idea how much I needed to hear it."

"It's the truth. I think you're wonderful, and even though I'm glad you're away from Kyle now, I think he's a fool for giving you up."

Michelle nodded, a tear escaping her eye. Without thinking, David reached out and wiped it away with his thumb. "Please don't cry," he whispered.

She blinked rapidly at David's touch, and although she didn't pull away, Michelle glanced aside. Her eyes settled on the clock on the microwave oven.

"Aren't you supposed to be meeting Shaunna for lunch?" She turned her attention back to David's attire and giggled. "You better make yourself presentable and go, or you'll be late."

"Are you all right?"

Michelle nodded and straightened to her full height. "Yes. I'm fine. Take my advice and don't keep that girl waiting. She can't stand it when people are late for their appointments."

He stepped back from her before making his way toward the door. "If you ever need anything, Michelle, let me know. Anything at all."

A look of solid consideration flashed across her face before her expression softened back into a smile that nearly matched the one in the photograph resting on the counter.

"I will, David. Thank you."

An hour later, David was sitting in the elegant main dining room of Masraff's. He was feeling slightly underdressed amid a sea of business suits. He was increasingly worried that Shaunna's intentions for their meeting were strictly professional. He wanted so much more than that.

He was alone at the table, trying to blend into the crowd. In particular, the eyes of the women in the restaurant kept resting appreciatively on the young actor's face. He pretended not to notice any of them, his own eyes traveling from one wall painting to the next, as though he were enjoying an afternoon at the museum.

He didn't see her entrance into the dining room as much as he felt it. The air thickened somehow, and his attention was pulled away from his artful distractions. When his eyes locked onto her, he momentarily forgot how to breathe the pulsing, heavy air.

The woman striding toward his table was not the Shaunna he'd met and become acquainted with at the Radisson Hotel. Her face was determined, showing no sign of playfulness. This woman was dressed in a black knee-length pencil skirt and a royal blue V-neck blouse. David had seen her look this way before, the morning she'd appeared in a courtroom. This time, her eyes showed no fear.

As she drew close to the table, David rose to greet her. He was unsure about whether or not to hug her. His instincts told him to hold out his hand, so he did. Shaunna grasped it and leaned forward to allow him to kiss her cheek, which he did gratefully, yet carefully. He was scared of pushing his luck.

He began to pull out her chair for her, but she beat him to the task. He waited awkwardly until she was fully seated before settling back into his own chair.

"Hello, David." She greeted him with warmth, and his tight posture relaxed.

"Hello, Shaunna," he returned. "You look perfect."

"Thank you. You too." She winked, and he grinned in relief.

"I feel like I should be dressed up a bit more."

"You're fine," she answered simply.

The waiter swooped in to take their drink orders, and Shaunna asked David if he would share a bottle of wine with her. He readily agreed. Once their waiter departed, Shaunna rested her arms on the table and leaned forward.

"So. I bet you're wondering why I picked this place."

"Kind of," he admitted, his gaze full of unanswered questions.

"Well, it's very simple, David. You need representation, and I need a new client. Whether you're ready or not, you're about to become the most famous new celebrity on the planet."

Chapter Twenty-Three

David was mesmerized by Shaunna's professional confidence. Her eyes sparkled with resolve, and her posture was self-assured without the presence of arrogance.

He sat up straight in the hopes of projecting a certain level of composure. In the process, David's mouth went dry, and he sipped his water as he watched her lips move in slow motion.

"Those photos of you and Michelle set something into motion, something I spent the better part of yesterday trying to side-step. But the truth is…the press, and more importantly, the fans, love the idea of you two together." She sipped her water and let a tiny ice cube nest on her tongue while it melted.

"They do?"

"You've been trending on Twitter since yesterday."

"That's good. Right?"

Shaunna flashed him the same smile he'd fallen in love with in the hotel pool.

"It's educational," she answered. "Yesterday morning, the paps got pictures of you going into, and then coming right back out of Michelle's hotel. But they only published the ones of you leaving. As far as the rest of the world is concerned, those images are the follow up to the photos taken of you two at the club. The paps know which story will make them more money, so they are very eager to paint this particular picture of you two together."

David sat back in his chair, stunned. "Are you suggesting we encourage that story to further my career?"

"No," Shaunna answered him quickly. "But you can't publicly deny it, either."

"Why not?"

"If you deny it, if you tell the truth, not only will they *not* believe you, they'll resent the perceived lie."

"Who are *they?"* he asked.

Shaunna understood his reaction. "The media. The fans. The studio. Everyone that matters to your success."

"Do we just lie, then, and say we're dating? Maybe pose for a few pictures?"

Shaunna laughed, but there was no humor in the sound. "You don't want to misdirect the press, either. If you're caught, you'll both be crucified."

"So what, then?" David's head was already swimming in semantics. "Start dating for real?"

"Hell no!" Shaunna's controlled demeanor finally slipped at the mere thought, and David was instantly relieved at her reaction. It meant there was still hope for them.

"Kyle has already used this story to set himself up as the jilted husband. The paps just did him a huge favor."

"But *he* filed for divorce before I knew either of them," David said, disgusted.

"Exactly," Shaunna said, pointing at him. "Kyle is spinning this his way, and we don't want him to get the upper hand now."

David looked up through the skylight in exasperation. He thrived in simplicity, and there was nothing simple about what Shaunna was presenting to him.

When David spoke again, his voice was filled with resignation. "Please. Just tell me what to do."

"Don't confirm or deny anything about you and Michelle to anyone. We're going to run with a 'no comment' strategy for now."

"But won't *they* just assume we're dating if we do that?"

"David, as far as the outside world is concerned, you and Michelle are a couple now. Whether you realize it or not, you're in a spotlight much brighter than you're used to."

He squinted at her statement.

"I can handle it." He uttered the words without knowing if he actually believed them.

"I know you can. That's why I'm speaking to you about this. But I need you to understand, they'll also hold a magnifying glass in front of the spotlight until they've burned you like an ant."

"Hmm," David pondered, in an attempt to lighten the mood. "Cockroaches burning ants."

Shaunna allowed herself to laugh momentarily in relief.

He leaned forward. "I need to know. Personally, what do you think about this strategy?"

Shaunna closed her eyes and decided to answer him honestly. "I hate it…but, it's brilliant." She opened her eyes. "And it's also our only option right now."

They were briefly interrupted by the waiter delivering their wine, and they ordered their meals, opting for the same thing: oven-roasted Nova Scotia halibut.

They sat in silence for a while after the server left, each processing the newest obstacle to their budding romance. Shaunna regarded the way his meandering hair hooded his ears, which were on the smallish side. David watched as a slight and mysterious grin began to form on her pretty face.

"Just out of curiosity," David mused while he was toying with his napkin. "How long do you think this will last?"

"It's hard to say." She shrugged. "Since everyone already believes you two are an item, it's just a matter of not correcting the media's assumption."

"Well then, if we're so popular together, aren't they all going to hate it when we break up?"

Shaunna thought once again how keen his mind was. "David, in this business, you can only afford to worry about one week at a time."

David crossed his arms as he leaned back in his chair. "There is one way to show everyone that Michelle and I aren't dating."

Shaunna's eyes betrayed nothing, but she knew what he was thinking. Frankly, it was about damn time he made the suggestion.

"If they saw us together," David continued, "the way I want to be with you, then they'd have to believe it."

She nodded her head. "True, but it could be solving one problem by creating an even bigger one for you."

"Why? Because it would involve you?" he asked pointedly.

"Exactly. I have a reputation of my own to repair. Having you seen in public with me right now wouldn't be good for you. My meltdown and arrest isn't exactly front page news anymore, but it's by no means buried. I'm still in damage control mode, and media outlets would pounce at any little thing I do if it helps resurrect a cash cow for them."

Shaunna elaborated before David had a chance to respond. "Think about it for a minute. Kyle and Michelle announced their divorce, and I made such a spectacular exit from his employ that it landed me in jail. Even if people know Kyle for who he really is, no one would blame him for filing charges against me. As far as everyone is concerned, Michelle is a saint for keeping me as her publicist."

David leaned forward in his seat and opened his mouth to object, but Shaunna held up her finger, requesting his continued silence.

"Now that Michelle has some distance from Kyle's shadow, the public is getting to know more about her. Having the two of you photographed together at that club produced unexpected results. Typically, people would scoff at a woman moving on so quickly with her life and wonder if the new man she was dancing with played a part in the breakdown of the marriage. But that didn't happen with the two of you. The public loves the thought of you and her together, and that story is only going to fuel interest in you."

Shaunna took a sip of water as she organized her final thoughts. "If you were to suddenly shift your attention from Michelle Cooper to me, it would end badly for us both. The story would be you leaving Hollywood's most popular actress to date the woman who stole from her former husband. Michelle would come across as dumb, but I guarantee you would come across as a likely two-time cheater, and I would've very publicly violated the trust of my client for the second time." She hazarded a look into his eyes and saw a future lover staring back at her with intensity. "I want to be with you, David, really. But the timing isn't right." As Shaunna shook her head, her brown hair fell in front of her shoulders on both sides, giving her a glamorous look.

"There has to be somebody in the media that you know and trust, and we can just talk to them."

"I understand," Shaunna responded. "But PR doesn't always work the way you want it to. Communication with the media doesn't mean control of the media. Right now, doing nothing and saying nothing is the smartest decision for all three of us."

Their conversation was interrupted once more as they were served their meals and began eating. Shaunna helped herself to David's lemon when he discarded it.

"Would I actually say *no comment?*" David asked, just before placing the first bite-sized portion of fish into his mouth.

Shaunna laughed playfully. "Not really. Nonsense like that is more appropriate for a Senate oversight committee. If you're asked on the street, just ignore the question. If it happens during an interview, just side step the issue with a joke."

They ate in silence for a while, each enjoying their food. "Can't we at least sneak around in private?" David blurted out, intending to ask a different question, but being suckered by his own lips and the influence of the mid-day wine.

Shaunna froze. She was thrilled he was flirting with her once more, especially after the awkward complication that had pried them apart the evening before.

"Maybe. When we get back to California."

They ate quietly for a while longer, allowing the weight of her last statement to work their hearts into a gallop. David breathed in through his nose while he savored butternut squash on his tongue.

He tried not to gawk at the slope of Shaunna's breasts too often, but he was fascinated by the way the firm scoops of flesh touched each other just before her blouse hid them. He recalled the image of her from the evening before, topless and underneath him. David wanted more than ever to undress her.

"We need to get your agent involved as soon as possible," Shaunna mentioned, casually changing the subject. "This development could land you some romantic comedies, and those are gold mines."

David took a long drink of water in a futile attempt to quench his lust-fueled thirst. "I don't have an agent," David admitted.

Shaunna arched an eyebrow. "I don't understand. How did you get the *Sling Shot* gig without an agent?"

"I had an agent before I left town," he clarified. "But she just passed along Nathan's offer. I was looking to get out of the business and hadn't been auditioning much. When *Sling Shot* came out of the blue, it made it possible for me to afford to go back home to Chicago. When I arrived here, I had no intention of returning to LA."

Shaunna turned pale upon hearing the news. He hadn't seen her look so distraught since she'd been arrested.

"My plans have changed, obviously," he added.

Shaunna exhaled in relief. "I have some news about the TV show by the way, but first you need representation. I can set you up with some good people. Folks who aren't looking for new clients, but who will take on someone for me."

"Can't you do it?" he asked sincerely. "You did such a good job with Gus."

"That's because it was Gus," she told him. "And because he was all discombobulated after seeing his daughter get thrown in the slammer."

"I like a girl who's not afraid to use a word like discombobulated in conversation." David chuckled.

"Can I make a few calls, then?" she asked with a sly smile.

David held his hand out, and Shaunna shook it. Much to his chagrin, it was to be the first of only two times he felt her touch the remainder of the afternoon.

She continued to speak to David about what she called "gaps" in his portfolio and quizzed him on the types of projects he might enjoy during his time off from filming the TV show. Shaunna nodded her head and took notes as he answered her questions. "I think I'm going to introduce you to Brandy Parlor…"

"Wait, her name is Brandy Parlor? Is she an agent, or a bar in West Hollywood?"

Shaunna gave him the stink eye. "She's a sci-fi nut who might already be a fan of yours and could keep you all gooped up in corn syrup for years if you want to continue making gross-out pictures. But like me, she'll wisely suggest that you try your hand at romantic comedy. You'd be a real draw."

David shifted uncomfortably in his seat. Fictional or otherwise, the only romantic interest he wanted to pursue was Shaunna Noble. Until he could distance himself from the scandalous mess of Kyle and Michelle's divorce and make Shaunna truly his, he wouldn't be finding anything comical about romance.

"All right. Introduce us," he offered in appeasement, "but I still don't know why you can't rep me."

Shaunna shook her head once again. "You don't want me, David."

David reflexively uttered a sensual, throaty groan that Shaunna acknowledged only with an undeniable reddening of her cheeks.

"I'm a publicist, not an agent. It's a language I don't speak, and I could get you into a lot of trouble. I was only able to haggle with my dad because I've been doing it my entire life."

"Did you say you had news from him?"

"Yes. We worked out a deal that I was going to turn over to your agent, but if you want…"

"I'll give you fifteen percent of whatever deal you made with Gus," he said firmly. "I'll work with whoever you suggest after this deal is done, but only if you accept those terms."

Shaunna nodded. "All right. Gus really liked you, and he always gets what he likes. It worked to your advantage, and this whole thing with Michelle certainly didn't hurt. Initially, he was firm on eight, but I got him up to two-point-five, plus a handsome bonus if the show gets picked up for a second season."

David paused in mid-chew with utter astonishment. "Two-point-five what?"

"Million," Shaunna stated matter-of-factly. "Even after my fifteen percent, you'll clear a deuce. That reminds me. You'll also need a finance manager." She returned her attention to her notes.

David heard every noise in the room amplify for a moment before he heard nothing but the crashing of waves in his ears. From underneath the table, he felt Shaunna grab his leg and squeeze.

"Stay with me, David."

It was the warmth and strength of her hand that finally lured him from the fog. He looked up, and she saw his eyes clear a little.

"How?" It was all David could muster as he reached for his wine.

"Like I've been saying, you're famous. Right now. Today. By the time the show airs, you'll be a household name. Gus understands he got you for a song."

"I don't know what to say." David was still overwhelmed and frankly was not out of the forest yet.

"Say whatever's in your heart, David."

"All right." He set his glass down and peered into it, taking one last moment to gather himself before he lifted his head and locked his gaze with hers.

"I was ready to give up on acting, to give up on myself. But you saw something in me I hadn't noticed in a long time. You saved me from having to go back home a failure." His eyes became as wet as his lips. "I'll never forget what you've done for me, and I don't know how I'll ever repay you, but right now…I just wish I could kiss you." He looked down again and spoke quickly. "I wish I could kiss you right here and now, and I know this feeling is only going to grow every day. I don't know if I can take this kind of happiness and sadness together at the same time."

"Just remember that I know exactly what you're going through," Shaunna whispered to him, resisting the painful urge to stroke his hair in reassurance. "And soon, we will be together, and we'll be alone."

The two exchanged knowing and hopeful looks before finishing their meals.

After a time, David was ready to return to business. "Do they have a script for me yet?"

"Yes. It should arrive later today. They want you to grow a beard."

"I'm too pretty to grow a beard." David spoke the words in jest, but Shaunna nodded enthusiastically and laughed.

"That's exactly what I said. But they want you to look more rugged. I told them to consider giving you scars instead, maybe work it into a more sinister backstory. After all, you *are* playing the villain."

"Chicks dig scars," David informed her.

"No, they don't," she replied. "That's a myth."

"Really? What about cars? Do chicks dig cars?"

"This one does," she answered with a playful smirk.

Shaunna informed him that her father's garage was full of muscle cars from the seventies and promised to arrange a tour.

"Can I bring Nathan along?"

"Absolutely."

"So let me just get this straight in my head one last time," David began. "If anyone asks about me and Michelle, I just play coy? I don't confirm or deny anything?"

"Can you do that?" she asked pointedly.

David's lips rose in a grin. "Actually, I think that's going to be the most fun part about all this."

Shaunna nodded. "Michelle said the exact same thing."

Chapter Twenty-Four

Two weeks later, Shaunna, David, and Michelle were on a flight back to California. They flew first class and had only unenthusiastic businessmen as company.

David sat next to Michelle. Shaunna was only across the aisle from him, but the physical distance from her was insurmountable. He held three magazines in his agonized grip. He'd seen and purchased the periodicals at the airport, the newest additions to his collection of covers. This trio brought his running total up to eleven. Tabloids, of course, didn't count.

Everything Shaunna told him over their lunch at Masraff's had since come true. When he wasn't behind closed doors or roaming a secure movie set, he was constantly approached by paps and fans.

She'd successfully found an agent for him, her friend Brandy "Sauce" Parlor, who had indeed already known who David was when she took Shaunna's call. When David first spoke to her from Shaunna's phone, they hit it off immediately. Brandy was busy lining up meetings with casting directors for the perfect hiatus project for David while he was busy memorizing the scripts from Gus's production headquarters. Technically, he was four days late for rehearsals, but was miraculously excused by the executive producer.

David rolled up his magazines so he wouldn't see his own face. The situation was odd. He wanted to keep them as a souvenir of his whirlwind experience; he just didn't want to have to look at them. He couldn't even explain it to himself.

As agreed upon, the actor and his publicist had led a chaste fortnight. They hadn't given in to the temptation, despite some steamy phone calls that left them both breathless at times. They'd adapted to the situation as well as could be expected, but clearly their nocturnal distractions kept them from thinking about some essentials.

Shaunna suddenly realized that David didn't have any place to stay once they landed and he hadn't mentioned anything to her about his plans. Presumably, he'd given up his apartment along with his agent when he flew to Texas. She felt ashamed that she'd let two weeks go by without thinking about where David was going to sleep until he could find a place of his own.

The last thing Shaunna wanted was for David to be stuck in another hotel for weeks on end, but she couldn't exactly invite him to stay at her house. Kyle and Michelle's divorce was still playing out, and it remained to be seen who would win the media in the settlement. Shaunna's outburst and arrest in Texas had mercifully ceased to be of any interest now that Michelle Cooper was likely dating her co-star. But if Michelle's alleged new boyfriend suddenly began to spend his nights at Shaunna's house, things would spin out of control in a hurry. It would be a disaster for everyone involved, except Kyle Petersen.

Not knowing what else to do, Shaunna covertly texted the actress sitting just two seats away from her.

Michelle felt her pocket vibrate and plucked her phone from her comfortable "traveling" pants.

Invite David to stay with you until he's settled. I'll explain later.

The actress shot Shaunna a shocked look, which was met with a pitiful stare that told her something else was at stake. It was all Michelle needed. She sent a quick text of her own and put her phone away before turning to David.

"Why don't you stay with me for a while?" she suggested casually.

David swallowed and immediately looked over at Shaunna. "Won't this only exacerbate the current situation?" he whispered.

He and Michelle were currently *The Hottest Couple in Hollywood,* despite the fact they weren't even in the state of California and had never kissed.

"Shooting a TV drama is going to kick your ass, sweetie. You need a safe place to relax and recoup at night. It's a nice big house with lots of room."

David waited patiently until she answered his question.

"Do I think it's going to complicate things? Yes, but we've been bailing water for weeks, and I'm already wet."

David's eyes twinkled as he considered her words.

"If you don't have any place to stay, then I really do insist, David. Frankly, I'd feel a lot safer with you around."

Ever vigilant about seizing chivalrous opportunities, Michelle's final words sealed the deal for David. "All right. Thanks. I don't know anything about buying a house, but I guess I should think about it."

"I'd be very happy if you stayed with me until you found what you were looking for," Michelle told him. "I mean it. I'll be sad when you go."

Somewhere over Arizona, Shaunna leaned toward David. "I just want to make sure you're really ready for what we're going to face when we land."

David's nervous chuckle was answer enough. "The Super Bowl, I know."

"Well, maybe not the Super Bowl, but if you think you can handle a stadium full of photographers, I guess you're ready."

"I'm just going to smile, wave, and say nothing," David recited.

Shaunna nodded her head. "What if someone asks, *Isn't it true that you make Michelle dress up like Princess Leia?*"

David laughed. "I'd say, *I might start now.*"

Shaunna shook her head and put her finger to her lips.

David nodded his head. "Okay." He made a mental note to just sing a song in his head or something. Maybe then he would be able to ignore the questions.

Shaunna wanted to touch his hand in comfort. She wanted to rub his back and tell him that all he had to do was get to Malibu and then she would take tender care of him.

Instead, she offered him her Chapstick.

He accepted it, but only because it meant he could pretend it was a kiss from her. It reminded him of eighth grade, and he felt goose bumps form on the back of his neck when their fingers brushed in the exchange.

"Are you staying in Malibu tonight?" David asked her causally.

"I'm going home first, but I'll be over for dinner," Shaunna stated plainly.

David grinned and whispered so only she could hear his words, "What about dessert?"

Shaunna turned toward him with ambitious eyes, but kept her voice low. "Dessert comes first."

Shaunna never considered LAX a special airport. Sure, it was always busy and even clean, but it wasn't memorable. Only the people passing through it were.

Photographers, reporters, fans, and the like were not allowed past security, but as soon as David and Michelle were fair game, the hunters came at them with clicks, flashes, and shouts.

"Michelle! Did you rebound with David? Or is it true love?"

She blinked at the man who asked the question, but didn't say a word.

David couldn't stop himself from formulating several responses that were neither confirming nor denying a relationship, but understood that the trap was giving the parasites any ammunition at all.

He began humming Roger Miller's tune "King of the Road" while the unnerving questions tripped over each other, each more invasive and insulting than the last.

"David! Have you landed a cougar to ride to financial freedom?"

"Michelle! How does David compare to Kyle in bed?"

"David! What was it like working with Kyle on-set while you were working on his wife off-set?"

"Michelle! I know he's young, but aren't you trading down?"

"David! What does your mother think about the fact that your new girlfriend is almost as old as she is?"

Shaunna walked slightly ahead of them both, clearing their path. She was pulling her own bag and trying not to cringe at the ruthless verbal attack on a "relationship" she knew the fans adored. Paparazzi were considered neither media nor fans (nor human, for that matter).

Still, David was green, and keeping one's mouth closed in situations like this was easier said than done. It took practice and, sometimes, medication.

He recognized the desperate nature of their questions, however. It was almost as if they knew that the only way to get celebrities to talk was to shock them into responding. This understanding made it easier for him to resist.

Being photographed within the confines of the airport was inevitable, but if the paps got no words out of their target, then they usually felt as though an opportunity had been wasted. David was thrilled to deny them any fodder.

Anticipating the airport frenzy, Shaunna had called her father the evening before and arranged for a car and his personal driver, Benny, to take David and Michelle to Malibu. She needed to retrieve her own car from the long-term parking lot, but hopped into the dark SUV with the duo to avoid a ride on the shuttle bus. She planned on a detour home before joining them at the beach.

"You did very well, David," Shaunna said once they were all safely enclosed in the vehicle. She'd been planning to offer him further reassurance, but her words were swallowed by the concern that swam into her eyes once she turned to Michelle.

"They were unfair and vicious, and you'd better not believe one word of their crap." Shaunna was in awe of Michelle's self-control and poise under such intense pressure. She believed that almost anyone else would've started bawling if they'd been peppered with such garbage.

"They failed." David's words carried the weight of a general informing his troops that the war was finally over. He looked at Michelle. "You are the best actress I've ever worked with...and the most beautiful fake girlfriend I've ever had."

He winked in her direction, and the car filled with giggles for a moment before the conversation turned to planning the afternoon.

David was quite willing to enjoy Michelle's invitation to stay with her, but insisted that he only occupy one room and be allowed to contribute to household costs.

Shaunna and Michelle rolled their eyes simultaneously, but agreed to his terms. As they dropped Shaunna off at her car, David sprang out and ran to the trunk before Benny had even turned off the engine.

Benny looked at David in his side view mirror and pushed the button to release the trunk with a grin and a shake of his head. The kid was just making his job easier.

"I'm that one." Shaunna pointed to a dark green Jaguar.

David's eyebrows sprang up so high that he might have interfered with air traffic. "Nice."

Shaunna crossed her arms. "They'll be coming soon, David. We'll want to be gone by then."

David's eyebrows landed, even though he was more surprised than ever. "What? It's not over?"

"Not by a long shot," Michelle added, popping her head out the rolled down tinted window. "Most of them will try following us through the city, but of course, they know where I live already, so we'll find a new batch of them sitting outside the gate."

"Yeah, well, they don't care about me much anymore," Shaunna said. "And I want to keep it that way. Good luck, you two."

David put Shaunna's bags in the trunk and closed it with a solid *thunk*. "I'll see you this evening, then?"

"Sooner," she cooed.

David drank her words like wine and climbed back into the car with a smile that quickly became a full-on dopey grin.

Chapter Twenty-Five

Shaunna returned to her home in Yorba Linda long enough to take a bath and change her clothes. She indulged in both bubbles and Ray Charles during her bath, but didn't stay inside the tub for more than a few songs. Her goal was to relax and unwind before leaving for Malibu, but she found that the longer she stayed away from David, the more anxious she became.

When she pulled up to the estate gate, there were three cars parked nearby. Men with obscenely large cameras around their necks and wrinkled pants were smoking cigarettes and ignoring her. She was glad. It meant her Texas tantrum hadn't truly transformed her into a celebrity, and therefore, she wasn't important enough to photograph.

Code punched and car parked, Shaunna began walking toward the carved wooden double doors at the front of Michelle's house. As she passed Kyle's car, parked right where she'd left it for him, her skin crawled.

The doors opened into a tall room dominated by columns that drew the eye up to a domed ceiling accented with snowflake-shaped skylights.

David was standing in the middle of the champagne marble floor, waiting for her. The skylights were trapping him in bars of thin light that swept over his skin in silent brilliance.

He'd changed his clothes. She would've expected for him to dress in shorts and a tee shirt, but instead, David was wearing his navy blue suit, complete with pinstriped vest. His outfit was complemented by shiny black wingtips that kicked sunlight back up at the walls when he shifted his weight.

"Michelle asked me to tell you that she will be in her room for the rest of the night and will see you in the morning for the meeting with Mr. Harper." David spoke with efficiency, but his eyes were wild with extra-curricular thought.

Shaunna closed the front door, and David began walking toward her. Shaunna held up her hand, and he froze.

"Stay there," she instructed him while dropping her purse on a wall table. "In the light."

She closed the distance between them with deliberate steps and pulsing, open lips. David actually braced himself for her arrival into his arms.

The first parts of their bodies to touch were their hands, and with fingers laced together, they pulled each other into a kiss.

David found a sprinkle of sunlight on Shaunna's neck and enthusiastically covered it with his mouth. She ran one of her hands up his strong back and rested it on his warm neck.

"I've been waiting for you for so long." Shaunna spoke the words and listened as they were returned to her by the faint echo in the room.

"Your wait is over."

His eyes were locked on hers, and his breath, sweet like candy, brushed her lips. He took her by the hand, leading her to an oval-shaped staircase that sank into the right half of the room. Before they began climbing, she pulled him in another direction.

"We have unfinished business. This way."

David played along. "Are you giving me the tour? Michelle only showed me the kitchen. That and my room. It's right next to yours. By the way, I didn't know you had your own room here."

"It started out as my office, but I spent so many late nights here that Michelle had a bed brought in," Shaunna replied simply. The two women had discussed David's living situation via several more texts during the flight, and Shaunna suggested that the exercise room would make a nice large living space for David. It even had its own bathroom and daybed.

"I'm sorry about the treadmill," she added after a few more steps. "We'll move it out together tomorrow. And get you a bigger bed."

David laughed. Once he got her undressed, he had no intentions of letting Shaunna put her clothes back on, let alone help him move a piece of exercise equipment. Still, he listened to her plan it all out as she guided him through hallways he'd never seen. Kyle had a billiard room with a train set up where the pool table should be. He also had a library that appeared to be half-empty. The occupied half was filled with what looked like entertainment magazines. It made him want to throw his own newly begun collection away.

The house was old. The walls were constructed with thick stone squares and reminded David of a castle.

Shaunna made one last turn, opened a heavy door, and revealed an indoor oasis.

"No way!" David was stunned. They were on the edge of a natural-looking spring, complete with a functioning waterfall.

"The water is a little on the cool side," Shaunna cautioned. "But you'll get used to it fast."

"No windows," David observed.

Shaunna had already thought heavily on the matter. "Actually, we're safe anywhere in the house except for the upstairs rooms that open to the balcony over the driveway." She began taking off her clothes. "But this is as private as it gets."

"This place is amazing!" It was clearly a product of the late eighties *inside out* craze that swept the decadent West Coast mansions, but he was grateful that the intimate lagoon was still available for their enjoyment.

When his eyes settled on Shaunna again, she was completely nude. Her pert nipples were beacons to the gentle valley between her round breasts. David's stare followed the path of least resistance all the way down to the tiny and tidy garden of brown curls that split the river of skin.

He suddenly realized how very, *very* overdressed he was and fidgeted slightly as he dragged his heavy eyes back up to hers. "Allow me to reciprocate," he murmured as he began to loosen his necktie.

"Let me," Shaunna offered as she stepped toward him.

David obediently dropped his arms to his sides, allowing the naked woman to undress him.

"This is a nice tie," she commented as she slid it from his neck. "You had it with you in Texas?"

David nodded his head. "I brought all my clothes with me."

"Of course you did," Shaunna said as she walked around behind him and removed his jacket.

She especially liked the way men looked in vests when their jackets were off. She admired how David's fit figure was accented by the almost corset-like nature of his pinstriped, three-buttoned special. Shaunna appreciated him as she completed her circle.

She then backed up to get, and give, a better view.

"Have a seat." Shaunna gestured to a custom rock bench near the edge of the black tiled pond. David sat, and she began removing his shoes.

He looked down at the nude beauty working the laces and willed himself not to be ticklish for the next thirty seconds of his life. Her touch, however, was too delicate, and he was just too tender-footed. David chortled and twitched, giving himself away. To her credit, Shaunna did not take advantage of her newfound knowledge until she had removed his other shoe and both his socks. She feathered the balls of his feet with her fingers before she allowed him to stand again.

"Don't worry," she assured him as she began unbuttoning his vest. "I'm ticklish too." She opened it and then pressed her firm body up against his while she claimed another kiss.

Shaunna began unbuttoning his shirt before she took his vest off, and when she reached the last button, her busy hands kept working down his body.

She unbuckled his belt and unfastened his pants with care. David was pressing so tightly against his boxer briefs that she had to pull the zipper away from the bulge first. She slid his trousers and underwear down his legs in a slow, steady movement.

Shaunna regarded his arousal. He definitely had plenty to work with, and more importantly, it was as appealing as the rest of him. He was smooth and straight and grew even harder before her eyes. She moved in to strip away his remaining clothes, and the moment his erection touched her belly, he closed his eyes and sighed.

She smiled and glanced down. "You like that?"

"Yes. You feel so warm."

She laughed. "I was going to say the same thing about you."

David eagerly took over removing his shirt while Shaunna gently caressed his thick shaft. She enjoyed the way it filled her hand.

She felt mighty.

David watched as she first looked at and then bent down to lick him. She was initially timid, tasting, sampling, but soon was swallowing with greedy grace. She knelt down on his jacket and swirled her tongue around his vivid pink tip until it was as shiny as his discarded shoes.

She paused briefly to admire her handiwork. Then she resumed pleasing him with her mouth. She took breaks often to allow David to watch her stroke him while she took in the results of her effective technique.

"We're going to get the first one out of the way, if you don't mind," Shaunna informed him matter-of-factly.

"Okay." David sounded like he was accepting an offer to help him out of a barn fire.

"Good." She turned her mind and her mouth back to her task, and David gulped before he sighed her name.

She liked the way he sank his hands carefully into her hair and called her name repeatedly as he spilled over. She adored the pulsing rush released in her mouth and milked all she could from him before he was allowed to withdraw.

"Now, let's finish that swim we started in Texas." Shaunna walked to the water, and he watched her round rear disappear into a reflection of itself.

"And then?" he asked somewhat breathlessly as he followed her.

"And then…you'll be allowed to reciprocate."

David caught up to her behind the waterfall. His hard, wet arms surrounded her, and she instantly felt like she was protected from the world. "Technically," he began in a low, determined voice, "to reciprocate would require no recovery time on my part."

There was a flat but worn rock ledge that sat just above the waterline, and he lifted her up onto it before she could protest.

Then, with his face at her knees, he asked permission. "Can I kiss you?"

His hands crept languidly along her calves, but waited for her command.

Shaunna arched her back. She then opened her legs to him and awaited the touch of his mouth on her soft flesh.

David moved his hands up and down her thighs as he delivered tiny kisses to the warm, pink skin she offered him. When he began to thoroughly explore her satin creases with his tongue, Shaunna moaned softly.

David clearly loved to kiss and suckle and flick and swirl. It was the satisfied grunts and moans emitting from his own throat that made her mercury rise.

He put his hands on her inner thighs and opened her legs farther as he immersed himself in her scent and her honey taste.

She wondered what David was thinking about as he worked so hard for her, bringing her closer and closer to what was going to be a frighteningly strong climax.

David was thinking about how much he truly wanted to satisfy her, body and soul.

Shaunna restrained herself for as long as she could. It was already the best any man had ever done for her in that regard, and she wished to savor the memory, but her orgasm was like a steamship: even if she wanted to stop it, its momentum would propel her into oblivion in mere moments.

Shaunna came with such force that she was still gasping for breath a minute later. David gingerly lifted her back into the refreshing water with him, holding her in his arms until she recovered her senses. They listened to the thundering waterfall nearby, and Shaunna thought it was probably the only thing that kept him from hearing her heartbeat.

She reluctantly left his embrace with a promise of a swift return. She swam away, and when she stepped out of the man-made pond, he observed beads of water racing down her round bottom. She fetched towels from a tucked-away cubby hole and held his out to him while diamonds of clear liquid clung to the bottoms of her breasts.

"Now we can go upstairs," she told him.

He left their oasis and took his towel. To Shaunna's pleasant surprise, he immediately began to dry her off with it. She wrapped her hair in her towel as he lovingly patted her down with his. Once he was satisfied with his efforts, Shaunna turned and produced two bathrobes, both pale green in color and very fluffy.

They gathered their clothes and carried them upstairs to Shaunna's room, which had a California King bed and an ocean view. David opened the sliding glass door, and a warm breeze plucked at the robe around his legs.

"If those photographers get themselves a helicopter, we could be in trouble," he wryly observed as he watched the outermost waves develop.

Shaunna pulled the thin white curtains in front of the open door. They billowed out, but blurred the horizon. "There. Now they need a helicopter and scissors."

David spun her around and pulled the towel from her hair. He then dropped his own robe to the floor, and they walked hand in hand to bed.

They lay on their sides and placed their foreheads together.

"I was in such a rush before, but now I just want this to last all night. I want to savor you." David spoke earnestly, his gaze locked firmly onto hers.

They kissed for a long time, learning one another's bodies with tongues and hands that moved leisurely over cool skin. After a while, David turned Shaunna over on her stomach and began rubbing her back and shoulders.

His caressing hands were wonderful, and she could have easily let him massage her to sleep, but she wasn't about to let this opportunity pass her by. When she was fully relaxed, Shaunna turned over and placed her feet sole to sole. Her knees were spread wide, and she looked at him with longing.

"I want you inside me, David."

"I'll be gentle," he promised her, his expression showing both his passion and his reverence.

"Not too gentle, I hope," she responded suggestively.

David laughed, but she saw concentration occupy his beautiful face for a moment. Then, as she felt his warm girth enter her, his face softened into bliss.

He felt so right inside her, and she wrapped her legs around the backs of his thighs to hold him firmly in place. She loved the sensation of him, plunging as deep inside her as anyone could go.

Soon, he began moving with determination, and Shaunna was certain that she was going to climax quickly. David was watching her soft body rock, and she liked that. He was also slowly losing control, and she liked that even more.

She wanted to know that he would respond to her.

Shaunna shifted underneath him, and David rolled from on top of her. As soon as she was free, she straddled him and sat down deliberately. David reached up and cupped her breasts as Shaunna began to rise and fall with a sweet and steady rhythm. She leaned her head back and felt her long, wet hair tickle her upturned feet.

David was feasting with his senses. The feel of her hard nipples against his palms and her warm tight body surrounding him; the sight of her naked figure deliciously looming overhead; the sound of the ocean, like distant applause; the scent of her soft skin and the taste of her silk that lingered in his mouth and memory.

Shaunna enjoyed his hands on her, and she seductively swiveled her hips and closed her wide eyes as he filled her over and over again. Her body and her heart were full of his love.

The light of the setting sun drifted over the couple twenty minutes later, peeking under the eaves of the house and brightening the room through the hazy curtained filter. Glistening with sweat, David was once more over Shaunna and thrusting into her. His strong hands were gripping her hips and pulling her toward him hard enough to cause her hair to flare wildly across the bed.

Shaunna treasured every movement, and the harder he pushed, the harder she came. She had never felt so cherished and yet so savagely desired in her entire life. She raptly listened to David, a passionate animal with an unyielding hunger.

He looked down and watched how his length disappeared inside her. He knew she must be growing tired, but he also recognized that she was stronger than she knew. He was completely focused on her pleasure. It was only when she begged him to come again that he obliged with as much haste as he could safely control. When his orgasm overtook him, he halted his movements so they could both feel him pulsing inside her.

It had never been like this.

She felt triumphant and exhausted.

David felt exactly the same way.

It was simply one of the many reasons the two had connected so quickly and so closely. Their minds, their hearts, and their bodies were tuned to the same frequency.

In the minutes after they made love for the first time, they held each other tightly and felt the sun heat the room all around them.

Chapter Twenty-Six

Kyle had no real reason to go to Malibu. He'd already gotten the stuff out of the mansion that he absolutely didn't want Michelle to lay claim to, and he could take or leave the rest when the divorce all shook out with the lawyers. He might've had no reason to go, but he was going anyway. Just to prove that he still could.

He did intend to give Michelle the house, or rather allow her to buy him out of his half, but she would have to sell everything else she got in the divorce to do it.

A studio car was provided for Kyle. He thought of how Shaunna would usually ride home with him on trips like this, to help him settle back into California life. He wasn't ready to admit, even to himself, that he wanted her back.

Heather was fine, but didn't problem solve like Shaunna could. She wasn't ugly, either, but having Shaunna around was like having a vase of fresh-cut flowers in the room, something small and vibrant. Fragrant, even, but subtle. Kyle had misjudged her loyalty to him, and although he was still angry at what he considered a betrayal, he knew he'd lost a lot more than his wife that miserable day in Houston.

It crossed his mind that Shaunna could be at the house. She and Michelle were inseparable now, when David wasn't around anyway. He grimaced tightly at the thought of dealing with both of them after the long flight from Houston. He almost asked his driver to turn around and take him back to Los Angeles, but then he remembered that his car was still in Malibu. He could have gotten anyone to pick up the car for him, but this was just the kind of the excuse he needed. Besides, he couldn't pass up the chance to intimidate Michelle if he could get her alone.

He laughed as the gate responded to his personal code. If Michelle had vacated the premises, he would have changed the code immediately; then again, he was the only one who knew how. He quickly spotted Shaunna's car, but decided to consider himself lucky that he didn't see some stupid Beemer or whatever the hell David might be driving.

There were a few photographers on the street outside his house, and they strolled casually over to the closing gate. Even they knew not to trespass on private property, but they readied their cameras for the only shot they could get: the driveway.

When Kyle got out of the car, his journey to the front door was recorded by snapshots. As soon as the photographers moved into action, the actor fully accommodated them. His posture was confident, his stride was slow, and his expression was smoldering and smug.

He looked down at Shaunna's Jaguar as he passed by. He imagined that she was probably up in her room clacking away at her computer and would no doubt wish to avoid him as much as he wished to avoid her. It wasn't that he was scared of her, exactly, but if anyone in that house could rattle him in any way, it was that girl.

The excited photographers hooted as he closed the door behind him. They had quite the interesting story in the making, even if they didn't know what it was. Ironically, at that moment, they knew more than anyone else.

Shaunna was in bed, lying on her back, trying to recover both her breath and her swirling emotions. Next to her and within reach was David, resting casually on his side.

She turned her head to look at him, if just to confirm that she wasn't imagining the whole evening. She even reached out tentatively with her fingers to trail them along his toned stomach. When she brought her brown eyes up to meet his, his face lit up brilliantly. She couldn't help herself and giggled in response.

David leaned forward and tenderly pressed his lips to Shaunna's forehead. "How are you feeling?" He asked the question without pulling away from her. The warm words deliciously tickled her skin.

"Loved." It was the only honest response she could offer.

David moved his body even closer to hers and fully enveloped her in his arms. He grew still, and as the moments passed, she realized he wasn't merely resting; he was contemplating something.

"What are you thinking about?"

David began tracing his fingers along her skin as he spoke, and Shaunna was instantly soothed by his movements.

"I was thinking about how I was done with California." He let the words rest on the sheets between them. "I remember how happy I was to get the hell out of here. I didn't know what life I was going back to in Chicago, but at the time, all that mattered was that I wouldn't have to come back to LA." David's fingers had drifted up Shaunna's body and now rested on her chin. He gently pulled her face toward his and looked deeply into her eyes. "I never saw any of this coming. I never expected to go to Texas and find you. You've changed everything for me."

Shaunna swallowed and leaned forward to kiss him softly, reveling in the luxury of their chests pressed together once again. David continued to hold her tightly as their lips remained content in their featherlight exploration. When he did pull back, there was a look of mild curiosity in his eyes.

"I'm thirsty. How are you?"

"Yeah. I guess I could use some water." She began to stir in his arms, but David's grip held her securely against his body.

"Let me. You wait here and rest up." He was out of the bed before she had a chance to blink.

Shaunna smirked. "You say that like you have more plans for us."

David merely winked. After he put his borrowed lime green robe back on and left the room, Shaunna sat up and pulled the covers over the lower half of her body.

The orange glow of the setting sunlight fell over her breasts like the warm breath of her departed lover.

The house was completely silent. Shaunna's purse was sitting on the table next to the front door. Kyle noticed it, but did not disturb it despite multiple thoughts of vengeance. He walked briskly to his master bedroom, hoping to catch Michelle undressed enough to upset her…and to please him.

She was fully dressed, unfortunately, and drinking white wine while she read her mail.

When she looked up at the doorway, Michelle wasn't startled, but she was surprised. "Kyle! What are you doing here?"

"I don't need a reason to be in my own house!" He wanted to begin things aggressively. It usually broke her down faster.

"Fine," Michelle said as she turned her eyes back to her correspondence. "But get the fuck out of my room."

Kyle blinked. "I came here to get my—"

Michelle stood up. "I said get the fuck out of my room! You're not going to sleep here, and you aren't going to stand there lying to me, either. Get out! *Right now!*"

He turned to leave, then turned back with determination. He wasn't going to lose to her.

Ever.

David walked downstairs and into the large kitchen with wooden floors and polished marble countertops. The rustic feel of the design was off-set by the very modern living room into which it opened.

The white leather sofa was temporarily made the color of orange sherbet by the setting sun, and the black glass coffee table reflected light onto the ceiling. It shimmered like water.

As David peered into the refrigerator in search of something other than soda to drink, he heard Michelle's muffled, but agitated voice carry into the room.

He stood up and cocked his head to the side like a curious puppy. He heard it again, but it was followed by something else.

A man's voice. Kyle's voice.

David looked like a green streak as he flew down the hallway toward Michelle's bedroom.

"I think you're forgetting yourself, Michelle. That new boyfriend may have filled your head with the notion that you're some strong, empowered woman, but he doesn't know you like I do. You *will never* speak to me like that *again!* Do you hear me? I will come and go as I please as long as this place is still in my name, and you will show me some *respect!*"

Michelle took a step toward him, and he flinched. It was instinctual, and she was amused when she saw it. "You're a worm, Kyle. And if you ever speak to me like that again, I will have Thomas draw up a restraining order so fast that you'll be served with it on your way out the door!"

"Thomas? You *would* bring that prick up. You hired him on purpose just to—"

"Of course I hired him on purpose! He's going to nail your ass to the wall and let me throw darts at your nards!"

"God damn it, Michelle! You shut your mouth!" He went to take a step toward her, but a strong hand on his shoulder stopped his progress.

Kyle turned around and found himself face-to-face with David.

"You heard the lady, Kyle. Time to go," David demanded. He was out of breath, and Michelle noticed his cheeks were flushed with anger.

"You!" Kyle snarled. "You dare to stand there in *my* bathrobe and tell me what to do in *my* own house!"

"Actually"—David was a stickler for details—"it was Michelle who told you what to do. I'll just be enforcing her wishes."

"You think you can take me?"

"I could take you like a free mint in a Chinese restaurant, Kyle. But let's not let it come to that, shall we? Get what you came here for and leave. We can handle everything else tomorrow."

"Or I could have you arrested," Kyle offered instead. "Then you could have something in common with Shaunna. I think Michelle must have a thing for felons."

David shook his head. "You really shouldn't have said that."

Kyle let him get close and then swung his fist with all his might.

Fortunately, he was such a bad actor that he gave something away in his face, and David managed to turn his head just as the balled-up fist came in like a baseball pitch.

Michelle heard the loud crack as Kyle's fist made contact with the side of David's hard head. David went sprawling to the floor, but it was Kyle who began howling in pain.

David was going to have a headache, but he was on his feet and grinning before Kyle had even torn his eyes away from his already-swelling knuckles.

"I'd say that you are at a disadvantage for the remainder of the fight."

David stepped forward and reached for Kyle's injured hand. Kyle jerked it back instinctively and smashed it into the closet door.

He closed his eyes in painful rage as he brought it back to his chest.

Michelle put a hand over her mouth. It looked like she was horrified, but her fingers barely covered the broad grin that desperately wanted to give voice to her laughter.

"Kyle." David spoke loudly and clearly. "If you go right now, I'll let you."

"I should call the police," Michelle said.

"No," David suggested. "Kyle wants to leave. Don't you, Kyle?"

With snot sneaking down his lip, Kyle cradled his wounded hand like he was Luke Skywalker in *The Empire Strikes Back*. "I need my car keys." He spoke with deflated simplicity.

"Shaunna left them in your car," Michelle seethed, her hand falling to the table. "Where she always does!"

Kyle walked to the door and disappeared down the hall without a word.

"I'm filing a restraining order with Thomas tomorrow morning!" Michelle called after him. "If you come back here, I'll have you thrown in jail!"

David walked behind Kyle, but kept his distance. The enraged actor left the front door wide open as he left, and David didn't immediately hear the distant cameras clicking. When he was standing in the doorway, however, he could see the flashes and heard the catcalls from the paparazzi on the other side of the gate. David projected a sense of calm, but inwardly, he was already worrying about the new mess Shaunna would be forced to clean up.

David closed the door and instantly went back to check on Michelle. Once he was satisfied that she was doing okay, he retrieved Shaunna's water from the kitchen. Then he went upstairs to apologize for his unexpected delay from having to take out the trash.

Chapter Twenty-Seven

Thomas Harper listened to Michelle's recounting of the previous day's events with his thick fingers laced together on top of his cherry leather briefcase. He shifted his gaze from his current client over to her publicist.

"Under the circumstances," he began, "I'm sure we can have a restraining order filed, but it will have to go through the police department. That means police reports, and that *will* include David's involvement, which, I imagine, you would like left out of all this?"

The two women looked at each other.

"Actually, it couldn't hurt," Shaunna said. "But it would complicate things, for sure."

"I just have to know that Kyle won't show up there ever again," Michelle told Thomas. "I don't care how."

"And you're sure David doesn't want to press assault charges?" Thomas asked.

"Not unless he has to," Shaunna responded.

Thomas nodded back at her. "Well then, I'm fairly confident that we will be able to handle this with his attorney."

"Does it make a difference that his attorney was my attorney until he filed for divorce?" Michelle had been struggling with the injustice of it since Kyle had her served with papers bearing a familiar letterhead.

"Actually…I love it when that happens. You see, your relationship with your former lawyer is already in his head and on his conscience. He will be predisposed to do something for you to make up for the fact that he took his pen and stabbed you in the back."

"Well, I wouldn't say that he stabbed me in the back…" Michelle looked at her hands.

"Ha! You see! You won't even let me call a backstabber a backstabber. Imagine how guilty he feels when he's the one who did the stabbing. He owes you one, and I'll make sure he pays retail." Thomas winked playfully at Michelle, who tilted her head to the side and smiled gratefully in return.

"You think instructions from his lawyer will keep Kyle away?" Shaunna's words were blunt, but necessary. David was meeting with his new agent, and she was relieved to have him away from the house while she sought reassurance from Thomas. Kyle's invasive visit had upset her more than it had David or Michelle. Kyle could've easily discovered her in bed with David, and the thought greatly unsettled her. She was anxious about the possibility of it happening again.

"We'll come to an agreement that will compel their side to hold up their end of any bargain we make." Thomas then opened his briefcase and spent the better part of the next two hours going through the assets and holdings the couple had amassed.

No doubt, Kyle hoped that his wife had forgotten the many money management options he took when his cash started flowing in. In truth, Michelle did not pay much attention at the time, but since Kyle always talked about himself, she heard about the assets over and over. He himself had imprinted the information in her brain.

Thomas asked all the right questions, and by the time he stood up to walk the two women out to the elevators, he had enough information to make Kyle think that they'd placed a bug in his phone.

"I'm sending over my *everything* guy, Sly, to change your gate code. Just to make us all feel a bit more at ease," Thomas told them as they waited for one of six pairs of shiny steel elevator doors to open. "He'll be the gray-haired fellow in the little Italian car. He'll get you set up."

"That's great," Michelle said. "But I still feel like Kyle will make another scene at the house."

"Well," Thomas elaborated, "Sly might have a few more tricks up his sleeve if that happens. But I'll make it part of the negotiations first thing, and I plan on putting it into terms that will scare the shit out of them if they fail to comply. Would you like me to send you the transcript?"

"No, thank you," Michelle told him. "Just...let me know how it goes."

"Will do," Thomas said as the doors behind him opened. He stood aside, and the two women stepped into the otherwise empty car. "I'll call around six thirty this evening, if that suits you."

Michelle looked at Shaunna, who shook her head as she reached out to hold the door. "You might not be done with your looping session by then."

Thomas stepped forward to take over door holding duties from Shaunna. To do otherwise would have been ungentlemanly.

"Can you make it eight o'clock?" Michelle asked.

"We'll talk then." Thomas let go of the door. As the elevator closed, they could hear him dialing his phone and whistling something from *Aladdin*.

"He's the best," Shaunna commented. She meant it, but she was also curious to hear Michelle's opinion.

Michelle nodded. "He is indeed."

"Is he married?" Shaunna couldn't help herself.

Michelle turned and looked at Shaunna knowingly. "No."

"Does he have a girlfriend?"

"Sometimes."

"Maybe you should be his girlfriend," Shaunna suggested boldly. "He seems very fond of you."

"He is very fond of me, and I'm very fond of him, and neither of us is interested in screwing that up."

The actress turned her attention to the lighted display above the door, monitoring their rapid descent to the lobby. Shaunna wisely read Michelle's action as the signal it was.

Case closed.

"We only have a few lines to replace from the picnic scene where the plane flew over and disrupted the shot, and about six pages of bridge dialogue," Nathan told Michelle as she settled into the sound booth. "All your harness stuff and the control room stuff sounded great."

Michelle used to hate ADR sessions. The thought of going into a sound booth and trying to reproduce her vocal acting performance seemed counterproductive. However, Nathan made the experience a revelation. He helped her realize that she could actually better her performance through inflection and articulation. He also reminded her that she now had more perspective on the character and could use that to her advantage.

She was encouraged to seize her second chance to alter the dynamics in her voice. The result was a more nuanced delivery while maintaining the right tone for the scene and the correct pacing.

"Okay," Nathan told her after they completed his checklist with time to spare. "We're all done. Thank you for another great performance."

"You're welcome."

Nathan moved to a work table, leaning casually against it to stretch his taut muscles. Michelle joined him, and the two stood comfortably side by side. While their time together as professionals was winding down, a new friendship had developed as a result of the larger-than-life events that had taken place on-set.

"Are you going to wait around to see David?"

"Does he have some looping to do, too?"

"No. He's taking me to meet a guy who has a car for sale."

"The *Teen Wolf* van?"

Nathan's eyes lit up with cheerful anticipation. "Yup. Wait, you know about that?"

Michelle nodded her head. "Mmm hmm. Shaunna told me."

"Ah, how is Shaunna? She's taking David and me up to see her father in a few weeks. He's got a whole museum of muscle cars up there at his place."

"He does. I've seen it. Shaunna's doing well. She's on her way here." Michelle's phone vibrated. "That's her now."

Shaunna walked into the recording studio a few moments later. David was a few steps behind her, and the two of them looked like they'd just shared a joke, or a secret.

"Hey, pal!" David declared as he shook Nathan's hand. "You ready to go?"

"Let me just say goodbye to the lads."

"When should we expect you back at the house?" Shaunna asked David.

"We're just going to Hollywood," he replied. "We could meet for dinner in town if you want to."

"No, thanks," Michelle said. "I'm going home to wait for my attorney to call."

"What about dinner?" David looked at both of them with mild concern. He was pretty sure the women hadn't eaten in hours.

"We'll find something," Shaunna assured him.

After the girls left, David drove Nathan to Hollywood. There were more size fourteen sequined platform boots in ten square blocks than there were chopsticks in China, and right in the middle of it all was his old apartment building.

When David had walked out of the old place on his way to Texas, he thought it was the last time he would ever see it. The reality that he could now buy the entire building nearly gave him vertigo when he looked up the stairwell.

The introductions went well, and the test drive went even better. As expected, Nathan overpaid for the car, but not by much, and when he tried to pay David the finder's fee he'd promised, the actor politely declined.

When Shaunna and Michelle arrived back in Malibu after dinner, there was a man with salt and pepper hair standing by the gatehouse.

"Hey, Sly's still here," Michelle said.

The slight man had arrived at Michelle's house that afternoon and changed the gate code, along with all the locks on the doors. He had a quiet awareness about him and was professional and prepared.

Michelle rolled down her window to punch the new code. "What's up, Sly?"

"I was just speaking with Mr. Harper," he answered. "I believe that he has secured your ex-husband's agreement to keep his distance." He tried not to let his mild disappointment show, as if he'd been hoping for the opportunity to confront the imbecile himself.

"Does that mean you'll get to go home soon?" Shaunna asked. He'd been there since before they'd gone into the sound studio.

"Yes, Miss Noble. Mr. Harper told me to see you both safely inside before retiring for the evening."

"Very well, sir." Shaunna liked talking to Sly. It brought out the debutante in her.

The gate opened, and Michelle drove in. It closed behind her with a solid *thunk*, and when she parked and got out, she noticed that there were no photographers lurking across the street.

"I encouraged them to disperse," Sly commented as he walked up the drive toward the women and his own car, a canary yellow Alfa Romeo.

"Is there anything you can't do, Sly?" Michelle asked over her shoulder as she and Shaunna approached the front door.

Sly appeared to consider this under the low California moonlight that was the same color as the smooth little car he stood next to.

"I can't sing." With that, he nodded his head and climbed into the car, waiting to drive away until after the front door had closed behind the two women.

Michelle asked Shaunna if she wanted a drink and began searching for a bottle of Bailey's Irish cream before hearing the answer.

Thomas's call came about two cocktails later. They had both kicked off their shoes, and Shaunna was standing at the wide window counting boat lights on the horizon while Michelle leaned forward to retrieve her buzzing phone from the coffee table.

"Hello? Thomas!" Michelle's voice was light and playful as she continued with a stream-of-consciousness greeting. "Thanks for sending Sly over. He's a miracle worker! I showed him around before I went to my looping session, and it took him forever to accept a glass of lemonade, but he changed the gate code and the locks and even hooked up my Blu-ray player properly. Did you know that you have to have special cables to hook your HDTV to your Blu-ray? Otherwise, you won't actually be seeing your movies in HD."

She listened as he told her that he did know about VGA cables, but agreed that Sly was indeed a miracle worker.

"What exactly does he do for you?" Michelle asked, the drinks aiding her bluntness.

After a pause, Michelle responded, "Well, he was a complete gentleman, and it looked like he stepped right out of a Charles Dickens novel."

Shaunna listened to Michelle's side of the conversation as she strolled to the kitchen and refilled her drink.

"Oh really?" Michelle said after a long pause. "Well that doesn't surprise me. Sly's very proper. Shaunna talked to him for a while and had to practically beg him to call her anything besides ma'am. In the end, I think she had to settle for 'Miss Noble.'"

Michelle finally worked up the nerve to ask Thomas about how things went with Kyle's attorneys and then listened for a very long time.

"So, he knows that we changed the locks, then?" she finally said, then listened some more. This pause was even longer than the first, and Shaunna marveled at how loud her swallows sounded in the hushed room.

"Apparently he had been squirreling things out of the house for months…Oh, just his stuff, shoes, suits, jewelry…Huh?…Art? No, he wouldn't care about the art…Okay, I'll check."

Michelle put Thomas's voice on speakerphone after asking his permission and waved Shaunna over to listen to the rest of his account.

"…They were like kittens after that. They guaranteed that Kyle wouldn't go back to Malibu and staked a very pending, very *public* restraining order on it. They even went so far as to suggest that our future meetings take place in my office."

"Is that a big deal?" Michelle asked. "Having the proceedings take place on your turf?"

"Oh yes," Thomas answered quickly. "Especially in this case. It'll be fun to show Kyle how much nicer my office building is than the circus tent his clowns hunker down in."

"When do we meet?" she asked.

"They left it completely up to us."

Michelle looked at Shaunna, who didn't need to consult her calendar. "You have next Wednesday and Thursday completely free."

"Let's do it Wednesday morning. Say…around ten?"

"That's fine with me," Thomas replied.

"Do I need to bring anything?"

"Just check the art, like I said."

Michelle looked at Shaunna. "Sure. Anything else?"

"Actually, there is one other thing."

"What's that?" Michelle's stomach clenched; she knew things were going too smoothly.

"Sly discovered something at your house while you were gone, and we both agreed that I should be the one to discuss it with you."

Both women wore twin expressions of worried curiosity.

"Go on," Michelle invited while outwardly cringing.

"What do you know about your home surveillance system?"

"What surveillance system?" Michelle asked in a small voice.

Thomas didn't hesitate. "That's what I thought you were going to say."

When David arrived an hour later, Shaunna grabbed him by the hand and led him quickly upstairs. He happily bounded up the steps, misinterpreting her intentions.

"Kyle had cameras in the house," Shaunna blurted as soon as the door to her room was shut.

David's eyes did all his reacting for him, first growing large with shock, then falling with dread.

"Thomas sent someone over to secure a few things for Michelle, and he found four cameras."

"Did the guy find a tape too?" David asked hopefully.

"It doesn't work like that. This system sends data to an offsite server that Kyle can probably access from his laptop."

"Did Michelle know?"

"Not a thing. He could have been filming her for years."

"Can't her lawyer do anything?"

"Since the cameras have already been disabled, I didn't bring it up to Thomas in front of Michelle. Unfortunately, this is still legally Kyle's house, so I don't know what Thomas could do, even if I told him about it. He is thinking about filing that restraining order though."

"Really?"

"He thinks it will help down the road by establishing that Kyle is no longer in residence and has been legally trespassed."

"Does he think that will work?"

"He does, but it'll take time."

"Where were the cameras?"

"One in the driveway, one out back by the pool, one in the master bedroom, and..." Shaunna hesitated and swallowed before finishing her sentence. "And one in the indoor pool. Where we were."

David's chest tightened, but all of his fear was for Shaunna. He knew what she was telling him and how devastated she must feel about it. But in his shock, he couldn't help but state the obvious.

"So, Kyle has a sex tape of us."

Shaunna nodded her head, the tears of embarrassment threatening to finally race down her cheeks.

"At least he doesn't know he has it yet," David supplied in an attempt to cheer her.

"What makes you say that?"

David remained silent for a few moments as he attempted to collect his thoughts. He didn't want to answer Shaunna's question with anything less than a reassuring response.

"If he had, it would be everywhere by now. Chances are he hasn't even checked the footage yet. What we need to do is not tip him off..."

"The system has been disabled. It's only a matter of time before he realizes that," she informed him.

"In that case, at least everyone will know that I'm not with Michelle," David half-joked.

Shaunna wasn't interested in making light of the situation. She thought of what her father's reaction would be, and that was enough to finally loosen the hold on her ever-mounting tears.

"I'll be humiliated if it gets out, David," she said quietly, "and your career will be over before it starts."

"Sometimes sex tapes actually help people you know..." David was grasping at straws for her sake, but Shaunna was too pragmatic to cling to false hope.

"If Kyle leaks that footage, you'll be nothing more than a punch line." She approached him, circling her arms around his waist and resting her cheek against his chest.

David held her numbly. He wanted to comfort Shaunna, but in truth, he felt just as defeated as she did.

Chapter Twenty-Eight

Kyle set himself up in one of the many overpriced and oversized rentals in Beverly Hills. He tried to get his new publicist, Heather, to take one of the bedroom suites for herself, but she constantly refused, each time more politely than the last.

He was served with a restraining order one week after his visit to Malibu, and his hand began to throb as he read the document. It was delivered by a court officer with a dozen photographers on his tail. This was a wicked and unexpected move, especially from Michelle, and Kyle was outraged to the point of having a tantrum. He stomped his foot hard enough to shake the chandelier and began shouting at Heather, who had gone pale. He was not going to rest until Michelle was ruined.

"You need to release a statement that says her little boyfriend talked her into this," he told Heather when he'd calmed down enough to think strategy. "Make him look like a pussy, and I'll look like the tough guy, like Colin Ferrell."

"I don't know, Kyle. That guy kind of grosses me out."

Kyle could tell that Heather wasn't on board with his PR angle. In his present mood, he found it to be a risky move on her part. By now, Heather should have known to approach all possible discord with him like a minefield laid by a chess master.

"It'll be worth the trouble if it toughens up my image," he said with surprising patience. He needed Heather to work the kind of magic Shaunna used to conjure on a weekly basis, and her gaze was becoming cold when he yelled at her.

She nodded her head, perhaps more savvy than she appeared. "I'll get right on it."

Heather's press release didn't blame David enough, and he made her rewrite it. The next draft actually complimented the young actor, and Kyle practically yanked her from her chair before sitting down to write his own statement. It was horrible, but he sent it off without even correcting the words underlined in red.

For the next week, he never failed to call Heather into his bedroom while he was in various stages of undress. From the hallway, she would take any new daily directives and retire to the shaded front porch where she felt safest. Kyle saw to his own breakfast—a bowl of cereal—but all other meals were sent out for.

Kyle talked about Michelle and Shaunna constantly, and the elaborate ways in which he envisioned sabotaging their careers were stunningly vindictive. Heather played no part in any of his "off the record" bashing. This usually took place while he was floating in the pool with his phone and giving daily exclusives to someone he called "his journalist friend."

The statements Heather made on his behalf were few, but always spoke highly of Michelle. Kyle took advantage of the excellent job she was doing by seeding the tabloids with things he would never say on the record.

Early in his professional relationship with Heather, Kyle determined that she was a good girl with a strong spine. She wouldn't be doing any of his dirty work. At first, this realization left him irritated, and his inclination was to simply replace her. Shaunna had been a master at her job, and her experience was showing now. But Heather had come out to Texas the moment she was hired and spent several weeks tirelessly working for him there. He felt like he owed her a bit more time to see if her good reputation could somehow benefit him. That decision was paying off.

There were still some things he needed to accomplish, things Heather would refuse to do, but Kyle had been thinking of getting more help anyway. Other A-list celebrities had whole teams of people working for them, and that's what Kyle wanted. He wanted to surround himself with more people, and then he wanted to watch as all his enemies were defeated by his army.

Shaunna's home in Yorba Linda was a cute, cottage-style residence that looked rather small from the outside, but in reality was a large, low complex of stylish and comfortable rooms. Palm trees stood like sentries around her lawn, a perfect emerald shade thanks to a timed sprinkler system.

The plan was for everyone to meet at her house and then travel together to her father's estate in Laurel Canyon. Nathan pulled up in his blue El Camino right on time. David and Michelle arrived together just as Shaunna was showing her first guest into the house. The duo greeted the newest arrivals on the flagstone path that led from the driveway to Shaunna's front door.

David and Shaunna tried not to make a big deal out of the fact that it was his first time at her place, but Nathan couldn't help but pick up on the nervous energy between them.

After a quick tour that included a small but stocked library and a sun porch that looked on to a spacious and blooming backyard, the girls wandered into Shaunna's bedroom to talk shoes. The boys gravitated back to the large cinema room, complete with custom shelves for a massive movie collection.

The television was big enough to make David feel like he was poised on the bridge of the Enterprise. Only the walls, which were covered with framed movie posters from the seventies and eighties, distracted him from the fantasy.

"Cool!" Nathan exclaimed after examining her limited edition *Matrix* box set. "What a woman!"

"Yeah," David said, distracted. He was standing in the home of the woman he loved and realizing he knew so little about the things that made up her life. "I had no idea she was so eclectic. Did you see the carved totem pole in the front room? And the stained glass dragon window in her kitchen?"

"You're right. Who has cool shit like that? Sounds like she's the one that got away?" Nathan tested him, attempting to subtly perceive David's reaction out of the corner of his eye.

David immediately tensed. "Look, Nathan, I know what it must look like—"

"Really?" Nathan didn't know until that moment how much he had been waiting for this conversation to happen. He approached David and pushed forward with enthusiasm. "Because it looks like you were falling in love with Shaunna until Michelle and Kyle called it quits. Then you jumped ship quicker than Molly Brown. And now, while the whole world is watching you and Michelle, you're flirting with Shaunna worse than *Big Brother* contestants the first night the producers give 'em booze."

David stood with his mouth open. He felt naked. Worse, he felt transparent.

"Relax." Nathan placed a large warm hand on David's shoulder. "I see now that you and Michelle were only ever playing at being in love, but you could have trusted me. In case you've forgotten, I have a vested interest in all of you."

"I know. And believe me, we aren't seeking to deceive anyone. Well, maybe Kyle at first, but then circumstances kind of…trapped us."

Nathan laughed loudly and turned to investigate an *Electric Dreams* movie poster. He waited for David to gather his thoughts while he strolled past Shaunna's collection. He passed by an *Enemy Mine* poster and paused in front of *Westworld* while David told him everything.

Nathan turned to face him, an uncharacteristically grim look on his face. "I completely understand about your living situation. In fact, I'm kind of glad Michelle has someone staying out there with her. Between you and me, I think Kyle has violent tendencies."

David pictured the constellation of stars he saw when Kyle punched him in the head. "Yeah. Lucky for me, he's as terrible at fighting as he is at acting."

Nathan wasn't surprised by Kyle's ever growing list of inabilities. Then he completed his warning to his friend. "Listen, if you're going to keep hiding your relationship with Shaunna, you'll regret it. It won't end well," he advised. "And she will resent you eventually."

"But it's her idea to keep appearances the way they are. Not mine," David informed him.

Nathan considered this revelation carefully before speaking. "Then you'll wind up resenting her. Either way, it's eventually gonna suck."

"Thank you for your honesty." David sounded stiff, but sincere. "Actually, I've been having second thoughts about it all, and I guess I needed to hear someone else say that it was a stupid idea to begin with."

"It is a stupid idea to begin with," Nathan dutifully supplied. "It's only a matter of time before the studio puts in their two cents about it. And I'm worried that Shaunna is already getting hurt by all this. She's been through too much as it is."

David shook Nathan's hand. "It means a lot to me that you care for Shaunna like you do. You're a good friend to her, and to me. I really owe you. Thanks, man."

"You're welcome, and don't worry. I'll play dumb about all this. It's my best trick."

David chuckled before responding. "Thanks again, but I will be sharing this conversation with Shaunna. She needs to know."

"I understand." Nathan sensed it was time to change the subject. "I admire you a lot, David, and I fucking *love* that Wolfmobile!"

"Good. Are you planning on making any deals with Gus?"

"Oh no," Nathan denied as he led the way out and into the front room. "But I brought twenty-five thousand in cash just in case."

Gus was in the back of his immense stucco mansion, tending a grill that looked more like a time machine. There was a wide assortment of burgers, dogs, chicken breasts, steak strips, and oysters available, along with what could only be corn on the cob wrapped in tinfoil. Gus was trying a new recipe with the vegetable in an attempt to replicate the chili lime corn on the cob that Shaunna frequently enjoyed at Disneyland.

His backyard was on the edge of a cactus-filled valley, but he had a large, leveled deck and a sunken hot tub that could seat the cast of *It's a Mad, Mad, Mad, Mad World*.

"Come on over, you guys!" he called out when he heard the patio glass door open. "Grab a plate and dress your buns!"

Michelle tried to look shocked by Gus's greeting. He flashed her one of his charming grins, and she accepted his proffered hug.

"I hear you're dating some young hot shot actor I just hired," Gus urged as he released Michelle and looked somewhat cautiously at David. Gus's responsibilities were such that he didn't have time to visit his sets often, and he'd actually not spoken directly with David since their initial meeting in Houston.

Michelle shook her head. There would be no lying to Gus Noble. "David and I are just friends. You know how it looks just because a young stud is living in my house."

Gus furrowed his eyebrows while Shaunna stepped forward and hugged her father.

"David and I are dating, Dad, but we don't want to make everything worse by adding me into the mix."

Gus looked surprised by Shaunna's quick exposure of her involvement with David. She usually refrained from discussing her boyfriends with him, particularly in mixed company.

"We have to keep it secret for the time being," she implored him. "I'm toxic right now."

David opened his mouth, presumably to object, but Gus beat him to the punch.

"That's not true," he said, warmly but loudly. "But I get what you mean. How did all this start?"

Gus casually nudged a few wieners and flipped a steak strip while he listened to his daughter retell a story the three of them were all sick of.

"It's simple," Gus announced. "David needs to get a place of his own. He can afford it. But as long as he's in that house, what do you expect everyone to think?"

Michelle frowned slightly, and the producer saw it. Gus turned his attention to Michelle. "Why don't you want David to leave?"

She looked down, but everyone heard her. "I'm lonely. Hearing his music at night and smelling his fancy coffee in the morning…It's the little things that keep me sane and feeling safe."

Gus nodded. "What all of you need is an exit strategy."

"I know," Shaunna muttered. "I'm still looking for one."

"It's not so difficult," Gus concluded. "When Michelle's ready to move on with life, she and David will need a breakup story. Preferably one that will make it look like Michelle actually set the two of you up together and one that would make sense to the outside world. I assume you're in Malibu a lot."

Gus looked at Shaunna, who blinked and broke eye contact with her father.

Gus inhaled sharply through his nose before finishing his thought. "If the public thinks that Michelle is genuinely happy for your new relationship and even encouraged it, she can step out while maintaining her dignity."

No one spoke.

"That's perfect!" Shaunna was relieved. Having been so mired down in the problem, she'd been struggling to devise a solution.

"Thank you." Gus turned and regarded first his daughter and then the director in the silver shirt, who was holding an empty plate. "I believe I have some cars to show you after we eat." Gus punctuated his offer with a wink.

"Yes, sir. Thank you."

Nathan ate fast and then opted for seconds. He ate that portion fast too. He was on his third Dr. Pepper and had already endured a *Forrest Gump* ribbing from Michelle when the conversation dulled. With plates emptied, everyone stood up from the patio table to stretch.

Gus and Michelle walked together, and Shaunna overheard her father telling the newly single actress that she was welcome to come by once she had formally ditched the pretty boy. Shaunna felt mildly uneasy by the idea of her father dating one of her friends, but calmed her nerves when she remembered Michelle's reaction to Sly a few days before.

Gus's car collection was colorful, and each car was perfectly polished and parked at a flattering angle. From the outside, his garage looked like a lackluster barn, but the cool air-conditioned breeze and the smooth cement floor resembled a museum. There were well over forty vehicles in the room, representing eight countries and just as many decades.

Still, there was no denying that Gus had a thing for muscle cars.

"Wow!" David was quite possibly more excited than Nathan. "I bet these are just the good ones too!"

Gus and Shaunna laughed together. "We'll show you the morgue later," she promised.

Gus glanced at Michelle. "Which one's your favorite?"

Challenge accepted, Michelle began strolling through the garage. She liked the 1970s brutes, especially the ones with flames.

Nathan peered inside a black Charger while David investigated a convertible Cougar that was the deep blue color of the early morning sky.

"What year is this Mercury?" he asked Gus. "Seventy-one?"

"You got it," Gus confirmed.

"Lucky guess," David confessed with a laugh. "I'm only consistent with Corvettes."

"He's got plenty of those," Shaunna said over her shoulder while walking off to sit in her favorite of the bunch, a 1965 Pontiac GTO. It was hers, given by Gus as a gift on her sixteenth birthday. It was only driven occasionally because, like her father, Shaunna cradled a good investment. Gus was also all too happy to keep it safe for her while it appreciated.

David followed in Shaunna's direction, slowly studying the cars as he went. He couldn't resist smiling at a bright green Chevelle, decked out with two fat black skunk stripes. He could hear Nathan and Gus clearly as he passed between a white Mustang and a red Camero.

"I hear you have a car collection yourself," Gus inquired of the young director.

"Yes, well…" Suddenly, Nathan felt silly about his small and quirky collection. "It's nothing compared to this…"

"Son," Gus interrupted what was surely going to be a ramble. "There's nothing like this outside of Leno's garage."

"I just have half a dozen cars that were in movies I like. That's all." Nathan spoke simply, not wanting to make a big deal out of it.

"Oh yeah?" Gus looked around for Shaunna with a smirk on his face, but he couldn't see her because she was sitting in her Goat. "Have a look around. Then we'll meet at that far door and head out back."

Black leather welcomed David with a squeak as he sat down next to Shaunna. "Hi there."

"Hey." Shaunna sounded deflated.

"Are you okay?"

Shaunna nodded her head, but lowered it at the same time. "I'm sorry I got you into this, David."

David nearly sighed in relief. In his mind, an exposure of their relationship, even in such a vulgar way, would ultimately end the stalemate with the press. He understood that no one would believe him if he told the truth, and lying would only get them in deeper. But he longed for a way out of the pulp purgatory he endured in the weekly pages.

"You knew it was a bad idea, and you almost talked me out of it," Shaunna continued. "I should have listened."

David was concerned once again. He dreaded the thought that Shaunna might want to walk away from him, that she might decide he really wasn't worth all the trouble she was going through.

"I don't regret anything," David stated, turning his whole body to face her, his knee resting on the seat and earning more squeaks. "I think it's time to change tactics anyway. Kyle may have something on us, but maybe it wouldn't be such a shock if everyone already knew that we were in love."

"In love," Shaunna repeated. She went to Texas, went to jail, and wound up in love. Now she was sitting in one of her favorite childhood places and listening to the noises of the garage outside her window. She couldn't hear the radio anymore, but Nathan's occasional hoots of excitement bled through.

"What do you want to do?" Shaunna asked.

"How about I take you to the *Sling Shot* premiere?"

Shaunna gaped. It was a flashy way of coming out, which wasn't necessarily her style, but given the circumstances, it might be exactly what they needed. "The only way we could possibly consider it would be if Michelle also had a date and we all arrived together as friends."

"Exactly what I was thinking." David beamed. "If Kyle is there, I don't want either of you facing him alone."

"Actually," Shaunna mused, "I think the restraining order will prohibit him from attending."

David's hands flew up, and he whacked the roof of the car. "I hadn't even thought of that!" He sat in thought for a moment. "He's going to be pissed."

"I know," Shaunna replied devilishly. "But he deserves it."

"So, will you be my date to the premiere?"

"It's still a long way off," she said darkly. "We could be a laughingstock by then."

"Then we'll laugh with them." He took her hand. "We'll get through this together. And the Malibu house will be just the protection we need for a while."

Shaunna shook her head. "The house doesn't give me protection. You do."

She rested her head on David's shoulder, savoring the moment until Gus began honking the horn of a gold Plymouth at the other end of the building.

"We're heading out back," Gus called.

Shaunna poked her head out the driver's side window. "Go on ahead. We'll be right there."

Gus responded with a grumble and led the rest of his guests out a white door with a heavy deadbolt.

The couple sat alone amongst the sleeping metal beasts. Shaunna flicked at the keys hanging from the ignition and felt like it would be a memorable moment if only she had something memorable to say. She took David's hand and squeezed it. A basketball game could be heard from the small radio near the big red mechanic's toolbox Gus used as a place to store his cigars.

"I'm hopelessly in love with you, Shaunna," David finally breathed into the still air. "Except it's not hopelessness I've felt since we met. It's faith, and joy, and a sense that I found a part of myself in your heart." He leaned his head back against the cool black seat, and his eyes gleamed with honest resolve. "I continue to find new ways to admire and adore you, and I know we can't go to Disneyland together right now, or even hold hands in public, but if that's the biggest problem we ever face, we'll be living very charmed lives." He took a breath and tightened his face in renewed focus. "I want you forever, and I'll do anything to make it happen. We can get through this."

"Thank you," Shaunna replied in a whisper. "I want that too. I've never wanted anything more in my life, and I love you, David. I've known that for a long time now."

With their heads cradled by the car seats and their eyes dancing in the dim space, Shaunna and David beheld each other and traded smiles.

"If we find our way out of this mess, we could go outside together." David stated what he had been thinking for the past month.

Shaunna nodded her head. "I think it's time we start going with your instincts."

"Is that a yes?" David was surprised at her response.

"Yes, but if we do this, we have to do it after we find Michelle a date."

"That shouldn't be too hard." David chuckled.

He leaned toward her, and they began kissing. Shaunna slid her chilly hand up under his shirt to stroke his chest. He breathed in quickly, but liked the cool rush along with the light touch of her fingers. He tested the temperature of his own hands against his cheek before dipping one under her shirt to cup a firm round breast. She sighed into his mouth and leaned her head back to encourage him to kiss her neck, as well.

The distant cheering on the radio and the occasional tick from one of the settling steel machines near them drifted into the car like smoke. Shaunna wanted to unzip David's pants and caress him, then take him into her mouth and suckle him until he exploded with pleasure and called her name against his steamy window. He was squeezing first one breast and then the other, but his kisses were tender. Soon, the lust she felt was replaced with the gentle romance of the moment. She scratched his back lightly up and down as their lips met again and again.

David's other hand found the back of her neck, and he began pressing her into him, intensifying his oral attack. She reconsidered her original position on where this rendezvous was leading, and when she stopped to look down at his slacks, she found a repressed bulge sticking up like a submarine's periscope.

She freed him quickly with both hands, despite his squawks of half-hearted resistance, and lowered her mouth onto his upright offering. She worked with purpose and used her hand to follow the progress of her lips, which led to awe-filled groans and a thunderous pulsing beneath her palm.

When the lovers in the GTO finally broke their embrace and joined the rest of the group, everyone was gathered around Nathan's newly acquired and moderately famous "crappy blue Chevy Nova." It had been referred to as such in *Beverly Hills Cop*, but was also the same car Lilly Tomlin drove in *9 to 5*. Nathan was actually dancing a jig about the twofer.

The late arrival of the disheveled couple was acknowledged with two sympathetic smirks and one cantankerous one. The group then went back to the house for drinks and discourse.

Chapter Twenty-Nine

Christmas came and went as David wrapped the first four episodes of his new TV series, *West of the Moon*. He was playing a complicated young ranch hand whose motives always seemed in question. Some of the crew had worked on the show *LOST* and took to calling him Sawyer due to his handsome shiftiness.

His directors asked him to play some scenes honest and likable, while in other scenes, he was encouraged to ooze arrogance and make snide remarks. This was music to David's ears. He knew that he wasn't a diverse actor yet, and the complicated character would be a nice addition to his credits. He was excited when Nathan mentioned that his performance in *Sling Shot* came off as intellectual and thoughtful.

David's new agent, Brandy Parlor, assured him that solid work was the best way to get solid work. He liked the sentiment and understood why Shaunna chose her for him. Brandy and David shared a goofy side, and neither liked to wallow in details. David frequently marveled at his abrupt change in status and tax bracket.

Thanks to the paparazzi, the world knew the constant whereabouts of Michelle and David. Any time either of them left Malibu, they were followed by unkempt ducklings with cameras. They tailed David to his studio set in Los Angeles and even down to his location shoots near San Diego. As annoying as it was to David, they were even more persistent with Michelle.

Michelle spent most of the holiday season reading new scripts in development and inquiring about directors and producers she admired. As a result, she'd been offered three separate roles, all paying her asking price and all of them offering short production schedules located right in Los Angeles. Shaunna and David were grateful for her choices. If Michelle had flown off to Tampa Bay to shoot a golf comedy called *Gulf Course*, or taken a part in *Astoria Waits*, a mother-daughter television series filmed in New York City, her absence would've only exposed Shaunna and David's relationship to penetrating scrutiny.

Michelle accepted a job which began filming immediately, and the role required temporary tattoos that progressed from her arms across the top of her chest. She loved how the body art helped her get into character. Thanks to time spent with Kyle, she already knew how to ride a Harley and became a sassy and seasoned rider named Bad-Ass Beth. The director was fresh off an Oscar win for one of his gorgeously gritty movies, and she was thrilled to play a part in his newest project.

She wore her Hollywood ink home most days and showered there unless she'd been instructed by the makeup artist to press shiny strips of stencil paper to her skin. This was done in order to preserve the work for quick turnarounds or night shoots. Shaunna and David loved the way she looked, and a few times, Michelle even wore her punk wig home in order to show off her character's full appearance.

Michelle and David developed a strong friendship. On the frequent week nights when Shaunna returned home, they played cards, watched movies, and practiced their western accents. David had a pleasant drawl he'd developed for his TV character, and one of the other roles Michelle secured was in an animated film about the Old West. Sometimes whole nights in the Malibu home would sound like an episode of *Gunsmoke*.

Michelle had wrapped all of her work on *Sling Shot*, but David still had a final sequence to complete. It was the climatic fight scene with Kyle, and it was the first time the two actors would be face to face since their altercation in Malibu. In the eight weeks since Shaunna realized that Kyle was in possession of intimate footage of the couple's first sexual encounter, the couple had been trying to brace themselves for the inevitable.

Although many despicable rumors about Michelle had surfaced, no tape had been leaked. As more time went by, Shaunna's anxiety bloomed. David hated seeing her in distress and did his best to comfort her, knowing that only resolution would bring her peace of mind. David had no illusions about convincing Kyle to do the right thing and, frankly, didn't want to tip him off in case Kyle hadn't yet discovered the footage. David was determined to maintain his professional dignity when he reported to the set.

Kyle arrived that morning in a foul mood. His head hurt like hell because he'd attempted to calm his own nerves the night before with drink. Since his squabble with David, the tabloids enjoyed portraying Kyle as the chump who got bested by Michelle's new lover. News of the restraining order against him did nothing to make him look like the tough guy he had hoped. This made his eyes quiver in his head whenever he thought about it, and he anxiously awaited filming the fatal confrontation between the captain and the pilot. Kyle didn't want his stuntman to have the privilege of choking David.

"Okay, gentlemen." Nathan cautiously greeted his two actors as they were getting their makeup done. David and Kyle were trapped, sitting side by side in dressing room chairs and stuck listening to the makeup artist's favorite country station. "We're going to do all the conversation today and all the action stuff tomorrow."

The director looked from one actor to the other. "I assume you guys have been working with Jonathan on the fight sequence?"

David was the first to respond. "He said since it's mostly wrestling in a closed space, he's just going to pose us from shot to shot and have us just bang around."

Nathan nodded his head thoughtfully. "That's fine. I'm doing this in jump cuts anyway, so the action can be pretty loose. It's gonna go quickly once it gets physical, so I need all your anger up front in your dialogue. Can you give it to me?"

"Yes," Kyle answered loudly.

David merely nodded.

Twenty minutes later, the two men were shouting at each other on camera. The tension between them was palpable and usable. Nathan didn't interfere much for the first couple of takes. Eventually, he asked David to open his eyes more and told Kyle that he was looking for something a bit more sinister. What he got from Kyle was merely an angrier performance, not exactly what he was hoping for, but at least it was consistent. Kyle was also doing something with his lip that

Nathan found fascinating. David seemed to be naturally repulsed by his commanding officer, and they finished filming an hour early.

Kyle's injured hand still bothered him at times, but the next day when he was instructed to choke David, all the pain seemed to disappear.

"I could squeeze your neck all day," Kyle whispered to David after the second take.

"Don't make me start squeezing things of yours, Kyle," Nathan growled from right behind them. He took both men completely by surprise. "You slip, I slip. Remember?"

David could have sworn that he actually felt Kyle's hands grow cold before they loosened from his throat.

Nathan walked away and joined the discussion his director of photography was having with the camera operator. Both Nathan and his DP put a tremendous amount of trust in the camera operators because they were actually the ones framing each shot. At the moment, they were considering a higher camera angle.

"What was that all about?" David asked Kyle.

"Nothing." Kyle sounded wounded already. "I hope you're getting the last few good miles out of my wife."

David tried very hard not to show his surprise. This was clear proof that Kyle knew nothing about his relationship with Shaunna. He couldn't wait to tell her.

"You poor imbecile," David said with hardly a trace of pity in his voice. "You threw away that woman thinking that you'd gotten the best of her, but all you got was the first of her. There's a big difference."

Kyle scoffed.

"Michelle is a dragon," David continued, "awakening from a bad dream. And she's going to burn you to ashes."

Kyle stepped toward David and leaned in close, their noses almost touching. "Fuck you."

David held his ground and smiled almost like an animal bearing his teeth.

The two men remained standing, eye to eye, their fists clenched at their sides.

"Let's set up for another take," Nathan called over in a deliberately casual voice.

Kyle sneered and took his mark, while David waited a moment longer before turning to his starting position.

With each new setup, the shoves became harder and the holds became tighter. The two actors were trapped between the rails of a catwalk and threw each other against the metal with increasing vigor. Once, when David's head was bent back over the green mats below them, Kyle put his thumb on his Adam's apple and savagely pressed down.

David responded with a quick, reflexive jab to Kyle's ribcage. The exchange was the final straw for both men, and suddenly, they were down on the walkway and fighting for real. Furious punches were thrown, and before Nathan could yell out the word "cut," Kyle was flipped on his back and defending raining blows to his face. David's patience had reached its breaking point, and his resentment of Kyle Petersen quickly consumed him.

"Stop it!" Nathan roared.

David instantly bounded up and stood over Kyle. He stepped back, but kept his infuriated eyes on the stirring man.

"Get up, Kyle," Nathan demanded, not offering his hand to the actor struggling to rise. "You're too beat up to be on film. Go home. You're wrapped. We'll have Deuce finish up for you."

Kyle was almost as livid as he was embarrassed. He shoved his way roughly past both David and Nathan, but kept his eyes on his feet all the way out of the soundstage.

As soon as Kyle stormed off the set, Nathan regarded David, more than ready to return to business. "The last thing we need is the shot of the captain pushing you into the plasma shield. We're going to use Kyle's stunt double and film over his shoulder. It should be fine."

"Okay." David kept his words to a minimum and concentrated on bringing his rage under control.

"He'll push you over the rail, into the mats a few times, and then you'll be wrapped too."

"Sounds great." David was now eager to finish the scene and call Shaunna.

Nathan completed his picture's principal photography later that day and had all the ADR dialogue in the can the week after that.

Chapter Thirty

Kyle was furious at having been so unceremoniously dismissed from the set of *Sling Shot*. It was a jolting departure on the movie's wrap. He was accustomed to more merriment when he finished filming. Traditionally, it was a day that was filled with hugs and handshakes and promises to stay in touch. He never bought into anyone's false promises, of course. Nevertheless, Kyle always looked forward to the extra attention, as he was frequently the biggest celebrity in the room.

Some directors had customs and speeches and made a big deal out of the last day on a set. Kyle didn't like any of that blather, yet the sense of loss at having been shooed away was as heavy as a boulder on his back.

Naturally, he took out his aggression on Heather, blaming her for everything, from the font size in *People* magazine, to the sunglasses he broke on the drive home. She dutifully endured his wrath while she labored on with his enormous press responsibilities. In her experience, big stars who underwent a fall from grace were in many ways more popular than ever, but the tone of the contact she'd had with outlets from around the world was combative. She was met with frequent snide accusations from online reporters and open mockery from radio programming directors. Everyone wanted to talk to him, but suddenly, nobody wanted to play by his rules. That, too, became Heather's fault.

"Please let me get something for your eye," she finally said after he wandered past her for the third time in as many minutes, attempting to poke holes in her self-confidence.

The genuine concern in her voice made him stop. "Go ahead," he said sternly and sat down in her chair when she got up. He glanced at her laptop, but resisted opening it. He didn't really like computers. He could never find the cursor, and nothing ever seemed to work for him, so he mainly kept to e-mails. When he was still living with Michelle, he would also occasionally monitor the home security system at the Malibu beach house.

Kyle straightened quickly, his eyes as wide as his mouth as a realization dawned on him. His time in Houston, along with the distraction of his divorce, had gotten him out of the habit of logging into the online system to review and purge the old surveillance data.

Before their separation, while he'd been sneaking his most prized belongings from the house, Kyle remembered thinking of the time when he could be in his new home and watch his ex-wife undress in hers. The idea had excited Kyle, and now he couldn't believe that he hadn't taken full advantage of his access yet. He nearly began bouncing with excitement in his chair. After such a shitty day, he finally had something to look forward to in the evening.

Heather returned to the room, carrying crushed ice in a cloth kitchen towel. Even though he impatiently moved to take it from her, she stepped forward and placed it gently over the whole left side of his swelling face. It was a kind act, like something a mother would do, and he almost felt sorry for yelling at her.

"Go lie down for a while," Heather suggested softly. "I can call your agency and see where they are in finding you a new manager. You don't need to spend your whole afternoon on hold."

Kyle was happy for an excuse to leave without coming up with one of his own and rose from the chair without another word. Passing by his bedroom, he went to his office. The towel he still held to his face was cold, but not uncomfortably so, and actually very soft. He wondered briefly if Heather was starting to fall for him as he opened his laptop and waited for it to respond.

As he logged into his computer and clicked on his security system's icon, he wished he'd installed a camera in the bathroom so he could watch Michelle take a bath. She took two a day sometimes, something he hated about her when they were together, but would've loved to take advantage of now. He smirked at the possibility of seeing Shaunna naked as well. It was something he'd often fantasized about and even attempted over the years to subtly engineer.

"What the fuck?" Kyle's security dashboard pulled up all four camera feeds, all of them totally dark. He had anticipated the usual quartet of angles of his estate, but the black denial was enough to make him almost re-injure his hand as he slammed it down on his desk.

Kyle's membership bought him a terabyte of storage space on the web site, which he hadn't come close to using. Even if that were the case, though, the screens should have been providing him with a live feed.

He began scrolling backward in time. First hours, then days, then weeks flew by with nothing to show for it.

"Are you kidding me!" He'd gone back months, and all four feeds were still blank. He mourned all the lost footage of his wife, who he'd so easily insulted, but now craved.

It took a while, but eventually, one stream sprang to life. It showed a bespectacled gentleman peering closely at the camera before walking away backward. One by one, he saw the same man's face as he discovered and disconnected the cameras in reverse order. According to the time stamp, the cameras had been deactivated within a few days after the group's return from Texas.

Kyle knew that one of the last events recorded by the cameras was likely to have been his other fight with David Quinn. That was absolutely the last thing he wanted to see. He slammed down his laptop screen and yelled in rage.

"Are you okay?" Heather followed her voice into the room, but the menace in Kyle's eyes sent her right back out like a slap in the face. She backed out in a move that reminded Kyle of the unknown man who had disabled his eyes into the house.

All he could think about was how Michelle now had two guys running around the Malibu estate with her.

As he continued to fume, Kyle also concluded that Michelle's delay in producing a restraining order had to be deliberate, which made him believe that Shaunna was behind the shady timing. They thought they had him, but he was still determined to come out of the divorce on top.

He told himself that whatever happened, they'd started it.

And he was going to fight fire with gasoline.

CHAPTER THIRTY-ONE

All Nathan had to do was spend the next two months cutting the film and filling in all the green spaces. He and his editor, Lauren, had a rough cut ready by Valentine's Day and sent it to the studio that morning. Nathan was extremely surprised to get a phone call before the end of the afternoon.

"This is gonna be *Titanic* in space!" was the exact quote, and Nathan had never been so happy to be on a conference call with a half-dozen suits.

Until they crashed him into the iceberg.

"We're taking a different direction with promotion." This was the president of the studio talking. Nathan couldn't remember his name, but his voice was unmistakable, and it was certainly a big deal that he was even in the room. "We want a summer blockbuster, but we want a red carpet movie even more. Your picture is just as gritty and tech-heavy as you advertised, but it's turning out to be unexpectedly sweet and human and dramatic all at once."

"Thank you," Nathan responded with guarded gratitude. He knew they weren't done yet.

"Also," the president continued, "we have the added wrinkle of your two lead actors and their impending divorce. I supposed you've heard that Michelle Cooper filed a restraining order against Kyle Petersen?"

"Yes, I heard," Nathan acknowledged.

"That means they won't be able to do any press together, and that requires us to re-think how they will be promoting your movie."

"Naturally," Nathan agreed.

"So, we're going to push your release date to the fall..." There was a sound of shuffling papers over the line that synchronized with Nathan's speeding heartbeat. "November sixth, to be exact. This will give you more time to complete your special effects, and I'm sure that can only please you, but...we're going to need to see only PG-thirteen cuts of the picture from now on."

Nathan was very glad he had not been driving, or holding something breakable, or standing near a cliff. He was actually in his editor's office, working on a scene in reel number two that seemed to drag. Lauren had been listening closely to his conversation with the studio boys, but now Nathan gave her a ghastly look she didn't understand.

A soldier might have recognized that look from his commanding officer.

Nathan took a deep breath and began with a deliberate smile in his voice, "Thank you very much for your belief in the film. I'm pleased that you think it could win awards, but if I may, I have a few concerns about that."

"By all means, we welcome your input." It appeared as if the president was going to do all the talking. Nathan really wished he could remember the man's name.

"First of all, this entire film has been shot and scored like a grindhouse noir piece, and for that alone, it will likely be ignored by any nominating committee."

"Tell that to Quentin Tarantino," came the quick retort. "I believe he's polishing two Oscars."

Nathan wrinkled up his forehead as he considered this. "Thank you for making my point for me. He doesn't make PG-thirteen movies, and neither do I." He took a breath and plowed onward. "May I also remind you that I secured final cut on this picture. Now, while I'll admit that it has matured, the material won't justify changes in the editing beyond pacing and personal preference. Doing otherwise will be as transparent as a toilet paper prom dress."

Lauren understood everything and looked like she was about to pass out. Still, she grinned at Nathan's joke and tugged on his pant leg to make sure he saw the thumbs-up she gave his monologue.

"Nathan, I admire the hell out of you." The president's response sounded genuine, but there was still an edge to his voice. "Your point about Tarantino and genre is a good one, but not as good as your reminder that you had final cut." He waited for the chuckle on his end to die down before he continued. "Make your picture. You clearly know what you're doing."

"Thank you," Nathan replied.

"Well, it's one hell of a ride already. That fight scene between Petersen and Quinn had me gripping my chair. And that scene at the end? I haven't cried that hard since I saw *The Green Mile*."

"He did cry his ass off at *The Green Mile*," came a distant, but nonetheless earnest, remark.

"Thank you," Nathan repeated. "Can I have more money?"

There were many laughs from the other side of the line.

Nathan was stunned by the turn of events. He was given a less crowded opening weekend and three more months to edit *Sling Shot*. While this news thrilled him as a director, he also felt concern for his principal actors and the delicate public relations scenario they were in the midst of navigating. The postponement of the movie's opening was a development not one of them had ever considered, but he'd have to indulge his worries later. He refocused on the conference call.

"I'll send you some of the scored stuff," Nathan offered. "The music makes a big difference. Oh, that reminds me. I still need you to clear 'Little Bit of Soul' by Music Explosion for the opening credits."

"We're already on it," said yet another new voice.

"Great!" Nathan gave an enthusiastic thumbs-up back to Lauren.

"Well…say…Nathan," the president began, "since you're going to persist with the R rating…ah…do you think you could get Michelle to show more skin in the shower scene?"

"I'm hanging up now," Nathan responded with a laugh.

Chapter Thirty-Two

Michelle threw a party on the weekend after Valentine's Day. She and Kyle had often hosted parties during their marriage, and she missed the buzz of the conversation and the delicious offerings her favorite caterer always came up with.

David was encouraged to invite any and all of his friends, many of whom asked him to play a song when he sat down at the long-forgotten white grand piano that matched the sofa in the living room. He sang the simple but sublime "Hallelujah" by Leonard Cohen, and the conversation stopped while everyone listened.

Michelle was mesmerized by the talent that flew from his lips and fingers. They'd been living together for the better part of three months, and she never knew he played until that moment. She glanced in surprise at Shaunna, who merely shrugged.

Shaunna had pleasantly discovered David's musical side early in their relationship. He'd taken to singing Shaunna to sleep after making love to her, and now the sound of his voice in the crowded space was enough to ignite her desire for him. As Shaunna turned her focus back to David, Michelle scurried off to mingle with her other guests.

David played an encore, a song by Billy Joel. Then he strolled out to the balcony for some night air to escape the admiration.

Shaunna desperately wanted to go out to him, but as agreed beforehand, the two acted like practical strangers, despite being known as business associates.

It was Nathan who went outside to check on David. "Hey, buddy. That was really good. I'll remember your pipes if I ever direct a musical."

David smirked. "Arc you ever going to direct a musical?"

"Fuck no."

Both men laughed and hugged. "It's good to see you again, man," David told him. He missed seeing Nathan almost every day.

"You too. Say," Nathan began shyly. "I haven't gotten a chance to apologize about the film getting pushed back. I know it's a sacrifice to live here rent free and pretend that you're humping Michelle, so I appreciate you taking one for the team."

David looked dubiously at Nathan.

"What?"

"We're not pretending to be anything," David told him, revealing a rare tone of exasperation. "And it's harder than you think not to show my love for Shaunna."

Nathan watched with unease as David stared pensively at the Pacific Ocean. "You're right. I'm sorry."

"It's okay," David relented and accepted the situation with a shrug. "The studio clearly has faith in the picture."

Nathan laughed. "They like that I'm playing the film as a straight grind job. They even think Kyle's stiff performance is part of the gag. They like you too, by the way."

David waved the comment away.

"No, seriously. They think that you and Michelle playing off Kyle is some kind of statement about mixed genres, and they say the bullet pace is 'an emotional crash cart of fun.'"

David nodded. "How's the final cut coming along?"

"Great. We'll have it in the can a month early. How's the TV show?"

"Good. We're going to wrap by April, and then we wait for the summer schedule to come out."

"Well, you'll have a hit on your hands, I'm sure."

"I don't know," David stated. "Some of the best shows go down before all the completed episodes even air."

"While crappy ones hang on for eight years," Nathan observed glumly. "That's why I like movies. Fun and done, and on to the next one."

"Ha!" David laughed. "I thought that was your love life."

Nathan shook his head, smiling. "Not even when I had one," he admitted. "I'm a film dork, remember?"

The men paused to enjoy the view of the Malibu beach and the comfortable silence between good friends.

"I'm casting *Bitch Slap* soon," Nathan mentioned, after a while. "I have a part for you if you want it."

"Really?" David was flattered.

"Yeah. I want to get you once more while your price is still low."

"Too late, but what's the part?"

"A psycho cross-dresser named Flavia."

"Played straight or for laughs?" David asked.

"Straight."

"Is there a death scene?"

Nathan looked at him, puzzled. "How'd you know?"

David shrugged his shoulders. "It just seems to me like psycho cross-dressers wind up getting the short end of the stick."

"In more ways than one," Nathan muttered.

David raised his eyebrows.

"But it's tasteful," Nathan added.

David's eyebrows rose a little more.

"Well, there's no nudity," he corrected.

David's eyebrows managed to achieve a tiny bit of extra altitude.

"No male nudity," Nathan clarified.

David laughed. "In just the death scene, or the entire film?"

"I have a script in the car," Nathan replied, deciding to let David read the part and fall in love with it on his own. "I'll get it for you before I take off."

Michelle came onto the balcony then and whisked David and Nathan back into the living room, where they danced with their friends, old and new, and drank champagne. Much later in the evening, a manuscript was pressed into David's hand and Nathan's voice was hurried in his ear.

"You're going to look gorgeous in pantyhose."

Sly had been invited to the party by Michelle three times before he finally accepted, but he showed up after the revelry was well underway. He confidently settled himself by the drink table, where he mixed exotic concoctions and offered them to partygoers who were running dry.

When Michelle saw him, she rushed over with rosy cheeks and bright, happy eyes.

"Do you think you could stop serving people long enough to dance with me?" She made the request before she had the opportunity to shy away from the idea.

"I'm not much of a dancer…" Sly began, but Michelle was already shaking her head. Her insistence surprised and flattered him.

"No, you told me when we met that the only thing you couldn't do was sing." She strolled in the direction of the dance floor, which had been set up near the piano.

Sly watched her walk away with interest. She didn't look back to see if he was following her, but he made sure that when she turned around, he was standing right there. He took her by the hand without another word and began swing dancing to the decidedly hip-hop song. Any other man might have made the moment awkward, but Sly made it work, and Michelle happily fell into his fluid movements. They locked eyes as Sly guided her through several fevered, yet elegant sequences that made her feel as young as the night.

That was the first of many dances and many drinks for the two of them. Michelle led Sly, gracefully and chastely, in and out of conversations and activities, but they remained together for the rest of the evening. David wondered if this would begin the speculation that he and Michelle were not romantically involved, but Shaunna assured him that it would never be that easy. Still, David felt the air lighten around him at the mere prospect.

Once the party wound down, he eagerly asked Shaunna to spend the night. Since realizing Kyle hadn't yet discovered their secret, they'd allowed themselves fleeting moments of optimism. She quickly agreed, and David was soon enthralled by a moonlit peek at her naked flesh, first displayed for him while he was in the shower washing off the heat and grit of the day.

When David returned to his room, he was wearing only his towel. Shaunna was waiting for him on the bed, lying on her stomach. She thought back to their flirtatious beginnings in Texas and offered an appreciative smile. He dropped the covering and walked over to the bed, regarding her with each step.

She bent a knee revealing more of herself, a movement she knew he enjoyed, and sighed into the cool, midnight sheets. David bent down to kiss her smooth back, and his damp hair tickled her deliciously.

He smelled like the forest after a spring rain, and she breathed him in as his lips greeted her skin over and over.

When he couldn't take it anymore, he gently rolled her onto her back and then hungrily devoured her shadowy nipples. When he released them, they glimmered in the delicate blue light that trickled in from the window.

As a boy in Chicago, David had always imagined there was something sinister about midnight. Now, he associated midnight with sensuality and felt nothing but joy in it. He'd found the friend he wanted to see the world with. He held the lover whom he would never let go. She was a living passion, a comfort for his weary soul.

"I've missed you so much," David whispered as he rested his head on her chest.

She wrapped her arms around his damp head. "I've missed you too. Do you have to be anywhere tomorrow morning?"

"Nope. The whole day is mine. Ours."

"Good," Shaunna breathed.

She pulled his face to hers and kissed him in a desperate, craving way that got him revved up all over again. When he pressed his body to hers, she opened her legs immediately. With an adjustment of his hips, David slowly entered her and closed his eyes with pleasure. Shaunna's eyes were wide open. She stared up at his strong chest as he became a part of her for the first time in weeks.

They moved slowly at first, savoring the contact, but it had been a very long day. Soon, they evolved into voracious lovers bucking against one another. They slid up and down each other's bodies, kissing and licking anything that was exposed. They flitted from position to position, each one causing Shaunna to climax faster than the one before.

David was strong but getting tired, so she pushed him down on his back and straddled him with a determined expression.

"Are you ready?" she purred. "I want you to come for me."

"Yes," David confirmed breathlessly.

Shaunna moved with purpose. David, jealous of the way the moonlight was caressing his lover's skin, reached up and cupped her slick breasts. She leaned into his hands and wiggled hard with him inside her. She climaxed twice more before she heard his soft blissful whimper and felt his hands squeeze her thighs.

"Rest," she told him as she settled back onto the mattress and pulled him into her arms. Her intentions were to look after him, to stroke his hair, but soon, she fell into a doze.

He was relaxed, but also excited for the time when he would finally be able to publicly declare their love. He fell asleep with a peace in his heart that all the money in the world could never have given him.

They didn't wake to make love again until the room was completely dark. Outside, the sky showed thin strips of purple on the undersides of low clouds passing each other like great puffy whales.

Their dawn lovemaking was silent and slow, and they didn't stir again until the house's air conditioning kicked in and the smell of Michelle's coffee snuck up the stairs to tempt them into the day.

Chapter Thirty-Three

Nathan played with the old Steenbeck editing machine Lauren kept in her office as he watched her cut his film together on a large computer screen. She was using a software called Final Cut Pro that had become the industry standard and could do things that the Steenbeck couldn't even dream of.

Yet, seeing a piece of film snake through the guts of the complex machine made Nathan think of a slower world, where one would get occasional whiffs of smoke and ozone. Those were tangible reminders of days gone by — the kind of smells and processes once the norm for his predecessors in Hollywood. He knew that even the flapping of film reels was disappearing as more and more theaters went digital.

Now, the film was practically cutting itself. Each scene was easier than the last, and even if he and Lauren had been under the old deadline to deliver a final picture, they could've taken the last two weeks off.

In a way, Nathan wished he'd never been told that the suits were assigning such a highbrow interpretation to his campy little pimp slap to the genre. As a result, he found himself pushing for things he normally wouldn't have, in anticipation of a specific critique. When he admitted this, Lauren gave him a proverbial pimp slap of her own and assumed full command over all five reels.

Nathan gladly let her. Her insistence to take charge placed his doubts on the cutting room floor along with the other dead shots. It was a relief.

"I want to drop in a close-up of Michelle here, but her eyes are just too intense," Lauren admitted, leaning in to her screen and admiring Michelle's pretty white teeth. "She's too good. Is that even possible?"

"Sure it is," Nathan stated matter-of-factly. "I hear they had a similar problem with Tobey McGuire in the first set of *Spiderman* pictures. I myself directed a young Cathy Marks when she scared the living shit out of my sound guy."

Lauren laughed, but sometimes, she still couldn't tell when Nathan was imparting factual information or completely making something up on the spot to entertain himself. Even after three productions together, she saw no limit to the processing speed of his mind. It was as admirable as it was infuriating.

"You're joking," she challenged.

Nathan punctuated the seriousness of his forthcoming statement by looking up from the editing machine for the first time since they started talking. "I had a beauty of a tight shot, with an admittedly indulgent Dutch angle, but Cathy's eyes ate through the film like a hot projector bulb. It was too intense."

"Why don't I remember this?" she asked, turning her chair to face him.

"I couldn't use it!" Nathan was already shaking his head at the memory. "She was supposed to be playing remorse, and instead, she looked like she had just won a hobo-killing contest."

Lauren turned back to her work, laughing, and spoke directly to the image of Michelle's frozen face on the screen. "I'll try to catch you when you're looking down or something. I'll only get a two-second cutaway, but it should give you some vulnerability, and that's all I want, hon."

Nathan liked it when she did this. Lauren once told him that it was her way of interacting with the characters because she wasn't on-set to see them in action. He respected her reverence for their efforts and how they'd be perceived by the audience. It's what made her such a smart editor.

As a smart director, Nathan understood that editing was by far the most powerful tool at his disposal. It also had the benefit of coming last in the film-making process. Every movie had three versions: the written version, the shot version, and the cut version. Nathan enjoyed all three stages, but he knew that it was the last step that could make or break a film like his.

Lauren thought of herself as a mother duck gathering all the scenes together like so many ducklings, keeping them safe and together in the right order.

Nathan wanted to help her find a resolution. She really wanted to bring out the most in the scene, so he thought back to all the other takes and angles that might have captured Michelle in a vulnerable moment.

He was suddenly excited. "Hey! Bring up that take where she couldn't get her hair to cooperate."

"The windy take?" Lauren had actually lifted Michelle's first few lines from that particular run-through.

"Yeah." Nathan walked around to the front of the editing machine. "If you go to where she's talking about the moon shield…"

"The wind blows her hair in her mouth," Lauren finished. "It's what busted the take because she stuck her tongue out to get at it, and *you* started cackling off camera like a buffoon."

"That's the one," Nathan confirmed.

They began watching the raw footage, and before the camera operator stopped rolling, Michelle was caught looking off into the distance with an ache in her eyes that melted Lauren's heart.

"That's it!" she exclaimed and pushed herself backward on her office chair. She zoomed over to Nathan on casters and was halted by his high-five. She then turned around, and he pushed her back to her computer in a well-practiced maneuver.

"I'm going to cut it in at half-speed," Lauren declared as Nathan went back to his tinkering with the Steenbeck.

"And if you get your thingy caught in that, I'm not going to help you get it out."

Those were fun days for Nathan, and they blurred together so seamlessly that when he looked back up, three months had gone by.

David was a bona fide star by the time Nathan turned his final cut into the studio for test screenings. The scurrilous photographers, who always seemed to show up fifteen minutes after he or Michelle went anywhere, were fixated on him now more than ever.

West of the Moon gained a massive and cheerful following, and the show was picked up for a second season after only half a dozen episodes had aired.

David's portrayal of Jonas Ravine, a son of San Francisco, was as funny as it was infuriating. The character was a pompous ass whose only concession was that if the world didn't revolve around him, it sure as hell did shake when he walked by. Still, Jonas was very intelligent and cared deeply for his family, comprised of an aging mother, three sisters, and a dog named Nugget.

His performance was widely praised in the same magazines that had once called him "a moderately talented, but extremely handsome extra."

Michelle was finished with all of her cameos and voice projects by mid-July, and by then, her tattooed alter ego made its silver screen debut. Bad-Ass Beth was easily the cherry role in the film, and her performance was hailed as "a perfectly pitched portrayal of gruff brilliance."

The cameras all turned her way again by the end of the summer, and David was especially happy about the fickle nature of the interest surrounding them.

Shaunna was happy about it as well because the movie only served to showcase Michelle's range. When everyone went to see their campy sci-fi movie in a few months, they would be sucker-punched with a savagely vulnerable performance from Michelle and a legitimate hero persona from David that all the girls would love. She easily envisioned the pair taking Hollywood (and the rest of the world) by storm.

The house in Malibu was still and peaceful most days, with David on-set for *West of the Moon* and Michelle juggling her various small film projects. Shaunna usually arrived in the early afternoon before either of them returned from their obligations. Depending on her mood, she would set up shop in various locations around the Mediterranean-style mansion and work until someone came home, usually around dinnertime.

Kyle's general lack of know-how had left the beautiful mansion in a state of casual disrepair, so Michelle made Sly a deal to tend to a few of the more pressing matters. She acknowledged, of course, that his arrangements with Thomas be honored first.

Sly had done his security job well, but his continued presence in Malibu was encouraged. Occasionally, Sly was at the house when Shaunna arrived, and the two would chat over iced coffees. As a car lover, Shaunna had already quizzed him about his pale yellow Alfa Romeo, and he'd told her with fond remembrance that he'd purchased it in Madrid.

He often dropped hints about where he was from and what he had done during his life, but the tidbits were difficult to piece together.

Shaunna did, however, hear about the people in Paris, the cuisine in Cairo, and the transportation in Turkey. Sly offered enchanting observations that spoke volumes about his vast cultural knowledge and his respect for the past, but he never hinted as to where his cradle sat.

He was sometimes at the house for three days straight and sometimes gone for weeks at a time. Thomas would call, and off he'd go. Sometimes when Sly came back, he had a tan, and sometimes he had a new pair of shoes. But he always returned cheerful and would remain bouncy for a day or two.

Michelle called him Tigger on one such occasion, and the resulting cranberry hue on his cheeks immediately gave his pleasure away. She called him Tigger from then on, even though the two maintained a professional relationship in all other respects.

But they were both thinking about each other.

Chapter Thirty-Four

It wasn't uncommon for unscripted occurrences to make their way into a picture. Unexpected vehicle debris during a stunt sequence or an actor bumping into a set piece were examples of things directors included. Sometimes it added to the realism. Sometimes it was funny, and sometimes it masked a flaw. For Nathan, it was all those things, plus sometimes it was like capturing a streaking comet on film.

When David's and Kyle's emotions finally bubbled over and they began fighting in earnest during the final hours of filming *Sling Shot*, Lauren and Nathan wound up with several usable shots. They were particularly intrigued by David's look of pure desperation. It was not what either filmmaker expected to see, but they were nevertheless drawn in for different reasons. Nathan admired the juxtaposition of savagery and fragility, which were conveyed at the same time. Lauren enjoyed that it made her think David's character was going to win. It would only serve to surprise the audience and add even more significance to his unjustified death.

Fortunately, Kyle took a punch like a water balloon and collapsed at David's hands almost immediately. It really did look like the good-hearted pilot was going to best the treasonous captain, but Lauren cut the film to make it look like David's character had relented, offering mercy. And that, in fine movie fashion, would become his downfall.

In truth, Nathan's approaching shadow had to be covered up in the last few seconds of the usable stuff while David was merely getting started. Nathan told only the studio of the decision to leave in footage of the on-set brawl, and they artfully leaked that information to the Hollywood press. When asked for comment, the studio played coy. The executives were ecstatic about any publicity that offset the on-set domestic drama that had plagued the project since the location shoot began.

Nathan couldn't help but admire the tactic, but also felt guilty. He wouldn't have told the suits if he'd known they would use the story as a teaser. He disliked any baggage a movie had to schlep and was known in the industry for getting frosty with interviewers who strayed from the art. In the past, if asked to comment on the social status of his actors, his answers would have been curt and sarcastic, followed by a request that the reporter speculate about the personal lives of his or her own co-workers.

Now, because he was the one who'd let the cat out of the bag, he felt obligated to acknowledge the rumors. Actually, he did more than acknowledge them; he confirmed them. He told a Los Angeles radio show that he had pushed his actors to be physical, and as a result, a few of the blows were real. He stressed that it was not uncommon for actors who insisted on doing their own stunts to get a bruise or two. He thought he had made it sound like a run-of-the-mill set scrape, but everyone saw right through him, and it became the talk of the town.

The real-life rivalry over Michelle would soon be played out on the big screen. Blog posts with headlines like *In the Fight of His Wife*, or *David vs. Goliath* were everywhere by that evening, and Kyle Petersen threw an absolute fit.

When Nathan's phone rang, it was Heather calling to inform him that her boss was stomping around so much he might make it rain.

"I'm sorry if it bothers him," Nathan said unconvincingly. "But he does know that his character wins the fight, right? You know, by actually killing the other guy? I don't think I could make him any more butch if I put him on a horse."

"Okay, I'll tell him," Heather said. She and Nathan had logged some real hours on the phone since her employ with his leading man. She was his shield against the temperamental actor, and he was therefore patient with her requests on Kyle's behalf.

"Did you hear about Michelle?" Heather asked, rather than hanging up.

"What do you mean?" Nathan hadn't.

"She got the court to amend the restraining order so Kyle can attend the premiere."

"He's going to be at the premiere?" Nathan paused. "Damn."

"I knew you'd say that, but I think it's sweet of her."

"It is," he agreed. "Are you going?"

"No!" she said, surprised at the mention of the idea. "He doesn't like me to attend the same events he's attending, but I suspect I'll be grounded for not talking you out of your decision anyway."

"That's not fair!"

"It's fine, and it's work." She said the next part like she was repeating a mantra. "I'm lucky to be where I am."

"Well, tell him no hard feelings and I'll see him at the premiere."

"I will. Bye, Nathan."

Heather slid her phone into her back pocket and then went to find Kyle.

He was in his office, sitting at his desk. All things considered, he took the news rather well. In fact, he had calmed down substantially. When he nodded at her, she gladly took the cue and left the room quickly.

Kyle was far more interested in what he had found on his computer. He'd suspected that Nathan would not change his mind, and the thought of an onscreen fight with David had returned his thoughts to the footage that he so recently hadn't wanted to view at all. In his old bedroom, he had once delivered a colossal punch to David's head, and he was looking for that footage. His resulting hand injury and subsequent re-injury were also caught on camera, but he would find a way to edit that part out.

He didn't know if he wanted to leak their private fight or just cheer himself up with it, but he found what he was looking for and watched it with fascination. Silently, he slugged his opponent, who staggered but righted himself and then tricked Kyle into striking the wall. It was not nearly as flattering as he'd hoped, but even in black and white, Kyle thought David looked ridiculous in that robe. He began scrolling back to see if he could find David in a more compromising position, or perhaps catch a glimpse of his wife topless.

Kyle was focused on the feed from Michelle's bedroom, but it just showed her milling around alone. She arranged the perfume bottles on her dresser but just wouldn't take off the bra she was wearing. Kyle willed her to take it off, never once connecting that since he was watching everything backward, she was more likely to put clothes on.

Movement in one of the other screens caught his eye, and what he saw made him cry out in shock.

"Holy shit!"

Shaunna and David were in the ground floor oasis, naked and kissing.

"He's cheating on Michelle with her," Kyle said to his astounded reflection in the screen. He rewound the pool room footage back to the beginning and watched as Shaunna knelt in front of David and worked her mouth on him. The camera was behind her, showing her round rear end, and David's stupid, satisfied face. When they went into the water, the falls distorted the action. It looked like David was returning the favor, but they could have been playing cribbage for all Kyle could really make out. When they eventually left the pool, they were pressed together like dictionary pages and kissed for a while before she disappeared from sight, only to return with the bathrobes that didn't belong to either of them.

"Heather! Get in here!"

Kyle was already reaching for a flash drive.

Chapter Thirty-Five

Having wrapped his TV show, David was finally free of his scraggly beard, and Shaunna was thrilled that his neck was clean-shaven again so she could kiss it.

He was too.

They found themselves alone in the house one early afternoon. Sly had gone home early because Michelle had appointments in Burbank. His side work on the Malibu estate had been completed for a month, but the cleanup was miraculously taking a long time. Neither Michelle nor Sly would make the first move, but David and Shaunna could surf on the sexual tension between them.

This day, however, belonged to them. The mansion had a colossal basement level that was cooler than any of the other rooms. Kyle had used the space as his den, but Sly and David had converted it into a fashionable private art gallery, where Michelle could properly display the paintings and sculptures Kyle had never had the sense to desire in the continuing divorce proceedings.

David and Shaunna walked into the room holding hands and, for a few moments, their breath. The pieces were quite exquisite. Michele had a fine, if bohemian, eye for art. Some paintings came from the French Realism period, while others came from the German Expressionism movement. Another half dozen came from America, and most of those were compelling examples of Luminism.

A round red upholstered bench sat in a sea of shiny black marble flooring. Since the day Sly and David brought it downstairs, it had always made Shaunna think of Mars floating in its big black expanse of space. She had also wanted David to make love to her on the tempting padded platform from the first moment she saw it.

David slipped away and dimmed the lights so just the art pieces were illuminated. Everything looked just as Shaunna had pictured it in her imagined gallery rendezvous.

David began unbuttoning his shirt as the determination in his eyes warned Shaunna that he intended to lose control. It was a thrill for her to see that look. Shaunna kicked off her shoes as she readied herself for his hunger. She was wearing a skirt, but he didn't bother taking it off and wasn't going to give her a chance to, either. She only just managed to slide something black and lacy down her legs before he embraced her, bare-chested.

When he kissed her, his mouth was hot and occupied her lips and tongue with a slow introduction. He then reached down and pulled Shaunna's blouse over her head, his long fingers moving to the back of her bra before the clothing even hit the floor.

"It's a front loader," Shaunna whispered as David slid his hand over the smooth fabric above her spine.

He knelt down in front of her with a grateful smile. "So it is."

He efficiently worked the clasp with a light touch, and the cups fell open, offering Shaunna a rush of cool air against her skin. David sighed contentedly as he beheld her liberated breasts.

He often stopped to stare at her before or after their lovemaking. It had made the shy woman uncomfortable at first, but after a while, she'd learned to accept the compliment for what it was. To David's enjoyment, she had even been known to pose for him from time to time as his eyes flickered over her like candlelight. David sighed again and took each soft nipple into his mouth until it was pert and wet.

He then stood up and began unfastening his belt until Shaunna took over. She liked doing this for him. When she unfastened his pants, an immediate display of smooth, stretched cotton told her that what waited beneath need only be exposed.

After she freed him, she gave him a soft squeeze that drew an appreciative moan from her normally mute lover. Shaunna felt immense satisfaction over David's immediate pleasure. In her book, sighs didn't count.

Shaunna released him, walked to the bench, and sat down, taking her breasts in her hands and pushing them slightly apart. David had never seen her do this, but he understood her meaning. He stepped between her open legs and nestled his solid form in her soft cleavage. She felt his warmth and even his pulse as she wound her arms around his body.

With her arms crossed, she pressed him into her, and he groaned yet again, fueling her excitement. When she began sliding her breasts up and down, she utilized her position and took him into her mouth in a great gulp that surprised him into a half-moan, half-yelp.

Shaunna was fascinated by the way that he always seemed hard in her hand, but soft in her mouth. She liked creating suction and moving her tongue around in a flurry. She prepared him long enough to hear his breathing hasten, and then she repositioned his slick organ between her breasts.

She kept moving like a determined motor, and whenever David's erection neared her parted lips, Shaunna eagerly kissed or licked him. Occasionally, she stopped altogether to slide him in and out of her warm and welcoming mouth.

David had stamina, but he wasn't going to be able to take much more of the ultra-stimulating gesture. Her intensity made him want to move on to something that served her fantasy more fully.

With a tremendous exertion of will, David pulled away from her and told her to lie back. He stepped out of his shoes and pants before parting her thighs with strong hands that had recently become rough with all the horse riding he'd done on-set. She admired his shoulder muscles and arms, which had grown bigger and more defined since they'd gone swimming together in Texas.

When he entered her, David closed his eyes and gingerly pushed in until he was as deep as he could go. His face was next to hers, and she sighed with completeness.

David opened his eyes and found a spot on her neck to kiss as he began moving his hips up and down with passionate thrusts that threatened to tumble his kisses into her ear—something he knew she loved.

Shaunna let her head drape over the side of the bench, and she peered at the paintings upside down as David's body spoke to hers. She was already close to climax, and when he grabbed her breasts and squeezed, she knew her orgasm was going to be especially overwhelming. David had learned well what made her body rush, and she was often seeing stars mere minutes after they began.

"Just like that," she murmured and tensed the necessary muscles to help facilitate the exquisite explosion. David maintained his movements, complete with kneading her breasts, until she filled the room with relentless gasps of his name.

Her reward for such a quick climax was David's gentle kisses on the hairline of her scalp before he redoubled his efforts and sent her over the edge again. He knew that with her, the first one was just the beginning. Where there was one, there were four.

He lowered his body to hers, and they kissed while their fast heartbeats pounded in and out of sync. David then gently placed his hands on her hips and pulled her body toward him so that her head came back onto the soft bench. He sat up then and lovingly placed one hand on her stomach, swaying his fingers back and forth in a stroking, tickling fashion.

She looked at him with soul-touched love in her eyes. "I'd do anything for you."

"You already do," he responded with sweet sincerity.

Shaunna sat up and regarded his arousal. "Lie back."

He did as she commanded, and as she straddled him, the shadow of her leg swept over him like a shiver. When she slid him back into her waiting warmth, he arched his back and whispered her name.

It began slowly, exquisitely so, and David murmured as she moved. He stretched his arms above his head and turned his face to the side. It was something she liked to do when he was above her because she knew he liked it. He was just trying to be cute by imitating her, but it was working. Shaunna gazed down at his submissiveness and began to understand why he stared sometimes.

Shaunna picked up the pace, encouraged by his sighs of satisfaction, but it was she again who cried out before she even got up to full speed.

David was, of course, invigorated by the sight of his lover's nearly continuous climaxes, knowing his own was a race horse still trembling in its gate. Shaunna leaned forward, and he watched her breasts dance before his eyes as she gyrated and grinded him into a frenzy. Her hair fell down and tickled his face, but he didn't dream of brushing it away.

He slid his hands down to her hips, savoring the feel of her power as Shaunna began lifting herself up a few inches and then dropping onto his body with taut, wet ambition.

His voice leapt out at last, and his eruption made his ears ring and his hands tingle.

She slid herself gingerly up and off of him and curled up on the bench. He immediately spooned up behind her and draped his arm over her waist. She took his hand and guided it up to cup her breast.

David had not had any idea how erotic the environment could be, and judging by the force of his sizable orgasm, he knew that something extra special had just taken place between them. Still, in that moment, the frustration of not being able to tell anyone the truth about his love for Shaunna seemed to bubble into genuine rage. He felt like a child, helpless to control not only the situation, but his reaction to it. He began to tremble.

"Are you cold?" Shaunna asked.

"I'm okay," he answered.

In response to what she perceived as a peculiar answer, Shaunna turned completely around and held him with her chin resting on top of his head and his warm cheek resting on her chest. She felt him begin to tremble even more.

Shaunna recalled one of the few memories she had of her mother. She'd been no more than five years old and sad about something. When her mother knelt down to pick her up, she began to cry harder, even though she was instantly comforted by the loving embrace. It was as if she hadn't allowed herself to fully absorb the whole emotion until she was safely in her mother's arms.

David's body communicated that he was being comforted by Shaunna. He let his sorrow out in the security of her arms before allowing himself to accept the relief they held.

"What is it, David?" Shaunna asked in a voice that softly commanded an honest answer.

He kept his eyes closed, sinking into her scent. Lately, there had been more and more of these frustrations for him. It felt like what he imagined a panic attack would be. He'd suddenly feel overwhelmed and consumed, like he was buried under miles of earth. The sensation came complete with a tightening chest and watering eyes.

"I'm sorry," David began. "This has been wonderful, and I don't want to bring us down. I'm just looking forward to when we can finally be a real couple."

"We are a real couple."

"You know what I mean. I'm just sick of all the lies."

"What lies? You don't have to lie to anyone, David."

"Easy for you to say," he responded quickly. "Every day on-set, I had to answer the same questions twenty times. 'How's Michelle?' 'How are you and Michelle doing?' 'What are you and Michelle up to this weekend?' My whole life outside this house is a lie!" He didn't mean to raise his voice, but he had, and the raw emotion made him quiver all over again.

"I know exactly how you feel," Shaunna soothed. "I cried in the shower this morning for ten minutes."

David immediately stiffened. "You did?"

"I'm fine, and so are you. It's just getting to us, that's all."

David sighed, and Shaunna slid her hand up his back and began rubbing his neck.

"You've been through a lot," she continued. "I admire the way you've held up, but it's okay if you're mad and want to vent to me. I understand."

"No, I'm all right, really. Making love with you was just so intense, and all my emotions rose to the surface."

"That's a good thing," she reminded him. "You can always be completely free with me."

"I know, and I'm glad I can trust you so effortlessly." He sighed again. "But that just makes me want to tell even more people about how I feel. I want to take you out and hold your hand on the beach, or make out at the movies. I mean, I haven't even been to Disneyland with you yet."

"I know," she agreed reluctantly. "I miss you every time I go."

"See? You have to go without me! Wait…you go without me?"

She shrugged her shoulders. "Dude, it's Disneyland!"

He laughed and finally began to feel the tension melt away. "I'm just selfish, Shaunna. I want to have my cake and eat it too *and* tell people how delicious it was."

She pulled back and admired his prone body. "I agree completely."

Shaunna rose gingerly to her feet and stepped into the downstairs bathroom. A few minutes later, she called to David, reminding him of the large marble shower in the lavish room.

David strolled in, and Shaunna giggled at the fit naked man with a mess of twisted hair pushing out from his head in all directions. While she appraised him, he studied the flecks of turquoise and gold in the midnight blue marble. It could only turn his attention from her for so long before she was back in the center of his gaze.

"Are you ready for round two?" he asked as he stepped into the chamber with her.

She was.

They washed each other's hair, then let the warm water rush between their bodies as they held one another in steamy silence.

David kissed her heated neck and smelled the shampoo in her hair. There was something nice about knowing that they'd both share the same scent for the rest of the day, even if it was strawberry.

When Shaunna leaned forward and set her hands on the bench, David didn't think he would actually be able to accommodate her. But to his surprise, and with only a slight ache, he rose at the sight of her inviting body. Her round cheeks were streaked with water that cascaded up her back and down her firmly planted legs.

David slid his ready length into her and proceeded to give them both the hardest, deepest sex of their lives. His hands were on a fervent expedition of her wet skin, and she came quickly. At first, she could barely breathe, but before long, she filled the shower with echoes of delirium. Her passionate cries only encouraged David. He had a good hold of her hips and moved his own in and up with each thorough penetration.

He was still holding back, though. He wouldn't dream of hurting her, but since she seemed to enjoy his efforts, he decided to give her a taste of his full strength. He used his arms to pull her to him as he pumped with hard resolve. He started grunting with the exertion, and Shaunna only screamed louder.

When they were spent, they simply stood there, holding each other until the water began to cool.

Chapter Thirty-Six

Shaunna was in her car by the time the street lights sprang to life like electric fireflies. With Michelle away for the evening, it would not look good for her to remain in the house alone with David after the dinner hour. They all wanted to find a way out of the situation, but Shaunna's spending the night wasn't the play to make.

She was feeling strong, yet sensitive, and chose to listen to her favorite Eartha Kitt album as she made her way toward home with the sun's last traces dwindling in her rearview mirror. She was singing along with "Sell Me!" when her phone out-buzzed her duet. She pressed a button on her steering wheel, replacing the music with the caller's timid voice.

"Miss Noble? Hello. Uh, this is Heather Lentz, Kyle Petersen's publicist."

"Hello, Heather." Shaunna was surprised, but not suspicious.

"I'm sorry to bother you," Heather said quickly. "But I was hoping we could speak."

"It's no bother at all. What can I do for you?"

"It's actually about what I can do for you, but I'm not sure how long I can do it."

Shaunna got a bad feeling about what was coming next. Heather's statement descended like a shadow that carried the weight of a horse blanket. "What do you mean?"

"Kyle knows about you and David." Heather delivered the news flatly.

"You mean David and Michelle," Shaunna corrected automatically. She assumed that the girl had gotten it wrong.

"No. You and David are a couple, and he wants to expose you." Heather sounded apologetic, but certain.

Shaunna was in denial. "Well, he's just grasping at straws. Kyle has—"

"I know it's true. I've seen it." Heather's voice was soft, but effective enough to stop Shaunna's words. "I don't expect you to trust me, Miss Noble, but I won't make you lie. He has footage of you two on his computer. He was going to leak it this afternoon, but I stopped him."

"How?" Shaunna's mouth went dry.

"I convinced him that the tape was worth too much money to just give away. He's letting me shop it around, but he won't give me much more time."

"Oh my God," Shaunna almost whimpered. She felt foolish for having almost convinced herself that the threat was finally behind them. She found herself wanting to ask Heather how she looked and then laughed with a bitter bark.

Heather finally spoke again. "I just wanted you to know that I'll stall as long as I can. But I can't stop him."

Shaunna sighed heavily. "All this time, and he can still reach into my life and hurt me."

"Does Michelle know?" Heather asked. "I don't want to her to find out this way."

"She knows everything. Michelle and David have only ever been friends," Shaunna admitted.

"Okay. Good." Heather sounded relieved. "I'll let you know if anything changes."

"Thank you." Shaunna was taken with how genuine Heather was. She had an admirable morality which Shaunna fully understood could sometimes be a liability in Tinsel Town.

Heather was about to hang up when she heard Shaunna say something else. "What was that?" she asked.

"I could help you get out," Shaunna repeated.

Heather was silent.

"I know what you're going through," Shaunna continued. "I know Kyle. You have been doing a good job of protecting him and remaining respectful of Michelle. Don't think I didn't notice. If you want out, I can set you up with a few lower-level, but very sweet clients."

"Why would you do that?" Heather asked.

"For the same reason you called me," Shaunna told her.

"I called you because you deserved a warning."

"Actually," Shaunna stated patiently, "you called me to give me a chance. That's what I want to give you."

Heather swallowed. "What do I have to do?"

"What do you mean?" Shaunna asked.

"Do I have to steal his computer or something?"

"No!" Shaunna said quickly. "I'm not trying to bribe you, Heather, and besides, taking Kyle's computer wouldn't guarantee anything."

"You're right," Heather said. "And I'm sorry. I just wasn't expecting you to spend your time worrying about me, after what I said."

"Do you want to set up a meeting at my office?"

"No. I want to stay right where I am for now. I'm the only thing keeping him from sending the video to *TMZ*."

"Maybe you could just sell it to me?" Shaunna inquired.

"Maybe I can," Heather mused. "But that would only buy you another week before he knew something was up. He wants to see this video everywhere. He wants the world to see you two."

"I bet he does. And if that's the case, I wonder how much we can really do to stop him."

Heather was silent.

"I'll be in touch," Shaunna said at last. "And thanks again. It was a big help that you called."

"You're welcome," Heather said as her goodbye and then hung up.

Shaunna pressed the button on her steering wheel, and Eartha Kitt's voice filled the car once more. She quickly turned off the music and found a place to turn around.

She might as well spend the night in Malibu now.

When Shaunna pulled back through the mansion gates, she noticed that the paps had all gone home for the night. It was ironic, since she didn't care at that moment how they discovered she and David were a couple, just as long as it wasn't Kyle's way.

David was in the living room, reading a Jeffrey Ford book that may or may not have been spooking him at the moment he heard someone enter the house. He definitely wasn't expecting Michelle, and Shaunna had just walked out, so it was Kyle's name that flashed through his mind like a movie credit.

Armed with a hefty but slender vase that sat on a lighted shelf near the television, he crept around the corner, but the entry hall was empty.

"David?" Shaunna's voice came from upstairs.

"Down here," he answered and put the vase back, relieved that he wouldn't have to explain to the cops why he broke it over Kyle's head. He assumed that Michelle would forgive him.

Shaunna came into the room and rushed into David's arms. She was relieved as well. For a time while she was driving back to Malibu, she worried that being close to David now would only exacerbate her paranoia and discomfort. She was thankful to discover that his arms offered her only peace.

"Kyle found the footage of us."

"What!" David stepped back and blinked once. "It's been months. How could he still even have it stored?"

"I don't know," Shaunna said, stepping back into his reach. "Heather called me on my way home, and it sounds like he just stumbled onto it this afternoon."

David didn't know what to say.

"She convinced him to shop it around instead of just leaking it, but that will only give us a few days, maybe a week."

"What should we do?"

"We need to talk to Michelle, but I think it's time for you two to break up."

They went out onto the balcony and sat in canvas chairs that tilted their views skyward. David was thinking about how, since he was the celebrity in the relationship, it would become *his* sex tape if it ever got out. On the one hand, he was glad that the charade that was never meant to be a charade was coming to an end, but his ultimate goal was to protect Shaunna, and he felt as helpless about that as a frog on the freeway.

"You don't really think we need to fake a break up, do you?" David asked.

"It wouldn't be very hard, and the media would do most of the work for us."

"Yes, but we haven't lied to them yet, and I don't think we should start now. What about just going out on a double date with Michelle? We talked about that once, and it still seems like the best way to go."

"It is," Shaunna admitted. "But now we have to do something in the next few days, and I'm just not sure it will have a big enough impact if we don't coax a little drama out it."

David shook his head. "Sorry, but we need to end this in the same way we began it, by going out and having fun together and letting them take more pictures. Except this time, we'll make sure that they get more pictures of you and me than they get of me and her. We could even go to Disneyland."

"No," Shaunna stated quickly and a bit too loudly. "I don't want any of this touching Disneyland. It's my special place, David. Hopefully it will become our special place, and I don't want the bad association."

"I get that." David had still never been to the famed park, but Shaunna promised him an inaugural trip that would blow his mind.

"If we do it your way, we just need her to agree."

"And her date?" David asked.

"With any luck, we'll see him before we see her again, and maybe we can appeal to his chivalrous side."

"Okay, wait. We're not talking about your dad, are we?"

"No!" Shaunna was already laughing. "You know she has a thing for Sly, and I'm pretty sure he feels the same way."

"Oh yeah, Sly likes Michelle, all right."

"Are you sure? We need this to work." Shaunna kept feeling little panic attacks that rose up and fell away like summer twisters.

"He's an old-fashioned guy. He practically talks about her in iambic pentameter."

Shaunna huffed. "Why haven't you told me any of this?"

"I thought you already knew. You just said so yourself."

She sat forward to think. "We can find a high-profile event, but not something too accessible. We want this to be a statement, but we don't want to spend all night talking about it."

"Obviously the premiere is out," David said. "But you could come to the Emmys with me."

"Too far out. We need this to happen tomorrow night, or the next."

He reached out and took her hand. "You know we're not really talking about the problem."

"There's nothing we can do about Kyle. That tape is coming out; we just need to be ready when it does."

"Can't we do anything to stop him? What about Thomas? Can't he do anything?"

Shaunna thought about it. "He might. Michelle should be home anytime now. We'll call him when she gets here."

"Why wait?" David urged. "He's your friend and lawyer too, isn't he?"

"Yes, but this matter technically pertains to Michelle's case."

David squeezed her hand. "Let me ask you something: if Michelle was here, and she called Thomas, would she explain the whole situation to him herself, or would she hand you the phone?"

Shaunna let go of David's hand. She took out her phone, but didn't dial the attorney's number right away. "Isn't it funny," she said while watching the phone tremble in her hands. "I'm embarrassed to even tell him about it."

"We can trust Thomas," David said comfortingly. "If we're lucky, he'll be the last person to ever find out."

David's statement got Shaunna moving, and she scrolled down to the last name Harper in her contacts. "He might not be able to help us at all, you know," she told David as she pressed the call button.

"No," David agreed. "But maybe he'll take us for a ride on his boat."

Chapter Thirty-Seven

As if David had made a wish on falling star, Thomas ended his conversation with Shaunna by inviting them all to a party he was throwing on his boat the very next day in Marina Del Rey.

Shaunna wasn't sure at first if she was on friendly enough terms with Thomas to call him up at the dinner hour and tell him about her private affairs, but he certainly felt like he was on friendly enough terms to bawl her out for ten minutes about not having told him about the possibility sooner.

He had explained that the law could be very sticky when it came to home surveillance, and he was reluctant to give her much hope about his chances to pull something together in a week. However, asking them to his yacht party was done in part so he could meet face to face and suggest an off-the-record solution that involved Sly.

So, as it turned out, Shaunna got her wish as well. Thomas would have a limited guest list, but any number of them would have their iPhones out in a jiffy if they spotted David Quinn chatting away with Michelle Cooper while his arm was around another woman. They wouldn't have to endure many questions, but would most definitely make a splash.

Michelle came home late, but David and Shaunna were waiting up. They started with the bad news first, but it was the good news, her official setup with Sly, that had her fluttering around the house the next morning like a trapped robin.

"What exactly did Thomas say?" she asked Shaunna for the tenth time over breakfast.

"He said that he would ask Sly to be your date to the party," came the consistent reply.

"Yes, but did he mean it was a *date* date? Or is it just like taking your mother to the Oscars?"

"I think it's sweet when a guy takes his mom to the Oscars," David added.

"It is," Michelle said. "But that's not what I want."

"Oh, I get it." David went back to eating his eggs, but Michelle's stare was a heat that he could feel on his hands and his cheeks.

"What do you think he thinks it is?" she pressed.

David paused long enough to regard both women. Shaunna knew from experience that they were going to get a thoughtful answer.

"I think he's wondering the same thing you are," he said, looking into Michelle's anxious eyes. "I think he'll take his cues from you tonight, so if you want him to think it's a romantic date, you'd better give him signs."

"What kind of signs?" she asked him and then gasped. Her hand flew to her mouth. "I'm sorry. You guys have so much real stuff to deal with—that's all my fault, by the way—and here I am, worrying about a date."

"It's not your fault," Shaunna said firmly, her cheeks puffy with pancakes.

David nodded his head. "Helping you actually keeps our minds off the whole mess."

She looked at both them with scrutiny, lingering on Shaunna. "You two are so full of shit, but you're lucky I'm gullible." She forked a peach slice from her plate and waved it at David. "So, should I just touch his arm a lot, or can I whisper that I'm not wearing panties?"

David began choking.

"Michelle!" Shaunna laughed in spite of her poor night's sleep and her knotted stomach.

David recovered enough to hold up his finger, earning another few moments to pull himself together. "For Sly, I think eye contact and arm touching is fine."

"Yeah," Shaunna said humorlessly. "And for the love of God, wear panties! The last thing we need is an upskirt of you getting on and off a boat!"

Michelle's face took on a horrified look and immediately agreed to reconsider her undergarment options. They were all drinking orange juice and kept reaching for their glasses at the same time. It was the kind of thing Michelle would miss most when David moved out.

Since it was a Sunday, they were all home until the party, and the day moved incredibly slowly. David called his parents in Chicago; Shaunna, likewise, dialed up her father and broke the news that Kyle was in possession of a compromising video of her and David. He was extraordinarily sympathetic, having only needed to hear that they didn't film it themselves.

Gus was no stranger to Hollywood scandals, but in his day, incidents were mostly drug-related. His rage for Kyle was not well-hidden from his daughter, who had to make him promise not to contact the actor. She actually did believe that he stood a chance of getting Kyle to reconsider, but she hadn't forgotten how he'd intervened in Texas and done something to compensate Kyle for her vengeful act of prissy watch flinging.

Michelle spent the afternoon trying on outfits and lured Shaunna into her bedroom by the time she had it narrowed down to four choices. David came in a few moments later with a soft knock, wielding Michelle's cell phone.

"Knock, knock. Are you ladies done with your tickle fight yet?"

"Come in, David," Michelle called after she had dashed into the bathroom. She was wearing only a translucent pair of undies, but came out a moment later in a short bathrobe that made her look like a karate student.

"Your phone chirped when I was in the kitchen," David told her, passing the device over.

Michelle scanned it, and she shifted her weight to one foot as she read with her lips moving. "I think Sly just sent me something from Shakespeare."

"Read it." Shaunna nudged her.

Michelle cleared her throat. "Love's not Time's fool, though rosy lips and cheeks within his bending sickle's compass come…"

"Love alters not with his brief hours and weeks," Shaunna continued with her eyes closed. "But bears it out even to the edge of doom." She looked at Michelle then. "Is that where he stopped?"

"Yes. How did you know that?"

"It's Shakespeare. Sonnet 116," she said, as if that alone should answer the question. After a moment and when David slightly bowed to her, she added, "It's like one of his most famous sonnets. It means that love can conquer anything. Even time."

"I think it's even more than that," David stated slowly, still mid-ponder. "It sounded to me like love can actually command time, even reverse it...well, as it pertains to how you view a lover."

Shaunna's mouth dropped open. "Wow, that's really insightful, David."

He shrugged. "I didn't write it."

"What do you think this means?" Michelle asked them.

"I think it means you have your answer about what kind of date he thinks this is," Shaunna said with a smirk that rounded her eyes.

Michelle nodded and began texting her response.

"What are you telling him?" Shaunna asked.

Michelle finished typing and walked into her bathroom without a word. A moment later, her white panties came flying out.

"What have you got?" Kyle demanded even before he'd even fully entered the room.

He had given Heather more than enough time to release the footage of Shaunna and David having sex. He couldn't figure out what the hell was taking so long. She should've been able to find an interested buyer with just a couple of phone calls.

Heather was sitting at her computer and swiveled to face him. "I ran into a problem. As it turns out, we really shouldn't sell it after all."

"Why the fuck not?" he yelled.

Heather maintained her composure as she answered. "Because it could be traced back to you, and that's the last thing we want."

"Come on!" Kyle whined, but with an edge. "No one is going to think I had anything to do with it!"

"They will if *I* send it, and especially if *I* auction it off to the highest bidder," Heather practically muttered.

Kyle threw his hands up in exasperation. "Then why did you bring the idea up in the first place?"

"I'm sorry," Heather said quickly. "I wasn't thinking, but then everyone I approached had all these questions about you, and I realized—"

"So some of them already know I have it?" He thought for a moment, a deep crease appearing between his eyes. "It's too late, then," he concluded at last. "Sell it today."

"No! We can't do that!" Heather stood up. She was face to face with him, pleading. "Mr. Petersen, please think about it. This could really backfire for you." She swallowed. "Look, I know I messed up, but I can fix this if you just give me a little more time."

Kyle froze. Within moments, his entire face displayed a struggle. He looked like he was about to cough, but instead spoke with deliberate softness. "What are you up to?"

Heather plastered a thoroughly confused expression over her nervous face. "I just need to set up a couple of go-betweens and— "

"No!" Kyle shouted, stepping forward and forcing her to sit back down. "Who have you been talking to about that tape?"

Heather blinked up at him. "*Insider* knows," she began timidly. "And *TMZ* knows, but they never want to pay for anything." Kyle said nothing, so she continued. "*Celebritits.com* knows, but I'm not sure he recognized my name, so maybe not. And *Playboy* knows, but they originally thought it was Michelle on the tape. They dropped out when they realized it wasn't."

Kyle regarded Heather for a moment. His opinion of her had always been that she was just north of stupid. This incident appeared well within the established pattern of her not living up to the standards Shaunna had set. "How long will it take?"

"Not long. A few days, maybe?"

Kyle wasn't completely sure, but it almost sounded as though Heather was relieved.

"Michelle and I have a divorce meeting the day after tomorrow," Kyle stated with no emotion. "You have until then."

Kyle turned to walk away and then hesitated. "I mean it, Heather. No more excuses. After that, I want to see that tape everywhere I look."

Heather didn't reply.

Chapter Thirty-Eight

Sly had arrived in Malibu to pick up Michelle, and the two of them were currently tiny versions of themselves in David's rearview mirror. Sly had texted Michelle several times during the day and finally requested the honor of escorting her to the party. She happily accepted, and Shaunna liked the exclamation point the gesture put on their message to the world. David Quinn and Michelle Cooper were friends and about to go public with their intentions to go home with different people that evening.

David drove Shaunna to Marina Del Rey in a muscle car he'd bought from Gus. She enjoyed the trip down the Pacific Coast Highway to Santa Monica. Cutting south toward Venice was a nice change of pace.

Thomas's boat was christened *The Culprit*. It was more like a luxury condo than a boat and easily held the forty people already milling around on its two sleek decks. Thomas was standing on the dock and offering his hand to the guests stepping aboard, even though it was hardly necessary. He greeted David and Shaunna warmly, and Michelle even received a kiss on the cheek. Sly merely nodded at his employer, and Thomas, knowing his friend all too well, returned the gesture.

"I hope you don't mind me setting you up with Michelle here," Thomas teased.

"I am delighted to be her date for the evening, Mr. Harper," Sly replied with dignity. "I believe it is her pardon you should seek."

"Oh, I think she'll forgive me," Thomas said, looking directly at Michelle and flashing a smile that even the twilight couldn't mute.

"They needed a nudge toward each other," Shaunna remarked. "You saved us another few months at least."

Michelle and Sly both looked down bashfully, and Thomas laughed as he raised his hand to still more approaching guests. "I'll catch up to you guys onboard."

The bay was small, and the vessel was out in the Pacific Ocean within minutes of being untied from the dock. Thomas wasn't piloting the boat that evening, but plucked Michelle and Shaunna delicately from the crowd on his way up to the wheelhouse, knowing that their dates would see and follow.

"This is Dale," Thomas told them as they filed into a room that looked as much like a lounge as it did a control room. "Dale, this is Michelle, Shaunna, Sly, and David."

Dale nodded. He appeared to recognize Michelle, but remained calm. It wasn't the first time A-list celebrities had been shuttled into the wheelhouse.

"Dale, will you give me a few minutes alone with my friends here?"

"Sure thing, boss." Dale leaned forward and checked a small computer screen, then a large log book before leaving the group.

Thomas stepped into his captain's vacated spot and looked out ahead of the boat. They were traveling south, with Vista Del Mar off their port side and the forthcoming sunset to starboard.

"Okay, gang," Thomas began. "This won't take long, and then we can all go enjoy the shindig. We have our final divorce meeting with Kyle in two days, but I don't want to tip my hand unless I know I've already won. And we're not there yet."

"Look." Shaunna sounded exasperated. "He could have hundreds of copies of that footage by now. The tape is going to come out in a few days." She looked around at them. "Heather texted me about an hour ago; it's going to happen. But by going public here at the party, we can diminish its impact, and that's going to have to be enough."

Michelle whispered something into Sly's ear, and when he nodded, she spoke up. "I have an idea that might work."

"What are you thinking?" Thomas asked. In his experience, simple plans were underrated, and at this point, any plan was better than none.

What Michelle proposed wasn't elegant, but it certainly was simple and didn't break any laws. Everyone agreed that it was the only thing that gave them any chance of success within the next two days. Sly seemed especially convinced that it would work, but he was biased toward his date. David likewise was overly confident, while Shaunna was trying to accept the inevitable embarrassment of Kyle's last act of revenge.

Thomas brought the boat to a stop off of Manhattan Beach, and they joined the rest of the partygoers well before the sun kissed the horizon. Electro-swing music played in the background, and it only took two glasses of champagne to encourage Sly to lead Michelle to the bow of the boat, where many couples were dancing.

David simply would not let go of Shaunna's hand. He knew she was sad, but he was all too happy to show his affection for her outside the sanctuary of the Malibu home. After all, a public display of devotion was their primary purpose in being there. He handed her a glass of something red and robust, hoping that it would relax her enough to look happy in any photos of them that might surface.

"Do you really think the plan will fail?" David asked her later in the evening, as his hand ran carefully through her hair. The music had switched to classic rock, and the lights on land twinkled like low-lying stars.

"Not anymore," she conceded. "But the timing will be key."

"I know."

"Either way— " she shrugged "—we're saving Michelle the hassle of being involved in the whole mess when it surfaces."

David glanced around the boat, seeking a distraction for Shaunna's woes. "There's this girl who keeps taking pictures of us from the upper deck."

"She must be tweeting them too," Shaunna told him.

"How do you know?" he asked.

She waggled her own phone. "We've been a recognized couple for the last half hour."

Shaunna grinned in an attempt to appear happy, but David knew her well enough to see through the facade.

Later that night, David drove Shaunna back to Yorba Linda, where they spent their first night together in her home. When they went to bed, they didn't make love. Instead, David held Shaunna while she rested her head on his chest. His fingers glided up and down her arm as he sought to ease her mood.

"We should use your den as a nursery someday," David suggested playfully.

"Slow down, cowboy!" Shaunna chided, but inside, she was warmed by the fact that he was already thinking about starting a family with her.

"I just don't want to have to choose between a full-sized *Donkey Kong Jr.* arcade game or a baby swing when the time comes," David supplied with a grin.

Shaunna lightly smacked his leg, and he was happy to see her playing along. "If we're getting an arcade game, it's going to be *Spy Hunter*. Or *Q*bert*. Or *Star Wars*!"

"The sit-down one?" David asked.

"Hell yes!"

"Great. It can double as a bassinet." David pulled Shaunna tighter against him as she laughed.

Problem solved.

Michelle and Sly were taking things slower, but they shared their first night together in her previously lonely bed, and she'd never felt so swept away by the experience of physical love.

Sly was gentle but passionate, and he whispered loving sentiments throughout the evening. Much of the time, he just held her. He gladly spent the night when she asked, and since they couldn't bear to be apart, he took the next day off.

A day off was a rarity for Sly, and he devoted all his leisure to Michelle. They stayed in bed with their bodies intertwined like the ribbons on a nicely wrapped gift.

Chapter Thirty-Nine

Thomas was waiting in his favorite conference room with Michelle sitting to his left. He liked the subliminal message that she was in the driver's seat and arranged it that way during each and every meeting. With any luck, this one would be the last.

During the past months, his superior knowledge of the law was a more-than-adequate match for Kyle's interchangeable trio of men, who never strayed from their Windsor knots and designer shoes.

The couple had been married before their immense wealth was acquired, so no pre-nuptial agreement had been drafted. Although their liquid assets had been split evenly, Thomas wanted insurance for the long-suffering Michelle. She'd already gotten the house in Malibu, with Kyle's interest being offset by the remaining money in an account worth almost four million dollars.

There were a multitude of smaller issues in the beginning, and Thomas paddled Kyle's lawyers like canoes. On one visit, Kyle had gotten so upset that he'd hit the table with his fist. Thomas had looked on impassively as Kyle cried out in pain and cradled the reawakened injury against his chest. Michelle had been particularly tickled but, as always, mustered the strength not to laugh.

Today, they were finalizing the figures on a few shared investments and some foreign real estate holdings, along with a rarely used bank account. Both parties seemed interested in spending as little time in the same room as possible. In Thomas's experience, that usually led to quick resolutions.

When Kyle's lawyers preceded him into the room, Thomas could tell by their gait that they meant business.

Kyle spoke first. "Where is the rest of the money in the vacation account, Michelle?"

"Whoa, whoa, whoa," Thomas objected in a booming voice. He then addressed his counterparts. "Please advise Mr. Petersen that addressing my client directly one more time will result in the immediate conclusion of this meeting."

Kyle's sleeve was touched by one of the three men, and he pulled it away angrily. "I heard! Ask her! Do your jobs!"

"Yes," Thomas encouraged, sitting forward and lacing his fingers together. "Why doesn't one of you, as they say, begin at the beginning?"

One of the men pulled on the lapel of his gray suit and spoke with a snooty cadence. "The West Cal Savings Union account was supposed to have a balance of one million dollars, but we have just discovered there is only two hundred thousand left."

"A majority of the funds were withdrawn on October twenty-first of last year," another man supplied.

"October twenty-first!" Kyle sneered, a sense of triumph surging through him. "The day after I served her with divorce papers!"

Thomas responded quickly. "Allow me to confer with my client briefly."

After a moment of silence, Thomas raised his eyebrows, a clear indication that he meant for everyone else to leave the conference room.

Kyle's attorneys slowly stood up, but the pained looks on their faces said it all. Having to leave the room at someone else's bidding was beneath them. Kyle's impatience was unmistakable as he followed after.

Thomas only spoke to Michelle for a few moments before summoning the visiting legal team to resume the meeting. He was more than satisfied with Michelle's explanation of the transaction and now had some questions of his own.

He was also smiling like the cat that ate the canary, along with a parakeet and two goldfish.

"Gentlemen," he said cheerily as the men came back into the room. "Please sit." He waited for everyone to settle into their chairs. "I'm so grateful that you brought this issue to my attention; otherwise, it might have gone completely unnoticed. First of all, I'll allow Michelle to explain what happened with the money in question."

She leveled her gaze at Kyle as she answered. She made sure to speak slowly so he could absorb it all. "I gave the eight hundred thousand dollars to Gus Noble."

Kyle looked confused at first, but then his hands clenched into fists. "Wait a minute!" He turned to his legal team. "She gave Gus Noble the money he gave me in Texas to replace my watch."

"And what time is it, Mr. Petersen?" Thomas asked, already staring at Kyle's naked wrist. "You were given almost a million dollars," he continued with deliberate slowness. "Yet, it didn't appear in any of your settlement paperwork. That, gentlemen, is a crime."

All three lawyers' eyes widened. "We didn't know," one of them squeaked.

"So," Thomas addressed Kyle. "Gus Noble delivered the eight hundred thousand dollars to you? And that was when, exactly?"

Kyle was reluctant to answer, but his attorneys were looking at him just as expectantly as Thomas was. "Yes, but she gave it to him from our account."

"The fact that Michelle gave Gus Noble access to the money doesn't matter here. You could have done the same, and she couldn't have done anything about it. However, if you are in possession of those funds, you owe half to Michelle."

"But it was *our* money he gave me!" Kyle whined.

"Thank you for proving my point," Thomas said, his voice stony.

Kyle turned to his befuddled team of lawyers. "This isn't fair!"

Thomas spoke humorlessly as he addressed Kyle's attorneys. "I don't see why I shouldn't report your firm's gross continuation of loose law practice to the California Bar Association."

"You can't say we hid it if it came from his own account," one of the braver lawyers tried.

"I can if he didn't know that's where it came from!" Thomas roared. "And he just admitted as much!" Thomas eyed each one of them and paused at the attorney with the most expensive tie.

"I've had enough of this," Thomas said in a dark voice. "Make us an offer we can't refuse on the remaining interests, and don't forget to include the four hundred thousand dollars on top of it."

"We need a minute," the lead attorney murmured.

Thomas nodded his approval and, after a few moments, raised his eyebrows again. Kyle and his legal team all rose begrudgingly to their feet and adjourned back to the hallway.

After a couple of minutes, only one of them returned to the room, and the lone attorney remained standing as he spoke. "Two million. One point six to buy out the remainder of the chattel and the other four hundred thousand to compensate for the honest mistake that we were unaware of."

"Five million," Thomas countered.

The man's mouth popped open before he disappeared back out into the hall. A few seconds later, the seated duo heard Kyle throw a muffled tantrum.

When the lawyer came back, he extended his hand. "You have a deal at four." His eyes were frazzled, but hopeful.

Thomas rose from his seat to shake the man's hand.

"Thank you," he said pleasantly. "Oh, and there is one other thing, if you could just ask Mr. Petersen to come back in, please."

The lawyer gawked at him, but exited and returned with the rest of his colleagues.

"As you will recall, Mr. Petersen," Thomas started talking the moment Kyle entered the room. "You gave up your interest in the house in Malibu beginning November of last year. If I recall, this was so you wouldn't have to contribute to taxes and utilities and so forth. Is this correct?"

Kyle looked at his lawyers, who only nodded their heads. "I guess."

"And this would be even before you had returned from your film shoot in Texas, correct?"

"Yes."

"In addition, the restraining order filed against you last November further establishes that you are no longer in residence?" Thomas didn't want to miss an opportunity to bring that up.

"Yes. What's this all about?" Kyle demanded.

"Good, then you'll agree that any video surveillance you may be in possession of from that house would not only be in poor taste, but also not legally yours to own."

"Absolutely not!" Kyle barked, standing up. He even dared to speak to Michelle again. "You're not getting that tape."

Thomas addressed Kyle's attorneys. "Surely you gentlemen can see the wisdom in prevailing on your client to reconsider."

"Not happening!" Kyle shouted.

"I'll give you a million dollars," Michelle said.

"Michelle…" Thomas began.

"No deal!" Kyle laughed. "You're not buying her way out this time! She's going to know exactly how it feels to have the whole world laughing at her."

"Actually, you'll probably make Miss Noble a billionaire," Thomas said offhandedly. "Not to mention the fact that your studio would drop you like a hot potato."

Kyle scoffed. It was a childish noise that carried the weight of an ember. "Yeah, right. Even if you could prove it was me who leaked it, why would they care?"

Thomas reached into his desk and pulled out a hefty stapled document. "This is the contract Michelle signed for *Sling Shot.* You will recognize it, no doubt, because you signed one yourself." He flipped through several pages. "Ah, here it is: the morality clause. Do you remember reading this portion?"

Thomas didn't wait for an answer, nor did he read from the stuffy text. He looked directly at Kyle's attorneys as he slid the papers across the desk. "If Mr. Petersen does anything to defame this production or any fellow cast members, he is subject to a host of nasty legal and financial repercussions. He would be sued for every penny he has been paid so far, and he would forfeit all of his back-end percentage."

Kyle's confusion turned into a sarcastic sneer. "So what? Shaunna wasn't even in the movie!"

"David was," Michelle pointed out.

Thomas took over again. "Mr. Quinn enjoys the protection of the studio on this matter, and I will gladly supply any assistance I can. That includes eyewitness testimony from the technician who removed the cameras from the house."

Kyle could still picture the face of the man discovering the cameras. He didn't want that face jeopardizing the substantial income he stood to make after the film's release, but he also knew something the rest of them didn't. Heather should be releasing the video in question as Thomas sat there making his threats. He really didn't have a choice but to back his own play, so he slowly stood up. "You're bluffing, and I'm leaving."

Thomas stood as well. His actions, not Kyle's, triggered those of his counterparts, who also rose to their feet. "If you force me, Kyle, I will have a warrant drawn up for the material and prosecute you with a result that could end in serious jail time."

Kyle looked at his companions, who had long ago learned to avoid his gaze. He briefly wondered if he could call Heather in time to stop her and actually felt his heart begin racing in his chest. With no other choice at hand and fueled with the desire to win just one confrontation with Thomas, he flashed his most brilliant Hollywood smile. "Fuck you."

Kyle walked briskly to the door and didn't look back. He did, however, hear Michelle's last words to him as she called after him.

"You should have taken the money."

When Kyle returned to his rented home, he immediately went looking for Heather. He'd just risked his career to burn Shaunna and wanted to make sure the effort was worth it.

Sunlight fell across the desk in the room she hibernated in most of the time, but she was nowhere to be found. Even her computer was gone. In its place was a piece of paper folded into a small square.

Kyle opened the note and read it all the way through before crinkling it up into a ball and throwing it to the floor.

Mr. Petersen,

Please consider this letter my immediate resignation from your vile employ.

Why you continually treat me, and most other people, like dirt is beyond my understanding. It makes you more than unlikable; it makes you despicable. You expect loyalty and respect while offering none in return, and this makes you untrustworthy. You genuinely think you're better than everyone else, and this makes you just plain stupid.

With any luck, you lost more than just my services today, and I caution you to think very carefully before you ever contact me again. If you choose to play another round, you should know that I've kept copies of all the e-mails you've sent to me in the last twelve months, and some of the stuff you wrote was crazy. (Like, batshit crazy, Kyle.) If any of it gets out, you'll be bowling with Mel Gibson.

I didn't take any of your possessions, so don't you dare suggest otherwise. However, I did hide your TV remote, just to piss you off.

No longer your fool,

Heather Lentz

P.S. Good luck finding your fucking remote.

Kyle ran upstairs to his office with Michelle's last words ringing in his ears. To his surprise, his computer was sitting on his desk right where he left it. Hope rose up in him like a song, but dropped away savagely when he went to access his security account. His user name appeared to no longer exist.

He smirked as he checked his e-mail, where he had sent himself a copy of the footage as a failsafe. Unfortunately, that too had been tampered with and he could no longer access his inbox. Someone had gotten to his computer while he was at Thomas's office, someone who obviously knew what they were doing. Kyle wanted to scream in frustration, but instead, a growing sense of relief crept in. He leaned back in his chair and wondered if he should pick a redhead as his next publicist.

Heather was on her way to meet Shaunna at her place. She had been promised a job and was in desperate need of someone who could overlook that fact that she wasn't going to get a very good reference from her last employer.

She was driven in a little yellow Alfa Romeo, whose chivalrous occupant walked her to the door and even stayed for a glass of strawberry lemonade.

Chapter Forty

Kyle didn't attend the premiere.

The previous two months had been almost unbearable for him. In the wake of Heather's departure, he'd been unable to hold on to any publicist for more than a few days. More than one replacement quit after an outburst. Others were fired when they refused his demands. Without someone in place to manage his public image, Kyle's erratic nature could no longer be kept a secret. When his divorce from Michelle was finalized, she won the public's favor like she won the Malibu home.

Kyle was increasingly ridiculed, and of course, he imploded. He made a series of phone calls to local radio stations that only served to make him look like a self-important prick with no shame and a propensity to say "you know" a lot. The DJs mocked him, and one morning host even played fart noises under Kyle's ranting and then asked him repeatedly to excuse himself.

All the calls ended pretty much the same way—a series of bleeps with Kyle taking breaths in between, followed by a dial tone and radio jocks laughing themselves into coughing fits.

The press crucified Kyle, and the late night talk show hosts were unrelenting. He lost not only his endorsement deals, but the leading role in his beloved film franchise. The studio informed him that they were going with a younger actor to attract college-aged girls, but no one was fooled. Not even Kyle.

No one was surprised that he declined to attend the premiere, and no one blamed him, either. It was kind of nice not having him around.

Michelle almost felt sorry for her ex-husband as she strolled up the red carpet with Sly on her arm.

Shaunna and David attended the premiere together, and the happiness that radiated from them was palpable. The mere fact that they were free to do something as simple as holding hands in public made them feel like they were flying.

Countless interviews had been held for weeks as the film neared its wide release, and both actors were prepared to expect questions about their altered relationship. It was mutually agreed upon that they would only acknowledge their continued close friendship and Michelle's role in bringing David and Shaunna together.

Nathan was planted near the theatre's main doors and welcomed attendees with handshakes and hugs. When Michelle and Sly reached him, Nathan told a nearby usher to take the couple to an assigned seat next to his.

He gave the same instructions to David and Shaunna and paused to hug the thin, dark-haired girl a second time. He told her how much he'd been rooting for her, then asked them to grab some Milk Duds for him on their way in.

The movie opened with a man installing gorilla glass roof tiles over a moon crater and followed his gaze to a trumpet-shaped spaceship that was landing on a platform nearby.

Kyle's character, Grant, exited the ship, and as he exchanged words with a ground crewman on the big screen, Nathan leaned over to Michelle to reveal a long-held secret. "Honey, you're in for one hell of a ride."

From the explosion that catapulted the recently decapitated crewman's head toward the well-dressed audience (who had all obediently donned their 3D glasses) to the reveal of Kyle as a murderous saboteur, the movie held on to its viewers like a determined dog with a heavy bone.

In many ways, the film was shot like a music video, with fast-paced edits and artistic lighting. But it also included long moments of tension-filled interactions between the actors.

Michelle had absolutely no idea that the movie was going to feature her so prominently, but it became clear early on that the narrative was centered on her character's experiences and reactions.

It was a fierce display of acting on her part, and David was extremely effective as the ambushed and sacrificed good guy.

Nathan thought it funny that he'd once worried the audience would resist seeing Kyle as a scumbag, but recent real-world events made his role match his public persona perfectly. His performance was also cleverly edited to keep him from ruining the picture.

When the film credits began to roll, an enthusiastic and genuine cheer arose from the crowd, and everyone involved felt very proud of their accomplishments.

There was no title card at the beginning of the film and no credits of any kind, so Michelle didn't find out until the end that her name was listed above Kyle's.

"Oh shit," Nathan said, as if he were just seeing it for the first time. "That's gonna piss him off."

Shaunna turned in her chair and addressed Nathan in a whisper. "Kyle has a rider in his contracts for top billing."

"Apparently not this one." Nathan shrugged. "He waived a bunch of his usual bullshit for a bigger paycheck. I verified it with the studio guys."

"I'm almost sorry he's not here to see it," Shaunna murmured.

Nathan met Michelle's eyes. "You were breathtaking, and I always believed you would be," he told her. "I'm completely in awe every time I see you in this film, and I've seen it a lot."

"It wasn't what I was expecting to see at all," Sly commented to Nathan. Their introduction had been brief, and this was the first time the two had really spoken. "Your decision to keep us focused on her character's point of view offered a valued human core and feminine reasoning to an otherwise horrific story." Then Sly added with a softening tone, "Plus, you captured her eyes brilliantly."

"Thank you." Nathan beamed. "You don't know how many times those eyes saved our ass in editing this summer."

David found that remark particularly funny and laughed so hard that he had to clutch his stomach while Shaunna hugged Michelle. "You turned this movie into a film," she told her friend earnestly.

Nathan looked for and found Lauren, who dropped by to tell the actors how great they were. Michelle, who now understood that her performance was pieced together like a quilting circle's spring project, took the editor's hands in hers and thanked her with a kiss on the cheek.

Before the group split up, Nathan joked that the studio was already hinting that there would be sequel money to spend.

Michelle laughed it off.

Shaunna eyed Nathan hard. "Not even you are that crazy," she said solemnly.

"One thing's for sure, though," Nathan observed. "Kyle would probably say yes. He needs the work."

Chapter Forty-One

David proposed to Shaunna at Disneyland. The two of them had logged hundreds of hours at the park, but she had not gotten him back on the Tower of Terror ride after their infamous first trip together. He imagined, but never truly considered, setting something up with the park wherein he could pop the question thirteen stories high in the creepy attraction and threaten not to let her down until she accepted. It was clever, sure, but decidedly unromantic and, in a word, tacky.

Instead, he did something simple and sincere. He resolutely got down on one knee and held out an open ring box with a shaky hand and asked her to marry him while they were at the Blue Bayou restaurant in the French Quarter. David loved how the sweet clean smell of the water from the Pirates of the Caribbean ride and the peaceful stillness of an animated twilight bayou complemented the Cajun cuisine.

They'd only been to the restaurant as a couple once before; they usually preferred to scarf down corn dogs on their way from Splash Mountain to the Matterhorn. David booked a waterside table, waited until dinner was ordered, and then stood briefly before genuflecting before her. She responded by inhaling deeply and covering her mouth in surprise.

"Shaunna?" David's voice was steady, but his eyes fluttered. "You know that feeling you get when you first sit down for a trip through Pirates?" He titled his head toward the boats of wonder-filled passengers drifting nearby in the bayou.

"You're excited because you know that not only is it going to be a good ride, but it's going to be a nice long ride. You start thinking about the exciting parts coming up. All the while you're floating through this stunning world, and no matter how many times you see it, it always fills you with awe." He looked around and then settled his eyes back on hers.

"What you don't know is that when you showed me this place, I already knew what that feeling was. You gave it to me a year ago." He blinked a few times and mustered his courage for a moment. "Since I met you, my heart has been filled with that sensation you get right at the beginning of a phenomenal adventure. Something you just know is going to take you places you never dreamed of and make your every wish come true. Well, I only have one wish, and I came to the Magic Kingdom to make it come true." His next words were gravelly with emotion. "Shaunna Noble…will you marry me?"

Her tears revealed her answer, and David slid the ring on her finger while nearby diners offered congratulatory applause. The excitement was also noticed by the boats of people in the bayou, who also hooted their approval for the newly engaged.

The drive back to their house was a quick one by LA standards, and it was a good thing, because the mix of fear and fun made them both surge with need for one another.

They made love slowly, and David took great care in brushing his lips over Shaunna's breasts and belly before he coaxed his way between her legs, delivering passionate and sometimes probing explorations.

His tender lovemaking and his occasional whispers of enchantment only added to her dreamlike state. There were two candles burning in the room—one on a tall dresser, and one near the bed on a small table that held mostly books competing for Shaunna's attention.

The two flames gave her two different silhouettes of David's back against the wall and ceiling. It was enough to keep her eyes open, as was the rising tide of pleasure in her body.

David was slow, seductive, but the animal need to just take her consumed him. He rose up on his knees and pulled her legs up to rest her calves on his chest. She was more or less in a sitting position, but her feet were pointed upward, and she wondered if this was how astronauts felt when they were blasting off into space.

This position sent David even deeper into her than before, and Shaunna tipped over the edge with ease, sighing at first and then quickly gasping for breath. He liked the feel of her smooth calves against his hard chest and pressed his cheek into the curve of her foot as he moved himself in and out of her.

He watched their coupling for a while, taking advantage of a perspective Shaunna often envied. Soon, he closed his eyes and sighed deeply as he slid his hands to her hips and urgently pulled her frame toward his increasing thrusts.

"Yes," Shaunna encouraged.

David leaned his head back and moaned toward the briskly turning ceiling fan. The cool air brushed the damp hair from his head as he remained one with his lover.

She could feel his release even as the rest of his body stilled, and when he allowed her legs to fall back to the bed, she curled around him and fell fast asleep.

David traced his fingers along her spine as he let the whirling of the fan carry him off to breeze-swept memories. Within a few moments, his limp hand fell to the bed and his breathing settled into a rhythm with hers that was almost musical.

Chapter Forty-Two

Michelle's Golden Globes invitation from the Hollywood Foreign Press included a handwritten note that smelled like the lavender ink it was written in. It informed her that she and Nathan would share a table reserved by the studio. Although neither the picture's writing nor its direction was being considered for an award, *Sling Shot* had received no less than five nominations, including Best Achievement in Editing and Best Actress.

The studio was thrilled to receive a trio of technical nominations and felt confident that it would snag a few trophies. The suits were ecstatic over the surprise announcement of its leading actress, and Michelle's nomination for a Golden Globe generated the single biggest buzz of the whole affair.

By the time the big night arrived weeks later, it almost seemed anticlimactic compared to the events that had taken place since the day of the nominations.

Sly had finally driven Michelle to his immaculate home in Riverside County. He lived in the wine country, just outside Temecula, and his home looked more like a castle, with its heavy stone structure and tall windows. There, he asked her to cast off the last trappings of her old life with Kyle and move in. Michelle accepted so readily that she sent movers for all her things and never set foot in the Malibu estate again. As a bonus, since it was a now-famous love nest, she put the house on the market for twice its estimated value in the divorce settlement, and her realtor quickly scheduled more viewings than a Jersey peep show.

Sly also fully revealed to Michelle the nature of his sensitive and secretive work. She wasn't surprised to learn that it sounded like he was some sort of crisis manager. Given the legalities of many of his dealings, he wasn't encouraged to discuss his work, which was fine since each job was usually an open-and-shut case, whether he succeeded or not.

Sly had no law degree, but his work had always been about getting two parties to see their similarities, rather than their differences. It was a skill that required a unique discipline and a broad education. His abilities ranged from psychological diagnosis, to speaking and reading fluent Mandarin. Sly was an ambassador and an advocate for his clients and sought only solutions that would help everyone. Simply put, he was one starship short of being the real Capt. Jean-Luc Picard.

Sly escorted Michelle up the red carpet with a suave confidence, but internally, his very bones were dancing with the excitement of seeing so many celebrities in one place. He may have led a life of intrigue, cutting logistic channels for Thomas Harper and the firm's other partners, but he had only occasional brushes with Hollywood types before he met Michelle and David.

Arm-in-arm with Michelle Cooper, he pondered the literal translation of "swinging from a star" as flash bulbs made his eyeballs smart.

Still, he was steady on his feet and stood aside whenever fuzzy microphones were waggled at Michelle. While she energetically explained who she was wearing and complimented the other actresses nominated in her category a dozen times over, Sly soaked in the warmth of her good heart while marveling at things like how the red carpet was actually violet in reality and how absolutely stunning Michelle looked in her dress.

Every picture of the duo captured the same polished calm. This, of course, only added to Sly's mystique. He was quite handsome, and his old-fashioned but flattering suit made him the talk of the morning shows the following day.

Shaunna and David didn't try to be inconspicuous. She wore a modestly cut, but brightly colored royal blue gown, while he wore a tailored pin-striped Italian suit with a silk pocket square that matched his date. They both felt like they were going to the prom.

They were several celebrities behind Michelle and Sly and were losing ground because every single entertainment reporter shoved interviewees aside for a chance to land a few words with David Quinn.

He was very natural when he spoke, and his answers were always witty as well as succinct. Shaunna thought, not for the first time, that he would have made a great lawyer or stand-up comedian.

She was largely ignored, which thrilled her to pieces and told her that everyone was well on their way to moving on to bigger and newer scandals. Plenty of photographs of her surfaced the next morning because she made all of the best dressed lists, but like Sly, she was content with being the silent chaperone.

Michelle and Sly finally escaped into the Beverly Hilton Hotel's International Ballroom, where Sly was introduced to directors, producers, actors, and agents for another ten minutes before they found their way to their table. It was located close to the stage — really close to the stage. Nathan and Lauren were already seated when Sly and Michelle walked up.

"Good evening, Michelle," Nathan greeted her after rising from his chair. Sly inwardly approved of the young man's adherence to good manners. "Boy, I couldn't help but notice how close they put you to the stairs." He gestured to the sweeping staircase immediately behind Lauren, who was rolling her eyes.

"It's almost as if they wanted to make it easier for someone to walk up there at some point."

Michelle gave Lauren a sympathetic look because clearly, she had been listening to this for some time. "Don't start. I'm nervous enough as it is." She directed her comment to Nathan, who had beaten Sly to the honor of pulling out her chair.

"Well," Nathan concluded with a wink to Sly, "I would've voted for both of you. Except I'm not foreign…or with the press."

When Shaunna and David arrived, the room was almost full and the collective murmur was like road noise on a highway. Every few minutes, another famous person would wander by and gush at either Michelle or David, or both, and move on. They were all served dessert and strong drinks while another half-hour demonstrated just how packed the room could get.

Of course, Gus Noble was there. He was to the Golden Globes what Jack Nicholson was to the Oscars — royalty. Even when he had no productions up for consideration, Gus was always welcome and often a presenter. His on-stage persona was engaging and popular.

He strolled through the room like the pope at a picnic until he reached Michelle's table. Gus sat down next to Shaunna. He was eager to catch up with his daughter.

"How have you two been?"

"We're good," Shaunna answered. "How about you?"

"I've been busy," Gus replied with a satisfied sigh. He pointed to David. "This one is going to keep me that way too. All four networks are fighting over my next series idea." He turned to Michelle and Sly. "It's nice to see you two again." Gus then leaned into Michelle. "I hope you wore sensible shoes. I have it on good authority that you are taking a walk up that very large staircase this evening."

Michelle waved his comment away as the two men nodded agreeably at each other.

Gus turned his attention back to Shaunna and David. "Have you picked a wedding date?"

"We were thinking about sometime in May," Shaunna answered. "But we don't know for sure yet."

Gus had known about David's proposal before Shaunna, of course. David wouldn't have had it any other way.

"Do you know what this guy did?" Gus asked, talking to Sly, but pointing at David. "He stopped by the house a few weeks ago to ask me, all formal-like, if he could come inside to discuss something important. I offered him a drink, which he accepted, and then he proceeded to tell me all these wonderful things about my daughter. All of them are true, of course, so I know he's in love…"

Gus looked over at David, whose slight nod simultaneously approved of his summation and encouraged him to continue.

"He promised me that he would only say and do things that would make her feel loved and treasured and said that he would never stop being her best friend in the world. Then he asked for my blessing to propose to her."

Michelle and Lauren looked at David adoringly. Sly was very impressed with the respectful and time-honored approach the young actor had taken by seeking the blessing of the father of the bride. Shaunna was also moved by the secret gesture David made to ask her father for her hand.

When the camera operators moved into position, all the industry veterans scurried back to their assigned tables before the lights dimmed. Gus made his hasty goodbyes, and as soon as the room was blanketed in a shroud of shadows, David leaned in toward Shaunna to kiss her cheek. His warm breath on her ear startled her.

The show was peppy and upbeat, with a host that chose not to insult every person in the industry. There were some excellent scripted performances as well, but Michelle just wanted to get the waiting over with.

As more awards were given to actors who were much farther away from the stage than she was, Michelle caught herself hoping that she wouldn't win at all. Lately, she realized how truly selfish she'd been with David for nearly a year. She'd put all their careers at risk for childish and spontaneous reasons, and if it came time to thank him publicly for his support, Michelle didn't know what she could say.

She hadn't written anything by way of an acceptance speech, and that became the reason she was suddenly overcome with the feeling she was going to have to give one.

Fortunately, she didn't have to go first. Several names from her table were called before hers. The sound guy shuffled up and collected his award, as did the director of photography. Then Lauren won, and Nathan banged on the table like a cartoon wolf. She spoke quickly and far more eloquently than Michelle felt capable of herself. Nathan was thanked for being a kind and creative friend and director, and then Lauren turned to Michelle and thanked the actress for being the single biggest inspiration she had while editing the film.

"Your performance made us re-think the whole picture," Lauren told her in front of the world. "Your performance is what got me up here tonight, so thank you. It was an honor editing your work."

Michelle sat with her hand over her mouth as Lauren wrapped things up, and then they all heard the announcement of another commercial break. After that, the award for Best Actress would be presented.

Sly took her hand, and his warm, rough skin soothed her racing mind.

"You know," he said softly. "If you lose, I bet we can be home in an hour."

Michelle smiled. That sounded fine to her.

She was not that lucky, of course.

Michelle's name was the first one called when the presenter listed all the nominees, and hers was the only one repeated.

The first thing she was consciously aware of was that their table instantly lit up with a spotlight like it had when her colleagues had won. Only, she hadn't noticed the prism of light left by the reflection of her champagne glass on the white tablecloth before. She was almost hypnotized by it while the room raced with sound.

Finally, Sly's voice cut through the chaos. "Time to start climbing, my love."

Michelle snapped out of it, turned to kiss him and then she was on the move. Her dress was, thankfully, not too cumbersome, so she was able to ascend gracefully.

Applause and whistles carried her to the glass podium, and she was handed the weighty award.

The ballroom was a sea of faces, more than she'd ever addressed in her entire life. That alone was enough to paralyze her voice, but when she considered the millions watching around the world, she was certain that even if she'd written a great speech, her throat was going to clamp shut before she uttered a word.

The room settled, and Michelle opened her mouth, hoping for the best.

"It's no secret that my nomination in this category was a big surprise to everyone, including me. I want to thank the Hollywood Foreign Press for that. I really needed it three months ago." A mixture of laughter and supportive applause gave her a brief moment to gather her next thoughts. "The other women in this category have long been heroes of mine, and the only reason I don't feel completely awful about standing here is that I'm pretty sure you all have one of these already." She lifted the sharp and shiny gold statue.

The room fluttered with laughter. She was off to a good start, but the conductor of the orchestra was already capping his water bottle.

"Shaunna, you never gave up on me, even when I did. Thank you."

The conductor checked his watch and picked up his baton, but Michelle wasn't finished.

"I would like to thank Kyle Petersen — " there were more than a few gasps when she mentioned her ex-husband's name; even the conductor's baton wavered for a moment " — for making me tough."

The room murmured.

"I would to thank David Quinn for making me brave. And finally, I would like to thank Nathan McPherson for making me win."

Nathan's eyes became as wide as cinnamon rolls as the audience swelled with applause that was clearly meant for him.

Fortunately, Michelle did not have to climb back down the stairs because she was escorted off-stage by a star-struck indie film actor while the room pressed on with its ovation. Shaunna patted David on the thigh and, after a quick kiss, left his side to escort Michelle through the gauntlet of press obligations.

When they all met up after the show, Michelle no longer wanted to go home. She felt like she wasn't going to sleep for days. They all went to the studio's after party, which was flooded with A-listers, all of whom wanted to congratulate Michelle and meet Lauren and David.

Shaunna gave Michelle her hundredth and final hug of the night at around two o'clock, when David insisted on leaving for their little Yorba Linda bungalow.

Sly was driving Michelle southeast to their home less than an hour after that. The soothing voice on the AM radio lulled Michelle into a comfortable doze.

Michelle's phone chirped, and she answered it without looking at the number. Only Shaunna called her so late.

"Oh, Michelle. I thought I would get your voice mail." Kyle's voice was quiet, but clear.

Michelle was stunned.

"Kyle. I…what can I do for you?" It only took a second for her voice to harden.

Sly tensed behind the wheel.

"Oh, well, I just wanted to congratulate you on your win tonight." He sounded like a child whose mother had forced him to apologize to someone for a transgression.

Michelle wasn't surprised that Kyle didn't understand that she'd insulted him in her speech and wondered briefly if he was going to thank her for the only good press he'd gotten in a while.

"Thank you," Michelle said caustically.

"That guy you're with is too old for you," he added.

"Actually, you were too young for me. It turns out I'm quite satisfied with someone a bit more mature."

"Well, he dresses like a professor."

"Can I ask you something, Kyle?" Michelle was exasperated, but not upset.

"What?" He sounded like knew what was coming. He didn't.

"Did you ever find your TV remote?"

It took a while but finally Michelle heard his answer, a soft and regrettable, "No."

"Well, keep looking," she said cheerily and hung up.

That was the moment Michelle finally felt free of him. Everything she had carried around inside her, all the power he'd ever had over her, flew out the convertible like a loose hat. It was an exhilarating rush of self-worth, and it made her quite ravenous in more ways than one.

She scooted as close to Sly as she could with the stick shift between them and recounted her favorite events of the evening as they sped through vineyards and sleepy homes.

Their laughter escaped into the open night and clung to the star-bound breeze.

The End

Acknowledgments

We wish to begin by thanking Becca, Elli, and Sue, all of whom volunteered their valuable time and talents. They read this story and provided feedback at nearly every stage in the writing process. From the beginning, their commitment and enthusiasm for this novel has been nothing less than amazing. They invested as many months into this story as we did, and did so from behind the scenes. This is why *Exposure* has been dedicated in their names.

Thank you to Nina for her guidance and support. She has been instrumental in the publication of this story and we extend our heartfelt appreciation. Thanks also to Mina Vaughn for generously providing advice early in the submission process. She steered us in the right direction, and we are grateful for her assistance. We also thank Carmen and Chris for their friendship and help during a critical time.

We have enjoyed our collaboration with Omnific and especially wish to thank Nina, Lisa, Elizabeth, Colleen, and Kimberly for their hard work. Special thanks go to our editor, Sean, for taking us on and showing us the ropes. We consider ourselves fortunate. We've enjoyed working with him and everyone at Omnific and look forward to doing so again in the future.

Writing has brought us closer together as husband and wife, but also required much of our time and attention. Our friends and family deserve more thanks than we can adequately provide. Over the past four years, there were moments when those closest to us raised an eyebrow or two, but no one ever discouraged us from the journey. For that, we will be forever grateful.

Finally, we wish to thank E.L. James and Sylvain Reynard. Their stories sparked our own creativity while their friendship and support have enriched our lives. Many thanks for all they have done for us.

Morgan & Jennifer Locklear

April 22, 2014

About the Author

Morgan and Jennifer Locklear met in 1989 as teenagers and became high school sweethearts. They have been married since 1995 and live in the Pacific Northwest region of the United States with their two children, a son and daughter.

Although both enjoyed creative writing in their youth, they have only been working as a writing team since 2010. Since then, they have created a dozen full-length and short stories together.

Jennifer has been employed in fundraising and development for a non-profit organization since 2000. She also enjoys participating in charitable activities, both locally and online. In her (limited) free time she is an avid reader.

Morgan has been employed in the hospitality industry since 1998. He has been active in the local performing arts community since childhood with many acting and directing credits to his name. He is also a musician and songwriter and has recorded six albums.

Facebook: Morgan & Jennifer Locklear
Twitter: @MJLocklear

check out these titles from

OMNIFIC PUBLISHING

Contemporary Romance

Boycotts & Barflies and *Trust in Advertising* by Victoria Michaels
Passion Fish by Alison Oburia and Jessica McQuinn
The Small Town Girl series: *Small Town Girl* & *Corporate Affair* & *Keeping the Peace* by Linda Cunningham
Stitches and Scars by Elizabeth A. Vincent
Take the Cake by Sandra Wright
Pieces of Us by Hannah Downing
The Way That You Play It by BJ Thornton
The Poughkeepsie Brotherhood series: *Poughkeepsie* & *Return to Poughkeepsie* by Debra Anastasia
Cocktails & Dreams and *The Art of Appreciation* by Autumn Markus
Recaptured Dreams and *All-American Girl* and *Until Next Time* by Justine Dell
Once Upon a Second Chance by Marian Vere
The Englishman by Nina Lewis
16 Marsden Place by Rachel Brimble
Sleepers, Awake by Eden Barber
The Runaway Year by Shani Struthers
The Hydraulic series: *Hydraulic Level Five* by Sarah Latchaw
Fix You by Beck Anderson
Just Once by Julianna Keyes
The WORDS series: *The Weight of Words* & *Better Deeds Than Words* by Georgina Guthrie
Theatricks by Eleanor Gwyn-Jones
The Sacrificial Lamb by Elle Fiore
The Plan by Qwen Salsbury
The Kiss Me series: *Kiss Me Goodnight* by Michele Zurlo
Saint Kate of the Cupcake: The Dangers of Lust and Baking by LC Fenton
Exposure by Morgan & Jennifer Locklear

New Adult Romance

Three Daves by Nicki Elson
Streamline by Jennifer Lane
The Shades series: *Shades of Atlantis* & *Shades of Avalon* by Carol Oates
The Heart series: *Beside Your Heart, Disclosure of the Heart* & *Forever Your Heart* by Mary Whitney
Romancing the Bookworm by Kate Evangelista
The Fate series: *Fighting Fate* by Linda Kage
Flirting with Chaos by Kenya Wright
The Vice, Virtue & Video series: *Revealed* & *Captured* by Bianca Giovanni

Young Adult Romance

The Ember series: *Ember* & *Iridescent* by Carol Oates
Breaking Point by Jess Bowen
Life, Liberty, and Pursuit by Susan Kaye Quinn
The Embrace series: *Embrace* & *Hold Tight* by Cherie Colyer
Destiny's Fire by Trisha Wolfe
The Reaper series: *Reaping Me Softly* & *UnReap My Heart* by Kate Evangelista
The Legendary Saga: *Legendary* by LH Nicole
Fatal by T.A. Brock

Paranormal Romance

The Light series: *Seers of Light, Whisper of Light* & *Circle of Light* by Jennifer DeLucy
The Hanaford Park series: *Eve of Samhain* & *Pleasures Untold* by Lisa Sanchez
Immortal Awakening by KC Randall
The Seraphim series: *Crushed Seraphim* & *Bittersweet Seraphim* by Debra Anastasia
The Guardian's Wild Child by Feather Stone
Grave Refrain by Sarah M. Glover
Divinity by Patricia Leever
Blood Vine series: *Blood Vine, Blood Entangled* & *Blood Reunited* by Amber Belldene
Divine Temptation by Nicki Elson
Love in the Time of the Dead by Tera Shanley

Historical Romance

Cat O' Nine Tails by Patricia Leever
Burning Embers by Hannah Fielding
Good Ground by Tracy Winegar

Romantic Suspense

Whirlwind by Robin DeJarnett
The CONduct series: *With Good Behavior*, *Bad Behavior* & *On Best Behavior* by Jennifer Lane
Indivisible by Jessica McQuinn
Between the Lies by Alison Oburia
Blind Man's Bargain by Tracy Winegar

Erotic Romance

The Keyhole series: *Becoming sage* (book 1) by Kasi Alexander
The Keyhole series: *Saving sunni* (book 2) by Kasi & Reggie Alexander
The Winemaker's Dinner: *Appetizers* & *Entrée* by Dr. Ivan Rusilko & Everly Drummond
The Winemaker's Dinner: *Dessert* by Dr. Ivan Rusilko
Client N° 5 by Joy Fulcher

Anthologies

A Valentine Anthology including short stories by
Alice Clayton ("With a Double Oven"),
Jennifer DeLucy ("Magnus of Pfelt, Conquering Viking Lord"),
Nicki Elson ("I Don't Do Valentine's Day"),
Jessica McQuinn ("Better Than One Dead Rose and a Monkey Card"),
Victoria Michaels ("Home to Jackson"), and
Alison Oburia ("The Bridge")

Singles and Novellas

It's Only Kinky the First Time (A Keyhole series single) by Kasi Alexander
Learning the Ropes (A Keyhole series single) by Kasi & Reggie Alexander
The Winemaker's Dinner: RSVP by Dr. Ivan Rusilko
The Winemaker's Dinner: No Reservations by Everly Drummond
Big Guns by Jessica McQuinn
Concessions by Robin DeJarnett
Starstruck by Lisa Sanchez
New Flame by BJ Thornton
Shackled by Debra Anastasia
Swim Recruit by Jennifer Lane
Sway by Nicki Elson
Full Speed Ahead by Susan Kaye Quinn
The Second Sunrise by Hannah Downing
The Summer Prince by Carol Oates
Whatever it Takes by Sarah M. Glover
Clarity (A *Divinity* prequel single) by Patricia Leever
A Christmas Wish (A *Cocktails & Dreams* single) by Autumn Markus
Late Night with Andres by Debra Anastasia
Poughkeepsie (enhanced iPad app collector's edition) by Debra Anastasia

coming soon from

OMNIFIC PUBLISHING

CPSIA information can be obtained at www.ICGtesting.com
Printed in the USA
LVOW11s1557090815

449426LV00002B/115/P